You're Still The One

Copyright © 2024 Claire Highton-Stevenson

All rights reserved.
ISBN: 9798335652612
Editor-Michelle Arnold
Proofreaders-Crystal Wren, Suzi Vilkman, &
Ali Medway
Cover Design-Claire Highton-Stevenson
This is a work of fiction. Names, characters, businesses, places, events, locales, and incidents are either the products of the author's imagination or used in a fictitious and positive manner. Any resemblance to actual persons, living or dead, or actual events is purely coincidental.

Dedication

To those who inspire us to be better, and those who are inspired.

- Claire Highton-Stevenson

Acknowledgements

Leah Goodwin - who reads all of this before it's made shiny for everyone else.

Chloe Flanagan – without whom, my blurbs would still be lacking.

Many thanks, I appreciate you!

Chapter One

2024 Manchester, Nova Plus Hotel

Natalie Shultz lingered at the bar and nursed a neat scotch on the rocks, restless fingers aimlessly twisting the glass. The complimentary bowl of nuts went untouched, even though, if she were to think about it for too long, she knew she was hungry.

The bar was empty, other than the bartender standing at the end of the bar, drying and shining glasses with a dish towel and a keen eye.

She swirled the glass again and listened as the ice clinked against the edges. It felt cold now as she fingered the condensation, but she barely noticed it, her thoughts unable to get past that one image that had been haunting her all day.

It was fleeting, a blur even, but she was sure that it had been *her* leaving the hotel just as Natalie's Uber pulled up outside that morning.

Raising the glass to her mouth, Natalie sipped and caught her reflection in the mirror.

She looked tired.

Lifting a hand to push her hair back from her face, and then instantly regretting it, she tugged the fringe back down again. In her mid-forties and still not as grey as some of her friends, she was pleased with that at least and hopeful of getting another decade out of the chestnut waves and curls that she used to hate back then.

Her thoughts drifted once more…another life, another place entirely.

They'd been so young, and foolish, and in love. Hours spent together, laughing and lounging in the fields behind her house.

Rolling naked under bedding her aunt washed without ever knowing the things they did with each other beneath the sheets.

Teaching each other, and themselves in the process. It was carefree and blissful – until it wasn't. Until she'd been forced to walk away.

Natalie smiled sadly to herself at the memory.

It had been Sadie; she was sure of it.

"Another?" the bartender asked, noticing her drink was almost gone. Just the ice melting and watering it down into a colour that no longer looked appealing.

She shook her head. "No, thank you. I should—" She stood up and collected her bag and coat from the back of the tall bar stool. "Thank you. Good night." She smiled at his polite nod and walked away.

Only her heels clipping rhythmically on the marble floor sounded until she pushed open the door and stepped into the foyer and its plush carpet. Quickly, she crossed the expansive space to take the lift to her floor, hoping not to get caught by anyone from the convention who'd want to waylay her with inane chit chat.

She wasn't in the mood for that.

She patted her pocket for the keycard and breathed a sigh of relief that she still had it, having had a bad habit of losing them when she'd been staying in hotels in the past.

This was her second night here, attending the Adult Intimate Gadget and Entertainment Convention. Her feet were killing her from walking between pitches and listening to each seller try and explain why their dildo or vibrating toy was better than the alternatives.

She thought once more about that straightlaced teenager she had been all those years ago and chuckled to herself. Who would have thought she'd have built her little empire around adult toys? But even that, she could lay at Sadie's door.

Glancing at the reception desk, she considered something, then made the decision and walked confidently towards it. This late, it was quiet as she stood smiling at the clerk.

"Can I help?" he asked brightly, remembering her from check-in. "Ms Shultz?"

"Yes," she glanced quickly at his name badge, "Brian, I was wondering if you could pass on a message to a guest I believe is staying here, I'm not sure of her room number, but her name is Sadie Swanson."

"Okay, let me just pull up the details." He continued to smile at her, clicking away at his keyboard. "I'm sorry, we don't seem to have anyone staying under that name."

"Oh, alright, well thank you."

"Sorry I couldn't help. Have a good night."

She smiled graciously at him, headed towards the bank of three lifts and pressed the button. It had been worth a try, she thought.

Stepping into the lift, she smiled quickly at the man who followed in after her and wondered what he'd think if he knew she made her living selling vibrators and anal beads to women around the world.

She almost chuckled out loud as the stainless-steel doors began to slide closed. She turned her attention on them and when they were just inches apart, Natalie stared through the gap and gasped.

Those eyes.

The ones she'd searched so many times back then, eyes that haunted her still after all these years. Heavy dark make-up, or not, she knew those eyes.

"Sadie?" The name was barely a whisper.

She was tall and slim still, long black hair pulled away from her face to hang down her back, much darker than it had been back then, and styled somewhat dramatically with the solid fringe. Pouting lips were covered in red lipstick and she wore a long black coat; the look was elegant.

Sadie Swanson, Natalie was sure of it.

In a moment of panic, Natalie furiously tapped the button to stop the door closing, realising too late that in her panic, she'd been hitting close. She switched and rapidly poked the open button, but it was too late. The steel doors had slid closed, and the lift began to move.

"Shit," she muttered to herself.

"Friend?" he asked, still smiling at her.

Exhaling her disappointment, she shook her head. "No, just—" Her mind was all over the place. "Someone I thought I used to know."

"Hopefully you'll catch up with her tomorrow then."

"Yes, maybe."

The lift jolted a little as it came to a halt and the doors slid open again, this time on the third floor.

He looked like he was about to introduce himself or offer an invitation.

"Well, good night," she said, dashing any hopes he might have had. She stepped out into the corridor.

"Yes, sleep well." He blushed a little and pulled an awkward Hugh Grant kind of face. "I mean—"

"Thank you, and you," she said with a wry smile. If she were interested in men, he'd certainly have been a candidate. Tall and rugged in a perfectly fitting suit. That level of quiet confidence to at least speak to her, even if he did feel a little awkward about it. But it was women like that who interested her. Self-assurance with just a hint of cavalier and swagger. Put her in heels and a power suit and Natalie might just have invited her in for the night.

Alas, it would be another night alone. Well, unless you counted the multitude of devices she'd been given over the last two days, to try out and potentially order in bulk for the stores.

Come Again had grown rapidly, from the opening of her first store in Brighton, to now having twenty-five nationally and an online presence that rivalled almost every other adult website in the UK, if not Europe.

She dropped her bag and coat onto the chair in the corner and sighed, kicking off her heels as she unzipped her skirt and let that fall to the floor halfway to the bathroom. Her blouse followed before she pulled the light switch and illuminated the small shower, basin and toilet.

Hot water soon peppered the tray as steam built in the room, and the minty taste of toothpaste filled her mouth. Once again, she looked at the image of herself in the mirror, naked now but for the underwear she would soon discard.

Many hands and mouths had touched her skin since Sadie. Women had come and gone. Some had stayed a while, while others just passed by in the night. None had ever really sparked her like Sadie had. Maybe that was because it was her first real love. Not just a crush, not just a fumble out of sight after sharing a bottle of cider on the swings at the park, but love, real and intense and passionate. It had filled her parts, every inch of her consumed with want and need for the one person who could turn her into molten lava.

Eight months of utter bliss.

She spat out and rinsed her mouth. Had Sadie realised it was her? When their eyes had met, had she known? She had to have recognised her. Had she too thought about her all these years and wondered what if?

Highly doubtful, she decided. Pulling the shower curtain back and stepping in and under the cascade, she allowed her body to relax. Heat massaged the tension away.

No, Sadie wouldn't have thought about her. Not after what she'd done.

Chapter Two

2024 Manchester, Nova Plus Hotel

Evelyn slipped out of the black cocktail dress and stood half-naked in the middle of the room in an expensive black lace ensemble that she knew was never going to be a disappointment to anyone.

The woman lay naked on the bed, eyes scanning every inch of Evelyn, attempting to contain her nervousness and failing dismally. Evelyn took note of where her eyes lingered before studying the woman a little more. A few pounds overweight and self-conscious about it, she thought as she mused how best to start.

The woman's lips parted, and her tongue darted out quickly to moisten them, her teeth worrying her bottom lip as she too clearly contemplated what would happen next.

Evelyn held back just a little longer, and allowed the woman to stare as she bent her arms behind her back and unhooked the bra, freeing her breasts. They were not overly large, but more than a handful. She could see the look of desire and embarrassment fighting for dominance on the woman's face.

"I've never—" she stuttered when Evelyn took a step towards her, the Louboutin's still on her stockinged feet. "I just thought, while the mouse is away—" She laughed uncertainly until Evelyn brought a fingertip to her own lips. "Me being the mouse," she said quietly, trailing to silence as requested.

"You don't need to explain," Evelyn said, her voice low and sultry. "I'm not here to judge you. My role here is to bring you pleasure. That is what you want, isn't it?"

The woman nodded furiously. "Yes, I—" Her face flushed. "I've always wanted…to be with…with a woman," she finally got out. "I'm married though." She glanced down at the ring on her finger and then out of shame, or guilt, she slid it off and placed it down onto the bedside table.

"We have three hours for you to explore anything you want to," Evelyn explained. "I can go down on you; you can go down on me. We can get adventurous and open my bag of toys, but whatever you choose, I can guarantee one thing—" She lifted her knee onto the bed and crawled towards the woman she knew only as Sandra. "You will never regret this evening."

"Oh, that's—" Sandra silenced at the touch of gentle fingertips moving between her legs, separating her lips and stroking across her clit.

Hovering above her, Evelyn smiled seductively. "So, where would you like me to start?"

"Uh, this is…nice," Sandra gasped again.

"You like that?" Evelyn asked, her mouth against her ear. She flicked her tongue out and licked the shell as her fingers moved more firmly and elicited a delightful groan.

"Y—yes, very much." Her hips began to gyrate rhythmically with the movement of Evelyn's talented fingers. "My husband, he's—" She gulped and pushed her hips into the touch, moaning softly. "He's not very hands-on."

"He doesn't know how to pleasure you?" Evelyn asked. Sandra was wet already, and Evelyn thought about how many other Sandras she had helped over the years. Women stuck in loveless, or uninterested relationships with people they felt unable to tell or show how to please them.

"No, I mean, he's good with…with his…you know."

"Penis?" Evelyn pushed two long fingers inside of her and curled them just enough to put pressure right where it would create the most delicious feelings.

"Yes." Sandra's voice hit an octave higher.

"But you fantasise about a woman, her mouth." Evelyn kissed the bare skin closest to her. "Her tongue, and fingers."

"Yes…always have. I just—" Sandra gasped and arched into the touch again. "I want—"

"Tell me what you want," Evelyn whispered, her digits teasing and thrusting enough that she knew Sandra would lose all sense of thought soon enough. "I want to know all of the things you fantasise about."

"I— Your mouth."

Evelyn grinned. "Relax, just enjoy it." She slid down, past the curve of her tummy, placing soft, gentle kisses against the plump skin. Sandra's thighs parted instinctively.

"Enjoy it. You can make as much noise as you want. I like it. There's nothing to be embarrassed about or to fear, okay?"

Sandra nodded. "Hm-hm," was all she managed before the most delicious sensation arched her back and raised her hips, and Sandra finally understood what she had been missing all these years.

The door closed with a gentle click behind her, leaving Sandra prone, sleeping on the bed.

Evelyn was shrugged off with every step, as Sadie Swanson walked with confidence along the corridor and waited at the lift, feeling rather pleased with herself. If there was one thing that she took pride in, it was her ability to bring someone a little happiness, even if they were paying for it.

But now, her thoughts moved elsewhere. It was the same lift she'd seen *her*.

Natalie Shultz.

It had been her; she was sure of it.

The same chestnut hair, the same style. She laughed to herself. Natalie Shultz; what were the chances?

She hadn't heard her name, but she was sure that Natalie said it.

The question was, why was Natalie here?

Sadie had known this week would be good for business, but she didn't expect to run into anyone she knew. The adult toy conference always brought sex-hungry men and women to the hotels of whichever town they were in. And Sadie had no issue with travelling when the jobs would be this lucrative. Return clients would book in advance, but half the time, she didn't need the website for bookings.

She just had to sit at the bar and eventually someone would offer to buy her a drink, or she would make the move first if she thought the woman had shown any modicum of interest. And one drink would lead to a discussion, it always did, just like Blanca had told her it would.

In the beginning, she'd found it awkward to steer the conversation towards fees. Now, however, she had it down pat. And the moment the drink was finished, she would put her terms to the woman.

Always, and only ever, a woman.

They would either take her up on the offer or decline politely and leave. Occasionally, they'd get upset, call her names or just gasp at the audacity. At least a quarter of those would seek her out later, once they'd thought about it some more.

Sandra though, she had been a website booking - far too shy to ever make a move in person. Sadie smiled to herself. Sandra had been sweet, and once she'd gotten over her nerves, she'd been quite an enjoyable lover. Which was always a perk of the job.

All Sadie hoped was that Sandra went home and used her newfound knowledge to demand her husband attend to her needs; otherwise, she could always book in again.

But now, as she climbed into the sleek new Audi she'd hired, and the stereo system kicked in and blared out the playlist she'd been listening to these past few days, she thought of Natalie Shultz again, and all those years since she'd done what she'd done, and wondered again: what had brought her here?

Chapter Three

1999 Bath Street Riverbank, Rainbow's Bar

Sadie gripped the wooden handle, polished to a smooth shine over the years with all the hands that had used it, and yanked it towards her, filling half the pint glass with the cloudy, gassy liquid. Ale seemed to be catching on with the local students and hip gay crowd who frequented the pub at every opportunity.

She was four hours into a six-hour shift and just about ready to take a break. She needed a cigarette and shot of vodka, and maybe someone to flirt with or a quickie in the loo if her luck was in.

Handing over the pint, she shouted over the music, "£2.10."

The short, stocky butch, twice her age with the girliest name on the planet, Tiffany, dressed in plaid and jeans, gave her a £5 note and a wink. "Get one for yourself, yeah, darling?" She gave her a smile that Sadie guessed she thought made her look cute and to someone else, maybe it did, but she wasn't Sadie's type.

Sadie blew out her cheeks and forced a smile in return as she answered, "Cheers," while thinking, *not in a million years*. She pocketed the change and turned away quickly, looking for the next customer waving money at her.

Glancing down the bar, she spotted a girl around her own age, maybe a bit younger. All fresh-faced and giggly, standing with a friend. Not a girlfriend, she decided, watching them interact. Sadie knew people. Could read them like a book.

She strolled down the bar, licking her top lip as she considered whether they would be her entertainment tonight.

It was so much more fun having to work if you could banter with a couple of people. Nothing serious, just a little fun, usually at the other customer's expense. Maybe a little flirting, and who knew where the night might take you?

"Hello ladies, what can I get you?" She leaned down on one elbow and looked the cute one dead in the eye and held her gaze as she drawled a sexy, "A slow, comfortable screw?"

The blonde friend giggled, but the brunette blushed.

"I – uh."

Sadie broke out into a laugh. "I'm just messing with you. Let me guess?" She stepped back and studied the pair. Pointing at the blonde, she said, "Watermelon Hooch? And you…" She turned back to the brunette, studied her a little more closely. She was cute. "Bacardi Breezer…nothing too exotic, orange?"

"That's impressive." Brunette grinned at her, now able to at least make eye contact.

Sadie reached for the fridge and pulled out the two bottles required. She popped the lids and pushed them towards the two girls. "So, not seen you in here before?"

"We thought we'd come in and check it out," Blondie said, taking a swig from the bottle while the brunette held out a fiver.

"New in town then?"

Brunette shook her head. "No, but we only turned 18 last week."

"Really? You look way older than that." Sadie leaned down on the bar again and put her face just inches away from her. "You know this is a gay bar, right?"

The blonde's eyes bugged, but the brunette kept her cool, and held Sadie's intense gaze as she sipped through the straw. "Yes, of course we do."

"So, you gay? Bi? Pan?" Sadie smirked, enjoying the way she blushed a little more.

She shrugged. "We just wanted to check out the bar."

Blondie held her hand out. "I'm Alice. This is Natalie." She pointed to the brunette.

"Well, it's good to meet you, *I'm Alice*." Sadie smiled at her and took the hand that had been thrust at her, then she turned to Natalie and waited for her hand. "It's nice to meet you too, Natalie. I'm Sadie."

"I need the loo," Alice said, putting her bottle down on the bar. "Be right back."

Natalie turned, still sucking on the straw and watched her friend until she was out of sight.

"Alone at last," Sadie said, continuing to smirk when the wide eyes returned to face her. "So, now ya friend's gone, gay?"

Natalie nodded. "I think so, but I'm not—"

"Don't worry, your secret is safe with me." Sadie smiled genuinely. "We don't out people in here, but it is mandatory that you have to kiss the bar staff, to prove it."

"That is totally not true." Natalie laughed. "But cute," she added coyly and sipped from the straw again.

Sadie noticed she was a little more confident now Alice wasn't hanging beside her.

"Sadie?" a voice at the end of the bar called her. "Customers?"

"Yeah, coming boss," she called back. Leaning into Natalie again, she said, "My shift ends at ten. If you manage to ditch your friend, I could buy you a drink."

"Or…" Natalie pulled a small notepad from her bag and scribbled something on it. "My number. Give me a call when you're free."

She took the number and slipped it into her back pocket. "I'll take that, but I still want to buy you a drink later."

"We'll see." Natalie winked, picking up Alice's drink and twisting away to grab a table that had become free.

"Yeah, we'll definitely see," Sadie called after her.

Chapter Four

2024 Manchester, Nova Plus Hotel

Always an early riser, Natalie was in the gym by seven. Thirty minutes on the treadmill wasn't quite the same as her five-mile run along the edge of the riverbank and around through Amberfield Park, then back to her townhouse, but it would do, and it would take her mind off the lousy night's sleep and the day ahead.

Day three of the trade show wasn't her favourite. Mostly boring talks on how the industry was evolving and how they all needed to be ahead of the game with regards to technology. *No shit, Sherlock*, she'd thought as she upped the speed and incline.

She already knew she could ditch halfway through when the talks being given were mostly by men, for men. That wasn't her bag at all. Come Again was a mid-to-high-end establishment catering firmly for the enjoyment of women. Whether straight or gay, in a relationship or single, Natalie wanted nothing more than for women to explore and enjoy the pleasures their bodies could achieve.

Sleeping that badly though, hadn't happened for years. Not since…her mind drifted back to the previous night. Those dark brown eyes, heavy with make-up and still filled with so much hurt, staring back at her as the doors to the lift slid shut.

She brought the speed down and let her legs gently slow to a jog before stopping the machine completely. Her heart was racing, though she wasn't quite so sure it was due solely to the exercise.

Sadie Swanson had been the love of her life.

When people talked about meeting the one, Natalie Shultz already knew she'd met hers, and she'd fucked it up completely.

Which was why seeing Sadie last night had caused such unrest within her. It was so unexpected. The last time they'd set eyes on each other had been back in Amberfield, in Sadie's bedroom.

Sadie's unreadable face had crumpled into a heartbroken mess that night, and for a split-second Natalie had wanted to tell her she was sorry; that she hadn't meant it. And she was sorry, that part was true. She hated herself, but her hand was forced.

It was all for the best, she'd eventually told herself. But best for who? Certainly not Sadie, or herself in the end.

She grabbed her towel and wiped her face free from sweat, dabbing at her cheeks before she took a long swig from her bottle of water.

Thinking about Sadie had opened an old wound. One she wasn't sure had ever closed, not properly. How could it be healed when it was so painfully raw any time she'd thought about it? She'd learned a long time ago to push it down, to not give it airtime. And that had been easy when she hadn't had to look into those eyes again.

But last night when recognition had kicked in... It was still there, wasn't it?

Twenty-five years later.

A quarter of a century had passed and they'd both lived different lives in that time. Natalie had married, and divorced, and built her empire. What had Sadie done? She'd wanted to believe that she'd been happy. That was what she'd told herself over and over, that Sadie would be happy. But the reality was, she had no idea. She'd turned her back, walked away without thinking it through properly. It didn't matter that she'd looked for her later; it was too late then.

She'd been a coward.

Chapter Five

2024 Manchester, Majestic Hotel

Snuggling down under the duvet, Sadie mewled and began to stretch as her eyes opened. One arm reached out and grabbed her phone. It was eleven already. She'd missed breakfast, but that was alright, she rarely ate it anyway, preferring to stick to a 2-8 window for food. And she was making up for the early start yesterday. Morning clients were not her favourite, but who was she to turn down another step towards her dream?

There were several messages waiting, and she smiled to herself as she opened the first.

Sandra: Hi Evelyn, I just wanted to say thank you for last night. It was everything I hoped it would be.

Of course, she wouldn't respond. There was no requirement to create a rapport after the appointment. Unless Sandra was planning to book again, which she doubted. £500 was a lot of money to spend on a few hours of fun, even if it did allow you to unleash your sexual fantasies without the guilt of emotionally cheating. The services Sadie provided were more...educational for women like Sandra.

The second message was more interesting, a notification from the website.

Davina: I saw your ad in the expo magazine. I hope I'm not getting my wires crossed but I wondered if you would be free this afternoon for some adult recreation. You can contact me at any time. I look forward to speaking with you.

Sadie flicked across to the woman's profile. There were several steps that anyone wishing to use her services needed to follow. Upload a recent image, contact information, and a brief description of what they were looking for. If Sadie decided to meet them, she would send her own photograph. Her fees were dependent on time and what they were wanting from her.

Davina looked to be mid to late fifties, attractive enough with short blonde hair and glasses that made her look intelligent and sophisticated.

"I'm a top. I enjoy toys," Davina had added as though an afterthought.

Sadie hit reply.

Sadie: Hello Davina, thank you for contacting me regarding a liaison this afternoon. I am free between 1-5, if that would suit. My fee would be £350 for two hours, £50 per hour after. To be paid before my arrival. Is there anything you would like me to wear/bring? If you can confirm time and let me know your hotel and room number.

Her bank balance was growing very nicely. The dream of packing it all in and buying a cottage by the sea was on the horizon. Every client was one step closer.

The response came quickly.

Davina: 1p.m. would be perfect. Dress elegantly, that's all.

"Pfft," Sadie muttered, staring at her wardrobe, "Elegant is Evelyn's middle name."

She got up and headed for the shower. She had an hour to get herself ready and grab something to eat before she'd need to make her way to whichever hotel Davina was staying in.

Sadie: I'll need hotel and room number.

She put the phone down. This was business, she told herself. "No more thinking about Natalie Shultz."

Not waiting for her client to respond, she got into the shower.

Standing outside of the Nova Plus Hotel again gave Sadie pause for thought. She didn't usually care about revisiting the same place so soon. Most people took no notice of someone who looked like she did.

She was dressed to impress, somewhat business style at this time of day. Her suit was made to measure and cost a pretty penny, the shoes even more so. Her clients expected nothing less. She walked in knowing exactly where she was going, and to anyone noticing, she was just a guest at the hotel.

But when she'd read Davina's message and realised, it was too late to back out of the appointment. Not that she wanted to. A job was a job, and the entire point of being here was to make the most of it.

However, the idea that Natalie was staying here made her feel a little out of sorts. An urge to run would need to be dealt with if she were to maintain her reputation and give Davina the afternoon of her life.

The only problem with that was, she couldn't stop thinking about Natalie, and the moments they'd shared and had the time of their lives. Together, entwined. Whispering promises and 'I love you' in the darkness of one or the other's bedroom or laid out on a blanket in the fields, under the sun, or under the stars.

"All so long ago," she told herself and climbed the steps. Sadie pushed through the revolving door and Evelyn took her place.

Chapter Six

1999 Amberfield

"So, you wanna hang out again?" Sadie asked as she walked Natalie up the street. This was the third night Natalie had come to the bar and waited around for Sadie to finish her shift, but it was the first time she'd been allowed to walk her home.

Natalie smiled as she turned towards her. "Maybe."

"Maybe?" Sadie scoffed and laughed at the audacity. Sadie Swanson had girls begging to hang out with her.

Stopping beside the post box, Natalie said, "It depends on what hanging out with you means."

"What do you think it means?" Sadie asked, letting her fingertips drag slowly down Natalie's arm.

"I don't know, but I've heard the rumours." Natalie giggled.

"What rumours and who said them?" Sadie narrowed her gaze and stepped in closer.

Natalie didn't move away.

"Oh, you know, that you like to show a girl a good time."

Sadie's tongue slowly slid around her bottom lip. "Only girls I like."

Natalie pressed her lips together, before tilting her head up and coyly asking, "You like me?"

A sexy smirk slid across Sadie's face. "Yeah, you're kind of cute for a newbie."

"A newbie?" Natalie pouted. "I'm not a virgin."

Sadie snorted. "Yeah, you are," she said, nodding slowly and holding Natalie's gaze. "Have you even been kissed?"

"Course I have," Natalie answered with just a hint of disdain. She shoved her hands into her jeans pockets and shrugged. "It wasn't very good though."

"No? Why not?"

"I dunno." Natalie sighed. "Because it wasn't a girl?"

Sadie looked around them. The street was deserted. Just a few lights still on in curtain-covered windows. She raised her hand up and cupped Natalie's cheek.

"Do you want me to kiss you?" she asked.

Shyly, Natalie nodded. "Only if you want to."

"Right." Sadie leaned in, but stopped to say, "Cos I'm really in the habit of kissing girls I don't want to." She smiled and leaned in again, but the firm pressure of a palm against her shoulder stopped her.

"Not here, I can't risk my aunt seeing."

"Your aunt see a lot of things that happen on street corners after midnight?"

Natalie shrugged. "I dunno, but I can't—"

Sadie huffed a little but took her hand and pulled her around the corner and out of sight. A short alleyway that led down the side of a house was dark and quiet.

"Are you really going to kiss me?" Natalie asked with all the curiosity of a child wanting to know if Santa existed.

"If you'd stop talking and let me," Sadie answered.

Natalie closed her eyes, lips parting just slightly, and Sadie thought it might be the cutest thing she'd ever seen.

When nothing happened right away, Natalie half opened one eye, but swiftly shut it again just as Sadie's lips touched her own.

Smooth, warm lips that moved gently and then more firmly, encouraging with each movement.

A soft moan escaped Natalie when she felt the presence of Sadie's tongue nudging past her lips and into her mouth. Sadie smiled into it, knowing that she'd just completely erased that bad kiss from Natalie's memory.

Fingers tugged her closer with her belt loops and she knew right there and then that Natalie wasn't that shy.

When she pulled away, she said, "So, you wanna hang out again?"

Natalie's dreamy-looking face beamed at her. "Yeah, I think I might."

Chapter Seven

2024 Manchester, AIGE Con

"AI-controlled, fully functional body suits will one day no longer be a thing of the future. Extremely sensitive, made-to-measure outfits that can be worn under everyday clothing, meaning the wearer can program how and when they want to receive their pleasure—"

The voice tailed off as Natalie discreetly got up from her chair and wandered towards the stand selling futuristic dildos that could adjust instantly to your body's heat signals.

It was a nice idea, but she couldn't quite get past the idea that sometimes less was more, and she'd never been one for toys that needed a mains supply.

"Can I interest you in a demonstration?" the chirpy woman asked as they made eye contact.

"Sorry, I—" Natalie couldn't quite work out how a demonstration could take place in such a public area.

"Oh, no, I mean…" She waved her over with her fingers towards a small screen. "You only need to hold it to see how it reacts to your heat and pulse rate." She eagerly thrust the very realistic appendage into Natalie's hand. "Now, as you can see, the heat from your hand is already reacting with it. You can imagine how hot it is inside—"

"Absolutely." Natalie cut her off just as the appendage began to vibrate. She wasn't a prude, but there was a time and place and right now, she really wasn't in the mood. Well, not for toys. It was times like this that she wished she were dating someone, but that seemed like a thing of the past recently.

"Are you looking for personal use or business?"

"Business. I own Come Again," Natalie said confidently, despite the now writhing pink dildo in her hand.

"Oh, that's awesome, been in there a few times," the woman said boldly enough, but she still glanced around to make sure nobody else heard.

It had always fascinated Natalie at how awkward it still felt for many women to say out loud that they had needs and desires.

She'd wanted to change that, to make shopping for pleasure just as simple as popping to the pub for a pint or running into town for dinner.

Sex wasn't something she was ashamed of, Sadie had seen to that, and she wanted that freedom for all women, but right now, she just needed to eat, and maybe take a nap.

"I'm sorry, I have to go, but I will come back and have a look another time."

"No worries. I'm Sandra, anything you want to know, just get in contact." She handed over her business card. "My company is offering exceptional deals right now."

"Fantastic." She pocketed the card and added it to the others she'd collected over the past three days.

"We'd love the opportunity to pitch to you—"

"I'm sure we can work something out." Natalie delved into her bag and pulled out a card with the number for the purchasing department.

It had, Natalie could admit, been a reasonably successful mission. She'd placed several orders for new stock and with the new sales drive coming up, things were looking good for an end-of-year upsurge.

Using the app, she booked an Uber and headed outside to wait. It wouldn't take long. They were buzzing around all day, shuttling people back and forth between the hotels and the expo.

"Natalie. I thought that was you," a familiar voice called out and Natalie turned on her heel to find a face she recognised.

"Davina. How are you? I did wonder if you'd make it this year."

Pulling her shawl tightly around her shoulders she said, "I wasn't planning to, but Yacob dropped out last minute and I figured, sod it, I could do with a break from the office."

Davina Gorman was CEO for one of the largest importers of vibrators into the UK. Although they did a lot of business together, Natalie had never really taken to her.

There was no reason for that, no argument or unrest between them; it was just something about her that Natalie didn't like. An arrogance maybe, the way she spoke to people. But Davina was always cordial, and they had an excellent working relationship.

"Well, I'll be sure to find your pitch and have a chat about the iVibe200."

"Sounds like a plan." Davina checked her watch and grimaced. "I should have ordered the car earlier," she complained and strained her neck to look down the street.

"Need to be somewhere?" Natalie inquired, small talk really. She had no real interest in Davina Gorman's life.

"Actually, yes." She smirked. "I have a date," she said before adding quietly, "Did you see the ad in the expo magazine?"

"There are a lot of ads in that. Which specific one are we talking about?"

Davina grinned. "Evelyn's," was all she said, just as her car pulled into the kerb. As she opened the door, she turned back and said, "You should check it out. Never know, you might enjoy it."

Natalie narrowed her eyes in confusion.

"I will," she called, but Davina was already in the car waving at her, and her own car had pulled to the kerb too. Shaking her head, she opened the door and got in, acknowledging the driver before settling back into the comfortable leather seats.

Seatbelt on, Natalie reached into her bag, pulled out the catalogue and started to flick through the pages of ads and offers until she found the one Davina had mentioned.

Evelyn's Services

Experience a discreet woman to woman intimate adventure.

Let me fulfil your desires and fantasies.

www.EvelynsDesires.co.uk

Chapter Eight

2024 Manchester, Nova Plus Hotel

Sadie checked her watch once more. It was almost ten past the hour and her client was still not here. Pulling her phone from her bag, she checked for messages and found one.

Davina: Running late, on way now. Get a drink on my room number.

This wasn't how she usually did business.

There were rules in place for a reason. It was how she liked it. You booked her services; she arrived on time and went straight to your room. She didn't hang around in hotel bars or lobbies waiting for you. She didn't want to be seen with you.

Sadie tapped her phone against her chin. She could just leave. She'd been paid, it wasn't her fault that the client couldn't keep time. Or had something else to do.

Huffing, she walked towards the bar. Right now, she needed the kind of session Davina had booked. A woman who would take control of her and fuck her senseless until all thoughts of Natalie Shultz left her head.

"Vodka tonic," she said, smiling at the girl behind the bar. "Make it a double and get one for yourself. Room 326."

"Thank you." The girl returned the smile and set about making the drink.

It was hard to believe that it had been over 20 years since Sadie had set foot behind a bar. Those days working at Rainbow and then after, when the shit had hit the fan and she'd needed to leave Amberfield, had been fun.

She'd spent four exciting years backpacking around Europe, working bars and clubs, until finally, she had reinvented herself as many times as she needed to and found who she was now and felt okay about going home.

Not to Amberfield though; she'd never lived there again. But returning to England and moving to Brighton had meant she could slip back into society and start making her own rules again.

"Thank you," she said quietly as the long glass filled with clear liquid and ice was placed in front of her. She lifted it to her lips and sipped.

She checked her watch again. "She's got until I finish this drink," she muttered to herself before taking a swig and gulping it down.

Pulling out her diary, she set about organising the next few weeks ahead. She was due in Eastbourne soon, at the InspoWoman business and tech event, and already had several clients booked thanks to word of mouth and returning clients from last year's event in Solihull, but before then she had time to fill.

"Evelyn?" A voice from behind her caught her attention and she swivelled around to find Davina smiling at her. "Let's go, shall we?"

Inclining her head, Evelyn replied, "Sure."

"I'm sorry for keeping you waiting. You wouldn't believe the wait for an Uber," Davina explained as they entered the foyer. "I'm very much looking forward to our time together."

"Me too," Evelyn said, following a few steps behind. She didn't like to appear to be with a client, unless a date was what the client was paying for.

She wasn't Davina's date.

Davina glanced up at the clock on the wall. "I realise we've wasted 15 minutes, so, shall we forgo small talk, and just get undressed as soon as we get to my room? I'd like that a lot."

"Of course. I am at your service. Do you have your own equipment?"

"Always. You never know." Davina turned back and winked. "You'll like it, I'm sure."

The lift opened. Davina stepped in and just as Evelyn was about to follow, she heard a voice call out.

"Sadie?"

Glancing back, she could see Natalie waving at her, trying to get her attention. Her eyes closed, blocking out the image in front of her. Refocused, she turned back to her client, who was grinning inanely at her, completely oblivious and out of view.

"I'm really looking forward to it," Evelyn said and stepped in beside her, hitting the door close button.

Chapter Nine

1999 Amberfield

"We can go back to mine," Sadie said when they'd finally flopped down onto the blanket. The field they'd strayed into was quiet and only the wind blowing gently through the wheat made any noise.

Natalie pulled a face. "No offence, but your flat mates are pigs."

Sadie laughed. It was true, they were.

"Okay, so where then? Because I don't want your first time to be on a blanket in a field."

Natalie shrugged. "Why not?" She stripped her summer jumper off and sat back on her heels, the vest top showing pink shoulders from the last time they'd been here, kissing for hours on a blanket until Sadie had needed to stop before it all went too far.

"Because you deserve better," Sadie insisted.

Natalie grinned at that. She liked the way that Sadie cared about stuff like that. It made her feel important and wanted.

"But what if I chose it?"

Sadie considered it. "Well, that's different."

"Why?"

It didn't take her any time to think about her response.

"Because I'd give you anything you asked for," Sadie said sincerely. "And you asked to take it slowly, so I have, and now you're all wanting to do it."

"I wasn't ready then," Natalie admitted. "I was scared and…you have this reputation—"

Sadie went to stand up, annoyed. "I don't have a-"

Pulling her back down, Natalie gripped her arm. "Let me finish. You have a reputation for being quite good in bed and—"

"Quite good?" The anger dissipated into disbelief, and she fell back onto the blanket in faux outrage.

Natalie laughed.

"I didn't want to be a disappointment," Natalie admitted.

"You won't be, it's not like that," Sadie reassured, "You can't get it wrong."

"I want—" Natalie began, and Sadie sat up quickly, ready to listen to every word. "I want it to be natural. Not planned, or a quickie in the loos at Rainbows. I want us to just be kissing and then do it."

"Do it?" Sadie winced. "So romantic."

Natalie nodded. "Yes, just do it. You know what you're doing, so just do it. You have my permission to finger me senseless." She chuckled and hiked her skirt enough that she could straddle Sadie's legs.

Smiling at her, Sadie said, "But Nat, it's going to be your first time. Don't you want it to be—"

"With someone who cares, and wants it to be special?" Natalie countered. She leaned forward and Sadie could see down her vest top, bra-clad breasts right there. "I want it to be you, and I want it to be natural," she said again, "and not with your housemates or Aunt Lina lurking and putting me on edge."

"Okay."

"Now, kiss me," Natalie demanded with a grin.

And Sadie did as she was told.

Soft, supple lips pressed against her own, moving together until they eased apart, and tongues slid effortlessly against one another.

Sadie's hand moved to lay upon Natalie's bare thigh, caressing the strong muscle, until Natalie adjusted her stance and created more space, taking Sadie's hand and pulling it to her inner thigh.

"Touch me," she whispered against Sadie's lips.

It was weird, Sadie thought, how in that moment, she felt like a virgin herself all over again. This was nothing like all the girls she'd drunkenly fingered in the toilets at the pub, or the girls who had begged her to sit on their faces in crappy bedsits and overcrowded dorm rooms after drinking too many pints of snakebite.

Tentatively, she reached under and let her fingers glide across the soft, damp cotton. "You're so wet," she said in amazement.

Nat sat bolt upright. "Is that bad?"

"What?" Sadie gasped, stilling her movement. "No, it's awesome."

A look of relief washed over Nat, the brightness of her cheeks diminishing just a little.

"Okay." She nodded, more to herself than to Sadie. Holding Sadie's gaze, Natalie reached under her skirt and moved her knickers to one side. "Okay? Or should I take them off?"

Sadie managed to nod, slowly moving away from the safety of the material until her fingertips were met with hot, wet, silky flesh.

"I think I can work around them," Sadie said, watching every feature of her face for any sign that this wasn't what she wanted.

Natalie's breath stuttered as she braced herself.

"It's alright, just relax," Sadie offered, gently teasing with the lightest of touches. Her fingertip rubbed back and forth and then circled around her now-lover's excited clit. "Like that?"

"Hm-mm." Natalie nodded. "Yes," she said, and Sadie smiled at her when she naturally undulated her hips to meet Sadie's touch.

"You're really wet." Sadie grinned. She wrapped her other arm around Natalie's waist as she found her opening and slid the very tip of her finger inside, inching in unhurriedly until she was knuckle deep. "Alright?"

"Yes." Natalie nodded again. "It doesn't hurt," she said with surprise. "I thought it would."

"That's only one finger. And you're really—"

"I'm wet, yes. Got that." Natalie grinned. "Is this it?"

Sadie laughed. "No, I'm just easing you in."

"Oh, good, cos I was thinking this isn't that exci— Oh, god," she said mid-sentence when Sadie curled her finger and found that perfect spot and sped up.

"You were saying?"

Chapter Ten

2024 Manchester Nova Plus Hotel

Natalie paced her room. If she didn't know better, she'd have thought that Sadie and Davina were walking together.

Conversing.

But that could only be polite small talk as two people walked in the same direction because Davina was meeting someone called Evelyn.

The idea of Davina having anything of interest to say to Sadie almost made her chuckle, until she remembered that she didn't know what interested Sadie anymore.

She'd heard her though, hadn't she? Sadie. She'd turned around and looked right at her. So, clearly two things were fact. One, it was Sadie, and two, she didn't want to speak to her. Not that she could blame her.

A quarter of a century.

The nap was now a thought of the past. She grabbed her purse and left the room. Forgoing the lifts, she took the stairs and headed for the bar. She needed a stiff drink.

Sliding onto a stool, she raised a finger and got the girl's attention. "Scotch on the rocks, please."

"Coming right up." The bar tender smiled and reached for a glass beneath the counter.

"Actually, make it a double, please." Natalie looked around the room, glancing at the clock. Almost three and she still hadn't had lunch. "Do you serve food by any chance?" she asked when her drink was placed onto the coaster.

"Sure, we have a bar menu, or you can wander through to the restaurant." She slid along a small, leather-bound menu with the hotel's name on the front printed in gold.

"The bar menu will be fine, thank you. I just realised I haven't eaten since breakfast."

"Of course. You have a little perusal then and I'll be back in a moment to take your order." She smiled quickly before turning to the next customer.

Opening the menu, Natalie read down the list of ciabatta and open sandwiches. Jacket potatoes looked interesting.

"Still skipping lunch, I see."

Natalie froze.

Every nerve ending in her entire body suddenly electrified at the sound of that voice and the perfume that wafted forward.

Something carnal and sensual.

"It's good to see you. Well, it would be if you turned around," Sadie continued confidently.

Slowly, Natalie placed the menu down and swivelled on the stool until she was face to face with the woman she dreamt about most nights.

"Sadie, I—"

It was hard to breathe when the image in front of her still looked so good. The messy hair of her youth was now a mane of almost black hair that hung loosely down her back. A more feminine version of the woman she'd known all those years ago. Looking at her, Natalie realised who it was she had been reminded of when she'd caught sight of Sadie previously. She had a Claudia Winkleman vibe with the heavy make-up and heavy fringe, and the dark clothing. It was all so…sexy.

"It's been a long time," Sadie offered, opening the conversation.

"Yes, it has. Too long." Natalie looked away, still ashamed of the way they'd left things. The way she'd left things. "I'm sorry, I—"

"All water under the bridge." Sadie waved the apology off and pulled the stool out beside her. "May I?"

"Yes, of course. I'd like that."

"Vodka tonic, right?" the girl behind the bar said to Sadie when she approached.

"That's right." Sadie smiled. She dropped her bag to the floor and slid elegantly onto the stool. "Sign of a good bartender, remembering customers' drinks."

"Thank you, though it was only a couple of hours ago that I served you, so probably not too difficult to remember." She turned to Natalie. "Did you figure out what you wanted?"

The question was one Natalie had been asking herself for years. And it didn't go unnoticed with the ironic small smile that crept up and then vanished from Sadie's face.

"No, thank you, I think I'll wait till dinner and—" Natalie stopped talking, aware that she was oversharing again. Something she'd spent a lot of money in therapy learning not to do.

She slid the menu back across the bar.

"It's good to see you again, Nat," Sadie repeated, meaning it.

The use of her old nickname again made Natalie's insides quiver the same way they had done a quarter of a century ago.

"Is it? I wondered if maybe seeing me had been something you'd want to avoid," Natalie said honestly, remembering back to earlier when she'd been ignored.

Sadie nodded. "I did consider that, I'll admit. But I guess curiosity got the better of me." She lay her card on the bar to pay for her drink. "You haven't changed much. Just the voice…it's a little…you always were well-spoken, but now—"

"I'm not posh." Natalie laughed. "I just sound it. Anyway, you can talk."

"Yes, I suppose I have learned to speak a little more nicely."

Natalie swallowed and caught the words in her throat before she vomited out something inappropriate. She turned at the approaching bartender with Sadie's drink in hand. "Add that to my tab," Natalie said when the girl went to take the card.

"You don't have to do—" Sadie was cut off from any further rebuttal.

"I insist. A drink is the very least I owe you after all these years." Her cheeks blushed again, but this time out of shame, not just embarrassment.

"You know, maybe it's time to forgive yourself and let that all go," Sadie said, and Natalie couldn't help but notice the way Sadie glanced down at her hand, the ring finger to be exact, before she asked, "Are you happy?"

Are you happy? Not *what are you doing here*, or *what do you do now*, or *are you married*? That was Sadie all over, always putting everyone else's happiness before her own.

"Define happy?" Natalie said with just a hint of humour and a smile.

Sadie appraised her. "Well, you look exhausted, but doing well for yourself, so, I guess that would mean you're throwing yourself into work and avoiding anything that might just ignite—" She pressed her lips together. "Sorry, old habits. It's not my place to tell you how you feel about anything."

"No, maybe so, but you're not far wrong. I am happy, life is good and I'm happy with that, but no, I'm not avoiding as such. I just haven't met anyone who ignites that spark…again," she said deliberately.

"That's a shame," Sadie said before taking a sip of her drink.

"And you…how…how have you been?" Natalie stammered as her eyes scanned Sadie. "You look well."

"I've made the best of whatever life has offered me," Sadie said with an assuredness that had always been there, but now, it was edged with maturity. Her voice was lower, and she spoke more slowly as though every word was carefully considered before she uttered a sound.

"And Manchester? You live here now?"

Sadie glanced at her watch. She had another client at six. "No, just visiting. I have a flat just outside of Brighton, but I seem to spend most of my time travelling at the moment."

"Not running a bar then." Natalie laughed and then suddenly stopped. "No, of course you're not, look at you." She pressed her lips together in an effort to stop herself from gushing, but it was inevitable. "You look amazing."

"I—thank you, that's kind of you to say." She didn't offer a compliment in return, but she didn't need to, not with the way her eyes were boring into Natalie's right now. Intense, like they'd always been.

Seeing her.

"I um—" Natalie swallowed, words caught in her throat and suffocated by the emotion of finally being able to speak them aloud. "I just needed to…to say…" She breathed deeply and exhaled slowly. "I'm sorry. I'm sorry for back then."

Sadie nodded. "What are you sorry for?"

The question threw Natalie for a moment. It was a valid inquiry. When she didn't answer right away, Sadie spoke again, this time with a little more aggression that hadn't been there previously.

"Are you sorry you did what you did? Or just sorry that you've lived with the guilt of it all these years and need to feel absolved?" She glared.

"Ouch." The barbed comment hit Natalie hard. "I guess I deserved that."

Sadie got up, her drink unfinished. "It was good to see you, and I'm glad that you're okay. But I need to get going if I'm going to make my next appointment."

"Yes, of course. Maybe we can—"

"No, I don't think that would be a good idea." Sadie smiled sadly. She reached down for her bag and lifted it onto her shoulder. "Take care."

Chapter Eleven

2024 Manchester, Nova Plus Hotel

"What the hell was that?" Sadie said to herself the moment her hotel room door closed, and she could toss her bag onto the bed. "All these years you've wanted to ask her and when she gives you the opportunity, what did you do? You ran." She flopped down onto the bed before instantly standing again.

She stripped out of her clothes and ran a bath. She needed to soak and ease the tension that had only gotten worse once she'd left Nat. And now, she was angry. With herself and Natalie.

The appointment with Davina had been everything she'd needed earlier. It almost felt embarrassing to charge the woman because Sadie was sure she got as much, if not more, out of it.

It wasn't often that a woman as dominant as Davina was who Sadie needed, but now and then, she was grateful for it.

She just needed to get out of her own head, stop thinking for a couple of hours and allow herself to breathe. And being fucked hard with a strap worn by a woman who orchestrated exactly what she wanted from the liaison meant that it was easy for Sadie to switch off from it all.

She became pliable. Moved when told to. Stayed in the moment and let herself enjoy the opportunity to totally give herself to someone else. There was something a little bit feral in being on all fours and taken from behind like that.

And she couldn't deny that the physical release had been somewhat powerful and multiple. Just like Sadie, women like Davina were experts at giving and taking pleasure.

Which was probably why she'd decided to stop at the bar on the way out. A quick drink to calm herself before this evening when the client would require a much more mellow and enchanting version of Evelyn.

She hadn't expected to find Nat sitting there all alone. Nor had she expected that she would stay once she had, but the biggest thing she hadn't expected, was to feel it still: love.

Knowing you'd always love someone and being confronted by it were two vastly different things. She'd wanted to touch her. To reach for her and take her in her arms again. Because Nat looked like she needed someone to do that - to hold her.

But to do that would just be too much. Her heart had never mended, not fully. To allow Nat Shultz anywhere near her again would just be asking for a mental breakdown.

She poured bubble bath under the water and watched as it frothed, and the aroma of the tropics filled the room.

Studying herself in the mirror, she groaned as she noticed a small bruise on her hip. Fingers that gripped and tugged had left their mark. If Davina contacted her again, she'd give her a discount but put boundaries in about marking her skin.

Turning up to any client looking less than perfect for them didn't sit well with her. She was sure they were not naïve enough to assume they were her only customer, but for the hours they were paying for, she wanted them to feel as though they were, and that she was there only for them and not the wedge of cash that it had cost.

She wasn't selling sex; she was selling an experience. The opportunity to enjoy a few hours alone with her. Some paid just to talk; lonely people away from home who just wanted company over dinner. She had sex with them because that was what she wanted to do. Whether it was her own basic needs or because pleasuring them allowed her to fulfil some kind of unhealed trauma, she didn't care. She enjoyed letting Evelyn take over.

Stepping into the tub, she sank down, slid under the water up to her chin and sighed. The conversation replaying in her head.

"You know, maybe it's time to forgive yourself and let that all go."

That's what she'd said to Nat. She laughed at herself and the audacity of that statement.

"Oh, because you're doing such a good fucking job of that, right?"

She was almost forty-six years old. How had just eight months of her life, when she was barely an adult, made such an impact on everything she'd done since? It was madness and yet, she knew without doubt, that Natalie Shultz had always been the one.

Chapter Twelve

1999 Amberfield, Aunt Lina's House

Sadie stretched out on top of Nat's bed, her hands behind her head, watching and laughing as Nat danced around with her hairbrush to Lou Bega's "Mambo Number 5."

The fun came to an end with the *bang bang bang* on the ceiling from downstairs.

"Your aunt is a real misery." Sadie laughed, grabbing for Nat when she flopped into the bed next to her.

"Yep. And I'm stuck with her for another three years." Nat frowned and rolled against Sadie.

"You know I love you, right? You could move in with me."

Natalie sat up and stared down at her with a profoundly serious look on her face.

"What is it?" Sadie asked.

"You love me?"

Had she just said that out loud, without even thinking about it? No big announcement, just a casual "You know I love you." She couldn't deny it.

"Yeah," Sadie said confidently. "I love you, I'm in love with you."

Natalie slid her fingers into Sadie's hand and watched as they interlocked and held. "Is that what this is? This feeling I have whenever I'm around you or think about you. Am I in love?"

"What does it feel like?"

She watched Natalie's face as she considered the question. The corners of her mouth turned upwards, her eyes sparkling with unshed emotion.

"Like the air around me thins and I can barely breathe. Like I'm embarking on something that will leave an imprint tattooed on my skin. Like my lips are magnets pulled only towards yours. Like—"

Sadie rushed forward and captured her mouth, an intense kiss that left them both breathless. And when she pulled away, Natalie was still, her mouth open, her eyes closed, as though she were trapped in that moment.

"I love you," Natalie said, not moving still, but her eyes slowly opened. The smile on her face widened. "I love you," she repeated, somewhat surprised by the second announcement of those three important words.

"So, move in with me then."

Nat laughed. "Pigs for housemates, remember? I do love you, but I must stay here. She'd—" She stopped speaking and licked her lip before biting it in deep thought. "It's not as simple."

"It could be." Sadie shrugged.

Natalie turned and leaned against her. "My parents put Lina in charge. I don't get to decide anything for myself until I'm 21."

"Decide what?"

"How I'll live my life," Nat said as though that were the most obvious answer. "Till then, Aunt Lina is in control."

"But why? Why can't your parents just let you be who you are?"

"It's just the way it is. Three years isn't that long to wait."

"I guess so." Sadie slid her leg around and over Nat's thighs and straddled her. "So, if we have no more dancing to entertain us…" She waggled her eyebrows, her hand already pushing Nat's skirt higher. "Can you imagine what your aunt would say if she knew I was…"

"Uh huh." Nat grinned. Grabbing said hand and pulling it away, she edged higher up the bed. "But I'm still liking the things your mouth can do."

"Oh, well in that case." Sadie dropped down onto her belly, legs hanging off the end of the bed. Easing aside Natalie's knickers, she blew lightly across her clit and enjoyed the way her lover's hips twitched. She gazed up and found Natalie leaning on her elbows, staring down at her, curiously watching, lips pressed tightly together in anticipation. "Now, remember…no screaming out my name."

"Stop torturing me then," Natalie whined playfully as a grin spread across her face.

"Torture? I'll show you torture…" Sadie's tongue flicked out. The barely-there touch had Natalie's hips raising to meet it.

"Sadie, please."

"What did I say about screaming my name?" Sadie giggled at the sight of Natalie biting her lip. "Okay, I won't tease…this time."

"I was thinking," Sadie said, pulling her jumper on. It was almost six and Nat's Aunt Lina would be banging on the door any moment announcing tea was ready, and that would be Sadie's first nudge to go. "What do you think about toys?"

Nat frowned. "Toys? I think we're a bit old for that."

Sadie snickered. "Not kids' toys, adult toys. Like a strap-on."

The furrowed brow grew deeper. "What's a strap-on?"

"You really have been hidden from the world, haven't you?" Sadie smiled and crossed the room to where Natalie stood. When Natalie gazed up at her she thought she might just be the most important thing on the planet to someone.

"It's a…" Sadie thought for the right word. She didn't want to scare Nat, or say a word that would describe it as being a man thing, cos it wasn't. "Basically, one of us would wear a special belt thing, and it has a space to attach a dildo, so we could have sex and be hands-free."

"Like a dick?"

"Kind of, but it wouldn't be a dick, it would just be a toy, something to play with that...I mean you don't have to; it was just a thought—"

Natalie thought for a moment before she said, "I trust you. If you think it would be fun, then..." She shrugged. "Why not?"

Sadie grinned at her. Nothing was ever judged or shamed. Just genuine curiosity and then a decision, usually a positive one.

"Have you got one?" Nat asked a little timidly.

Sadie's shoulders shrank. "Nah, but we could go into Brighton one day. There's a shop there that sells them."

Natalie considered it a little longer before she asked quietly, "Will it hurt?"

"I don't think so. Why?"

Nat flopped onto the bed. "It's just something Aunt Lina said."

"What did she say?"

Flushing pink, Natalie moved closer to Sadie. "She sat me down one day and said I needed to know about sex. That it was dirty, and only bad girls enjoyed it."

Sadie bit her tongue. "Go on."

"She said that sex is for making babies, and that if it hurt, it just meant the baby would be stronger, braver and more wanted. I know it's different with us, you're not a man so..."

Sadie grimaced. "I think your aunt is a bit..." She twirled her finger around by her head. "Does it hurt when I use my fingers?"

"No, I mean, well, it was uncomfortable sometimes, in the beginning, till I got into it."

Sadie sat down beside her and took her hands in her own. "Promise me something."

She waited until Nat looked at her and nodded. "Okay."

"No matter what we do, if it ever hurts or you feel in any way uncomfortable, you'll tell me, and we'll stop."

Natalie looked horrified. "But I don't want to stop! I like what we do."

"I don't mean stop forever. I mean…sometimes maybe your body isn't as ready as I think it is and it just needs more time to relax and—"

"You're so sweet, you know that?"

"Only to you. Everyone else thinks I'm—"

The banging on the door made them both jump apart instantly, just in time before Aunt Lina swung it open.

"Time your friend was going home. Dinner's on the table." The German accent sounded as harsh as the scowling face suggested. She walked away but left the door open.

"How come she's got an accent?" Sadie asked.

"My family are Swiss," Natalie answered with a shrug.

"Swiss? But how are you so English?"

Natalie laughed. "Boarding school. And now, college."

"So, your parents sent you away to secondary school and you picked up the accent?"

Natalie shook her head. "No, I went when I was four."

"Four? That's so young."

"I guess so." She sighed. "I came here at four and attended a private nursery and then I went to boarding school and only went home for holidays. For some reason, my father decided I would do local sixth form, so I stayed here again with Lina."

"So, you're not English?"

"Technically no, but I can claim citizenship and as soon as I am twenty-one, I will do. I don't want to go back there. I don't know them."

"Wow, that's so…I like it," Sadie said. "You being different I mean, not the whole arsehole family stuff."

Natalie kissed her.

And then there was the bang on the ceiling.

Chapter Thirteen

2024 Manchester, Nova Plus Hotel

As conventions went, this one had, in the end, been quite productive. She had several new contacts and a small suitcase filled with all kinds of gadgets for her team to have a look at and discuss.

The big late summer/early autumn promotion was already in place. Come Again was about to be splashed all over late-night TV and magazine pages.

The iVibe2000 was looking like a great product to use for that too, if she and Davina could come up with an arrangement that worked, and Harry could work it into the ad campaign at such short notice.

Now, though, she was ready to head back home. Bags were packed and the car taking her to the station had arrived. All she had to do was sit back and let the train take the strain.

But that was easier said than done when her mind wanted to wander back to Sadie at every opportunity. All these years later and she still felt the same way about her.

The sound of her phone ringing in her pocket stopped her head from going over it all again, and she smiled when she answered and Harry said, "When are you back? I've missed you."

"I'm on the 11.15 a.m. train to Euston and then I'll change onto the Gatwick express and get a taxi from Gatwick to Amberfield. I'm not expecting to be back in the office before Monday, Harriet." She dragged her case on wheels behind her down the hall. "I intend to fully relax this weekend."

"Oh, that many new toys, huh?" Harry laughed and Natalie considered it.

"I'm sure I can find what I need in my little box of playthings."

"I'm sure you can, but back to work, are you bringing anything exciting in for us to use during the promotion?"

The room four doors down from her opened and Davina stepped out. With a little nod of the head, she fell into step beside Natalie, ignoring the side-eye glance that questioned that decision.

"Yes, I might have the perfect product for the ad. I will spend some time over the weekend putting a plan together and do a presentation at ten on Monday. Email all concerned and make sure everyone attends."

She came to a halt at the lift.

"Will do, safe journey and have a good day."

"Yes, you too. Okay, buh-bye." Natalie rushed to close the call out. She never liked having someone listening in, even if they weren't trying to.

"All set?" Davina smiled, chewing gum. Clearly, she had been listening.

Natalie pushed her phone into her bag and nodded. "Yes, it's been a long week." The doors opened and they stepped inside. "How was your date?"

Davina chuckled. "Fantastic. Sometimes all you need is a willing woman ready to bend over and—"

She stopped speaking when an older couple appeared just in time to squeeze into the lift with them, and Natalie couldn't have been more grateful.

Davina leaned in and whispered, "Worth every penny. Seriously, you should consider it. Very discreet."

This was exactly why she found Davina difficult. What should have been a private liaison always became something to brag about.

"I'm sure *she* is, and I'm glad that it worked out so well," Natalie said in response.

"Seriously, that woman was a hot piece of—"

The lift came to a halt and the couple stepped out. Natalie turned quickly to Davina. "I think we can both agree that we can respect a woman's choices and not degrade her, right?"

"Oh, sure, sure," Davina answered quickly, trying to keep up as Natalie headed towards the front desk to hand in her keycard. "I didn't mean anything by it."

Natalie raised a brow at her. "I would hope not." She dropped her keycard into the slot before turning back to Davina. "Give me a call next week to go over that order, okay?"

"Absolutely," Davina said enthusiastically, apparently already moving on from Evelyn. "Do you need a lift to the station?"

"Thank you, but—" Natalie's phone beeped. "My car just arrived."

She waved over her shoulder as she walked away and pushed through the revolving doors and out to the waiting vehicle.

Settled in the back, she closed her eyes for a moment and when they opened again, they had already moved along the road and were passing the next big hotel.

As she stared out of the window, she recognised the woman lifting her bags into the boot of a fancy black car.

Sadie.

Chapter Fourteen

2024 LNER train, Manchester Piccadilly Station

The express train would take just over two hours of vomit-inducing rocking that, that no matter how often Natalie travelled on it, she would never get used to. It was the same whenever she was a passenger in a car on long journeys.

She'd already taken her travel sickness tablets, and booked a seat where she would be travelling backwards. That usually helped.

With her laptop open on the table and her phone plugged into the wall socket, she started to write up her notes.

"I'm so sorry," a man's voice said to someone along the aisle behind her. "Big old feet." He laughed and then there was a response that left Natalie mid-tap on her keyboard.

"Don't worry. It's a tight squeeze, isn't it?"

Natalie turned a little to her left just in time to see Sadie walk past her, looking up at seat numbers on the other side of the aisle.

"Which seat's yours?" Natalie said as confidently as she could manage. She didn't take her eyes off Sadie for a second, watching as she slowly turned.

She looked immaculate in a camel-coloured knee-length coat over a pinstriped suit and heels, all of which looked expensive in an understated way.

The smile on Sadie's face was one of irony and acceptance as she turned to find Natalie looking at her.

"32," Sadie answered.

Natalie pointed to the one directly opposite where she was positioned.

"Of course it is." Sadie sighed. "Thank you."

Sadie pushed her case into the luggage rack, slipped off her coat and then took her seat, slightly ahead of Natalie's seat and facing the other way. Meaning they were virtually face to face across the aisle.

Natalie could imagine Harry waffling something inane about the universe putting things together.

But then she remembered their earlier conversation, when Sadie had been clear that meeting again would not be something she would entertain. So, with just a hint of disappointment showing, Natalie turned her attention back to her laptop and began to type and delete, getting frustrated with herself and the lack of focus she had with Sadie sitting so close by.

She smelled so good.

There were still a few minutes to go before the train was due to depart but it didn't look as though first class would be filling up today. Natalie was grateful for that. The last thing she needed was a chatterbox sitting opposite from her; plus, she could use the entire table to spread out her notes and brochures.

"Would you mind watching my things while I go and get a coffee from the—"

Natalie looked up to find Sadie standing awkwardly in the aisle.

"Sure, yes, of course." Natalie nodded eagerly. *Anything you want*, she wanted to say, but held it together.

Sadie turned to walk away and then changed her mind and turned back. "Do you want me to get you anything while I'm there?"

"Oh, uh…sure. I'd love a tea. English Breakfast?" She was reaching for her bag and rummaging for her purse. "And maybe a pain au chocolat?" She held up a ten-pound note.

"I think I can afford that." Sadie smiled with a little more ease about her. "Still taking one sugar?"

The question hit Natalie hard. Sadie still remembered something so trivial about her, but then she considered, didn't she remember everything about Sadie?

"Yes, never managed to kick that habit."

"Well, it's not going to kill you and clearly hasn't done you any harm." Natalie's eyes widened at the compliment, but she didn't respond before Sadie said, "I'm gonna…" She began backing away and Natalie was reminded of the Sadie of old. "Tea and pain au chocolat, got it," she repeated.

Natalie smiled as she walked away.

"Breathe," she said to herself just as her phone rang and the train began to pull away from the station. "Harriet?"

"Nat, we've had Davina Gorman on the phone wanting to connect next week. I know she's not your favourite—"

"Goodness, she's eager. I literally left her at the hotel less than an hour ago. I said to call me next week." She huffed to herself. "It's fine. Yes, I want to speak with her regarding some new products, but make sure it's Wednesday or Thursday. I really don't want to ruin my weekend."

Harriet chuckled. "Of course. I'll make sure Bina organises that."

Natalie looked down the aisle to make sure Sadie wasn't returning. "H, you know I told you about my younger years and about—"

"The one?" Harriet said instantly, and Natalie had to wonder how often she'd talked about Sadie over the years for that to be the first thing Harry thought of.

"Yes." Natalie smiled as she leaned out into the gangway and checked to make sure she wasn't going to be overheard by the woman in question returning. "Sadie."

"That's the one. What about her?"

"She's buying me a cup of tea and sitting opposite me on the train, and I may have had a drink with her earlier in the week."

"Woah, what the fuck? Natalie, that is insane. It's like you've manifested her."

Natalie rolled her eyes. Harriet was a great friend but her penchant for believing in the weird and wonderful was often over the top.

"I'm not sure about that, but I will admit that it is a coincidence I'm happy about."

"So, what ya going to do?" There was just a hint of a Scottish accent when Harry got excited about something.

"I've no idea," Sadie admitted.

Chapter Fifteen

1999 Train to Brighton

"Have you been to this shop before?" Nat asked, staring out of the window as the drizzle hitting the outside and the condensation on the inside set about racing each other to the bottom. So far, the condensation was winning, due to the rain being blown sideways.

"No, but a friend has and said they've got a lot of things there we might like."

Natalie turned to face her. "Like what?"

Sadie checked who was listening before leaning forward. Natalie mirrored the move. "Like vibrators and stuff."

"Stuff?"

Sadie shrugged and sat back in her seat. "I think there's a lot of things we might not be interested in yet."

Natalie thought about that for a minute.

"Like what?"

Leaning forward again, Sadie whispered, "Like bondage stuff. Handcuffs and whips."

Natalie's eyes bugged, and her mouth gaped open.

Sadie chuckled. "Don't worry, we're not—"

"Handcuffs?" Natalie mused. "Why would anyone want to use those?"

These were often the moments Sadie loved best, the innocence and curiosity battling to understand something that Sadie knew would make her blush.

"It's a control thing I guess." Sadie shrugged, trying not to sound like she knew too much about it, because she didn't. Only what she'd read in magazines or overheard people at the bar say. A lot of people were into it apparently.

She never wanted Natalie to feel inferior, and equally didn't want to scare her off with the things she kind of knew about.

She watched Natalie's face as she considered that.

"Why would you want to control someone? Is it a bad thing?"

"No." Sadie shook her head and moved across to sit next to her. "It's a trust thing, I suppose. Like, let's say…" She twisted around in her seat and faced her. "If you couldn't escape and I had permission to do anything to you, anything we've agreed to do, then you could just…let yourself go, in your head I mean."

"Okay, but you already have permission, so..." She frowned at Sadie.

"True, but I guess when you're unable to move it makes it a little more…I dunno, erotic? It doesn't have to be handcuffs. You could use a belt, or rope, or—"

"I get it," Natalie said before following up with, "Do you want to do that to me?"

"Tie you up?" Sadie asked, before shrugging. "I dunno, do you want me to?"

"I like everything we've done so far, and I do trust you, so…" She shrugged too. "I'd let you, if you wanted to."

Sadie nodded. "Let me know if you ever decide that you want to."

"The next stop is Brighton."

Sadie stood up and held out her hand. "Come on, this is us."

Walking through the lanes hand in hand felt exciting and illicit to Natalie. Far enough away that her Aunt Lina wouldn't see or hear about it, she felt free and happy.

"What are you smiling about?" Sadie grinned, pulling her closer and wrapping her arm around her shoulders.

"Just this, being here with you and being able to be me."

"Your aunt is a tough cookie."

Natalie shrank away.

"Hey, she's not here. This is Brighton, we can do whatever we want here. Look." She pulled her close and kissed her on the mouth quickly. "See, nobody cares."

"I wish I could be—" Natalie looked away. "I want to be like this always, but I can't, not yet."

"Well, right now, it's just us and sex." Sadie laughed, pulling her to one side of the road where a single-fronted store stood with a big red light flashing in the window. "This is it."

A look of fear flew across Natalie's face.

"You wanna do something else?" Sadie asked, looking around to see where else they could go. "Milkshake?"

Natalie rolled her eyes. "I'm 18. We could go to the pub, but…" She shrugged and moved closer to Sadie. "I want to get the…so we can…"

Sadie grinned. "Come on then."

She pushed the door open, and they wandered in, a little unsure what to expect.

Three men turned to face them. One was reading a magazine with a photo of a woman with huge breasts. He leered at them both and slowly let his hand drop down to his trouser pocket. The other two sneered at them and whispered to each other before they started kissing aggressively.

"You sure this is a place for women?" Natalie whispered, scooting closer to Sadie.

"Doesn't matter. We know what we want, and we're just as entitled to be in here as them," Sadie said loudly enough that at least the one reading the magazine could hear. "Come on." She dragged Natalie to the counter and with her chin held high, she waited until a woman old enough to be her mother swanned out from the back room looking like she worked the bar on Coronation Street.

"If you kids are here to piss about, you can fuck off," she said, looking from Sadie to Natalie and back again.

"That's not very polite, is it?" Sadie said. "If you must know, we want to buy something."

The woman pouted at them until Sadie pulled a rolled-up wodge of cash from her pocket. "Alright, what d'ya want?"

"Strap-ons."

"Fuck yes," the dirty mag man said from their right. He'd moved closer and was eyeing them both up like a lecherous creep. "Which one of you's the man then? Can I watch?"

Sadie turned to Natalie. "Come on, let's go." She took her hand and went to walk away but was tugged back. "Nat?"

Natalie was glaring at the man.

"Nat, come on."

Turning to Sadie, Natalie said, "We came to buy something, and we're going to buy it." Rotating back to the woman she said, "Where can we find the strap-ons?" Then she turned to the man. "And you can take your filthy paws and keep them in your pocket."

Chapter Sixteen

2024 LNER train en route to Euston

With her head in her laptop, Natalie didn't notice Sadie's return until the waft of her perfume hit and the shadow of someone standing beside her caught her attention.

She looked up and smiled at Sadie, who was holding out a cardboard cup and a paper bag.

"Thank you," Natalie said, taking it from her. She tried not to think about how close their fingertips were to brushing against each other.

Itching to touch.

"They were all out of pain au chocolat, so I got you a croissant and flirted with him until he handed over a pack of Nutella." Sadie smirked. "There's a plastic spoon in the bag," she finished as she took her own seat again. "They didn't have a knife, so you'll need to make do."

"I am grateful for your initiative." Natalie opened the bag and with her fingertips, she inched out the flaky pastry and placed it on top of the paper bag. "Would you like some?" she offered.

Sadie had settled back with her coffee cup and stared out of the window. Now she turned her head slowly to face Natalie. "No, thank you. I don't eat until two."

"Oh. Should I not…"

"I'll be fine. Please, enjoy your breakfast." She reached into her bag and pulled out a book, opened it, then closed it again and placed it down onto the table. "I wanted to say something, if I may."

Natalie stopped, spoon poised to spread the chocolate onto the piece of pastry she'd torn, her heart racing.

"Sure."

Sadie placed the cup down and pressed her lips together before she looked at Natalie again.

"The other day I said something I'm not proud of and I wanted to apologise for that. I was out of line to question why you said sorry. I should have been more gracious and accepted the apology."

"Well, I don't think you said anything that wasn't true." Natalie placed the spoon down onto the paper bag along with the piece of croissant. "I don't have many regrets in life. I learned my lesson on that the hard way." She smiled sadly and looked away towards the window.

The train had slowed.

"I thought this was the express train, straight through to Euston," Sadie queried.

"It is," Natalie responded with curiosity. They'd now come to a complete halt. "Probably a signal issue."

Sadie chuckled to herself quietly. "Do you remember that day we went to Brighton on the train?"

Natalie smiled at the memory too. "Yes."

"God, I thought I was going to have to fight our way out of that store."

"Well, he was a foul creature." Natalie laughed. "Reading dirty magazines in the shop…who does that? Buy it, take it home and read away to your palm's delight."

Sadie laughed properly then, and Natalie thought it just as beautiful now as it was back then.

"He's probably dead now," she added for a punchline.

"You're probably right," Sadie said, still finding it funny. "I've still got it, you know."

Natalie eyed her quizzically.

"What we bought. I kept it. It's in a box somewhere," she admitted. "Isn't that crazy?"

"Probably." Natalie smiled, but the thoughts and questions and ideas that swam around her head at that nugget of information were mind-blowing. She needed to say something equally as thought-provoking. "But we all have a memory box, don't we?"

The driver's voice crackled into life over the Tannoy. *"Ladies and gentlemen, just to let you know that we are currently held up due to a points failure along the line. We should be on our way again quite soon. If you'd like to take the opportunity, we have a café car at both ends of the train. Otherwise, sit back, relax and let the train take the strain."*

"I guess that answers that question then." Sadie's smile dropped, and much to Natalie's dismay, the previous conversation seemed to be over when Sadie picked up her book again.

Almost an hour had passed, and the train still hadn't moved. Natalie was busy typing away her report.

Sadie sighed and peered into her empty coffee cup as Natalie instantly looked up at her.

"Time for another?" Natalie asked.

Sadie considered it, checked her watch and then nodded. "Yes, why not."

Grabbing her purse, Natalie jumped up. "My shout." She was about to ask if Sadie would watch her things, but considered that was probably a given.

"Chai latte, if they have it. If not, I'll have a plain latte. I guess."

Natalie smiled down at her. "Coming right up."

With Natalie gone, Sadie picked up her phone and scrolled through the numbers until she found the one that she wanted and dialled.

It took less than three rings before it was answered.

"Darling, where are you? I was hoping we'd have lunch."

"Sorry, sweet pea." Sadie smiled and let her head fall backwards at the sound of the Portuguese accent that still lilted the perfectly spoken English. "I'm stuck on the bloody train."

"Oh no, that's horrendous."

"I know, so we'll probably have to skip the lunch. We've been here an hour now, and god knows how long it will take."

"Okay, that's not a problem. I can wait, and we can have dinner, yes, if these old bones can last that long."

"Oh, enough of the old and the woe is me. You're as fit as a fiddle."

"I'm retired, Darling, I'm entitled to a little woe is me."

"Well, I will be home at some point. Shall I order in, and we can watch that show you keep yapping on about?"

"You'll love it. Gillian Anderson, I know how much you love her." Gillian Anderson was indeed an attractive prospect, but the reason she was so attracted to her would be situated not more than three feet from her when she returned with their drinks.

"Alright, I'm game for it. Oh, and don't forget I'm away again soon, though I could probably commute."

"You know they'd come to you if you insisted."

"Maybe so, but I like the travelling aspect of my work," Sadie answered. "And I like my privacy when I'm not at work."

There was a deep laugh down the phone. "You like the getting off aspect of your work."

"That too. Now, I must go. Chai awaits."

"Bye, Sweetie."

She closed the call just as Natalie arrived back with her drink.

"No chai I'm afraid," Natalie said, handing her the cardboard cup. "They've run out."

"Well, isn't today just full of disappointment." Sadie huffed. "Thank you though."

Natalie tried not to speculate as to whether she was part of the disappointment.

Chapter Seventeen

1998 Geneva

The summer holiday was supposed to be fun. At least it was for her friends at school. With it being their last year of A-levels and most of them already eighteen, they were partying and going on exciting vacations, unlike Natalie who still had several months to wait.

Instead, Natalie had been summoned to see her father.

Her mother was of course not here, choosing this week to sun herself in Monaco, no invitation to join her. Not that Natalie wanted to be there among the elite of her mother's circle of so-called friends. More like her audience. People she could enjoy showing off to. Once upon a time that had included Natalie. But she'd grown too big and "too opinionated" to be trusted around the grown-ups, who "didn't want to hear what a child had to say."

She'd been waiting for fifteen minutes already when finally, the double doors opened, and the manservant stepped in to wait for her father's entrance.

She often wondered what it would have been like to grow up poor. Poor but loved, and not an inconvenience to her parents.

"Natalia. You've come home," he said as though that had been a choice she'd made all by herself. It wasn't. This wasn't home. This was a summons, and one she knew she couldn't ignore, not if she wanted to continue living in England.

"Yes, Father," she said compliantly. She'd learned a long time ago that arguing with him only ended badly for her.

He studied her for a moment. "You've grown."

She imagined her friend Alice quipping, "No shit, Sherlock," but held her tongue and smiled instead.

"Come, sit." He pointed at a chair opposite. "Lina tells me that you are doing well. School is good, yes?"

She nodded. "Yes, I enjoy it very much, and I am hopeful that I might be able to attend university. I've applied—"

"Good, that's what I wanted to talk to you about." He nodded and read something on his desk. He picked up the phone and rattled off a swathe of instructions to do with the paperwork he'd just read. "Oxford, Cambridge, St Andrews, Geneva."

It took a moment to realise he was talking to her. "But you said I could go to Chichester."

He sat back and steepled his fingers. "It wasn't a negotiation, Natalia. My daughter will attend a prestigious university, or she will return home and begin an internship within the company."

"But…I'd be able to stay with Aunt Lina and—"

"Don't argue with me, young lady," he snapped. "You are educated because I say so, and I say where and when."

She bristled and tried not to cry. Just over three years and she would be free; until then, this was who she had to deal with.

"You'll apply yourself, get the grades you need, and you will attend one of those universities. The applications have been sent. In the meantime, you may return to Lina." He stood up. "I have a meeting to attend in Bern, so I need to go. Your flight is booked for this evening. Hans will take you to the airport."

"And Mother?"

"She's staying in Monte Carlo." He waved her off.

She watched him leave the room. No hug. No kiss goodbye. No term of endearment. Just a list of instructions on how her life would be for the next three years and five months.

Sighing, she thanked every star above that she still had almost another year in Sussex with her friends. She would at least get to celebrate her 18th with them, unless she was summoned back again. And maybe, she would be able to persuade him to let her stay where she was.

Keeping on side with Aunt Lina was imperative, even if she was hard work and no fun.

"Miss Shultz, your car is ready." Hans, the tall, blonde, bespectacled groveller her father employed, smiled at her from the doorway. "I've already had your bags loaded."

Of course he had. She didn't know why she'd bothered to pack at all.

"Thank you," she said, walking past him out into the huge marble foyer. She'd always hated this house when she'd been little. If she never saw it again, it would be a day too soon.

Walking outside, she got into the car and closed her eyes. She liked Geneva, she really did, but it wasn't home. It had never been home.

Chapter Eighteen

2024 LNER train en route to Euston

From her vantage point, peering from behind her book, Sadie watched Natalie go about keeping herself busy. It was obvious that she found the entire situation as awkward as she did.

"You know she's a curious little creature. She's desperate to talk to you, to ask about your life," her internal monologue said, creating a back-and-forth conversation only she could hear.

"Maybe so, but I'm not ready to divulge my secrets just yet."

Her life before and after Natalie was two vastly different adventures.

She turned a page. She hadn't read it, but she needed to look as though that was what she was doing. Natalie's left hand came up and she pushed a strand of hair behind her ear, only for it to fall again.

"No ring."

She'd noticed that the other day at the bar too. In all the years they'd been apart, she'd always assumed Natalie would get married. The way her family were, it seemed the logical conclusion.

It was strange also, that in all those years, Sadie had never taken a moment to find out. It was easier not to know. It would be simple nowadays, with social media and everything that ended up on the internet. Natalie would surely have an online history, but then, she reminded herself that she didn't.

No social media. One email for personal use, one for business. One website that didn't contain details of who she was. Sadie Swanson was a mystery if you wanted to find her.

Now though, as she watched the woman who had been, and if she were honest, probably still was the love of her life, she realised that she wanted to know everything about her.

She glanced down at her phone. *"It would take a few seconds to pick it up, open the screen and type in Natalie Shultz and see what popped up,"* she thought. *"But that would be dangerous, wouldn't it?*

That would open a can of worms that potentially, you don't want to deal with."

"Because the more you know about someone, the more you will get attached and you already made that mistake with Natalie, didn't you?"

Every so often, she'd catch Natalie glancing at her from the corner of her eye.

"She wants to talk to you," Sadie said to herself, *"You'd get to ask all the questions you have, maybe get the answers to understand it all."*

She really did want answers. She'd never understood, not really. They could have made things work, couldn't they? Or was she so naïve and optimistic that she couldn't see the bigger picture, the landscape from which Natalie had been making her decisions?

"All you'd have to do is put the book down and look at her. She'd be willing to talk the moment she noticed, and she would notice."

She closed her eyes and let her head fall back against the seat.

"This isn't the place for the conversations we need to have."

Opening her eyes, she scanned the train carriage again. Three men in suits, all on laptops. A younger couple off to somewhere exciting were chatting and laughing about something nobody else could hear. A woman much like Natalie, in business attire and working.

"Ah, so you admit there is a conversation you need to have."

"There's always been a conversation needing to be had."

"If an opportunity arises, I might take it. But I'm not initiating it."

Her phone chimed.

A message had come through. The sound caused Natalie to look over at her with a half-smile. It took everything not to let herself get lost in the greenness of those eyes again.

A client.

Instantly grounded.

Chapter Nineteen

2024 LNER train en route to Euston

The heavy sigh made Sadie look up and stare as Natalie rubbed at the back of her neck.

"You alright?" she asked.

Turning to Sadie, Natalie smiled slowly. "Sorry, yes, I'm fine. I was just thinking about something."

Sadie placed the book down open on the table and slid her glasses up into her hair. This was the opportunity, wasn't it?

"Wanna talk about it?" she asked in a tone that said she was genuinely interested.

Natalie considered that.

What she would have given to have heard those words every day of her life for the past twenty-five years? And she wanted to talk to her, didn't she? Wanted any excuse to start a conversation. To show Sadie the woman she had become and how that had happened, and how she would never do again what she'd done back then.

But nerves got the better of her and she asked, "You want to listen?"

"Got nothing better to do," Sadie answered, clasping her hands together and turning slightly in her seat, giving Natalie her full attention. "Only if you want to share, of course."

"Alright," she said slowly as she considered what to say. "I was thinking about the last time I saw my father."

"When was that?"

"Fifteen years ago." She stared impassively.

"That's a long time to not see him."

Natalie nodded. To anyone with a normal upbringing or good parents, she supposed it was a long time.

"I never felt…safe with him or my mother, or Lina. I'm not sure any of them ever had my best interests at heart, and I didn't see them often anyway, so..." She let her words drift away as she was reminded how safe she felt with Sadie. Even now, she was eager to share and let her walls down.

"That must have been a lonely existence." Sadie's voice brought her from her thoughts.

Natalie shook her head. "No, I was never lonely. Not once I went to boarding school anyway."

"I remember you said you were four when you were sent to the UK to go to school."

Natalie smiled, another snippet of information Sadie remembered about her.

"Aunt Lina came and collected me. Took me on a plane to England and I started school the very next day. That was kind of fun. Until then I'd been at my parents' home in Geneva by myself."

"Your parents weren't there?"

"No. The staff cared for me mostly."

Sadie looked genuinely sad. "That's awful. I wish you'd told me."

Natalie smiled. There was so much she wished she'd told her. So much of each other's lives they'd missed out on because Natalie had made the biggest mistake of her life.

"I was loved more with those people paid to care for the house than I ever was by my own parents. The staff spoilt me, played with me, read to me. I had more parents than I knew what to do with." Natalie smiled at that memory. "With Lina, it was less fun, but school meant friends and playing. I liked that."

"How is the delightful Aunt Lina?" Sadie asked, trying not to grimace and failing.

"She died, 12 years ago."

"Oh, I'm sorry to—"

Shaking her head, Natalie said, "Don't be. Nobody else was. She wasn't a nice woman."

"No. I remember." Sadie leaned forward. "So, going back to your dad, why haven't you spoken to him?"

"He ruined my life, so I ruined his."

Sadie sat forward, grinning. "Well, that sounds like a story."

Chapter Twenty

2009 Paris, Cheval Blanc Hotel

It had been a decade since she'd seen him. Ten whole years where she had worked and focused and gotten herself into the position she was right now. And she couldn't be happier about it.

Her parents would both be at the hotel. She hadn't seen her mother, other than in magazines, in over ten years, but she was easily recognisable by the loud voice making demands on staff.

Natalie followed the waiter through the restaurant and took a seat without waiting to be asked. She wasn't that scared little kid anymore. Her father couldn't threaten her. He had nothing to hold over her now. His grip on her had vanished the day she'd turned twenty-one.

"Natalia," her mother said loudly, grinning and glancing around to see who was looking in their direction.

"It's Natalie. I took the English version when I was twelve," Natalie said, pulling her gloves off and dropping them into her bag. She smiled tightly at them both. "I assume I've only got a few minutes of your time, so I'll be quick."

"Natalia, there is no need—"

Ignoring her mother, she looked into her father's cold, steely eyes. He was in Paris schmoozing a member of the National Rally, the French version of the National Front in the UK. She felt sick just looking at him.

"I wanted to tell you both face to face," she began, holding his gaze for the first time in her life. "I'm a lesbian," she said loudly enough for the tables around them to hear her.

His face grew red instantly. Her mother's mouth gaped open.

"Shut your filthy mouth," he hissed at her, eyes darting around to see if anyone else heard her. She hoped they had.

She smiled. "I'm 28 years old, Father. I don't have to do what you tell me anymore. I don't need you to support me. In fact, I have used Grandmama's money wisely and invested in starting my own business."

He wiped his mouth and threw the napkin down onto the plate, hissing his words through gritted teeth. "You will do as I say."

Ignoring him, she continued, "I've opened a store. Selling sex toys. And I'm going to be opening more. I'm building an empire of dildos and vibrators, and I'll be sleeping with more women, and making sure that the entire world understands that I'm your daughter."

She pushed her chair back and stood up.

"You insolent little bitch," he said venomously.

Pausing just long enough to unsettle him some more, she said, "You ruined my life more times than I can count. You won't do it again."

"Natalia…" her mother said with no real interest.

"And we will never see each other again," Natalie said, turning on her heel and striding away.

Outside, Harriet leaned against the wall, waiting. When she saw Natalie, she pushed off and grinned.

"Well, how did it go?"

"That was the scariest, and most exhilarating thing I have done in the last decade," Natalie said, letting Harriet hug her.

"I'm so proud of you. Now, are we going to get some lunch? Because I am starving, and you promised a fancy restaurant and a boat down the Seine."

"Natalia!" Her father shouted her name as he ran from the restaurant to confront her outside. "You are dead to me, you hear? Dead."

The words hurt, of course they did. It was finally confirmation that there was no love lost here.

"I've been dead to you since the day I was born. What makes you think anything you say now has any impact on me?"

Harriet linked arms with her.

"You disgust me." He sneered at them both.

"Good." She smiled, remembering back to the time she'd told that old pervert off when she'd been with Sadie. She'd felt empowered then, like she did now. "Because you've disgusted me my entire life, and now, I don't have to think about you ever again."

As they walked away, the emotion of it all began to creep out. Every step, she gripped harder at Harriet's arm. Her friend held her up.

"Head up. Keep walking, babe. You can cry, but you keep walking, and you keep your head up."

"I will." She sobbed.

She was finally free of them all.

Chapter Twenty-One

2024 LNER train en route to Euston

Sadie's eyes widened and she now understood why she should have let curiosity get the better of her and look Natalie up online.

"You own Come Again?" Sadie asked. "All of it or a franchise store?"

Natalie chuckled. "All of it."

"Wow, I'd never—" She tilted her head at Natalie. "No, that's a lie, you absolutely would."

"I admit that it was satisfying to totally embarrass my father, but he wasn't my reason for creating the business."

"Okay, are you going to tell me how the most sophisticated, privately educated young woman got herself into the sex trade?"

Now Natalie laughed wholeheartedly. It wasn't often anyone described her as a member of the sex trade. She kind of liked it; anything that would bring shame on her father's political ideas was a good thing in her mind.

"It was you, actually," she said. "I really did remember that day in Brighton, when we went to buy the strap-on and how awful an experience it was." She lowered her voice for politeness. "And what stuck with me most was how, I walked in there with the most confident girlfriend. Someone I wanted to explore things with, and in a moment, it was all shattered." She kept her gaze on Sadie's face as she spoke. "The way you seemed to shrink and asked for us to leave."

Sadie remained passive. Just listening.

"I wanted to create an experience where women never had to endure that. Where they could walk inside and know they wouldn't be shamed or judged or leered at."

"That was why I wanted to leave, to not have you feel that; it was bad enough that I felt it, but you…you were so much braver than I was." Sadie smiled as she cottoned on to something unsaid. "You bought that Brighton store we went to, didn't you?"

"Yes, I knew it had to be the first one. To remove that other place from existence and make a point." She found herself smiling again. "And every time I open a new store, I take out a full-page ad in my father's favourite newspaper."

Sadie put her hand to her mouth to cover the laughter. "That's hilarious."

"I'm planning to open a store in Geneva next year for his 70th birthday gift. Not that I hold a grudge." She smirked. "It makes good business sense."

"Wow, you are…" Sadie's lips pressed together as she thought about what she was going to say next. "I always knew you'd be a success. You just had that fire in you to keep fighting." She looked away suddenly. "I guess that's why it was so hard when you wouldn't fight for us."

It was a fair statement, Natalie concluded, but it hit like a bullet train racing through Tokyo. She felt the shame of it all over gain and closed her eyes.

"I'm sorry, I didn't mean to upset—"

"It's fine. It does upset me. I made a hash of things but even now, I know that I had no other choice. The alternative wasn't something I was prepared for."

"Ladies and gentlemen. We would like to thank you for your patience today. I can now happily inform you all that we will be moving in the next few minutes. The issue has been fixed and there should be no further delays. We are expecting arrival at Euston to be 2.56 this afternoon. Again, we would like to apologise for the delay."

Natalie smiled at the news.

"I want to talk about this with you, if you want to, but not here," Natalie said. "Have dinner with me next week. I'll cook, and we can talk, and I'll explain everything and answer any questions you have. I owe you that much."

"It's not that I don't want to, but—"

"I get it. You don't need to explain, honestly." Natalie smiled sadly. She'd had a glimmer of hope for a moment.

"I just can't do next week; I'm busy with work, but I can do this weekend, if you have some free time, or the weekend after."

"Oh. I—" Natalie reached into her bag and pulled out her diary, flicking through the pages until she found today's date. "Is Sunday too soon? I mean, I can do Saturday at a push. I just need to move some things around and—"

"Sunday would be fine," Sadie said quickly. "Shall we say three?"

"Yes. That works." Natalie jotted it down into her diary. "I'll cook lunch…if it's after two, so you can eat then, right?"

"I can." Sadie smiled.

"You're not…I mean, are you vegetarian or anything now?"

"No, but I am allergic to shellfish."

"Ok, good." Her eyes bulged as she realised how that sounded. "I didn't mean good that you're allergic, I mean…I wasn't planning to cook shellfish." She took a deep breath. "I'm sorry. You must think I'm an absolute idiot. It's just…I've wanted this moment for so long, I can't actually believe it's happening."

"Yes, it certainly wasn't what I was expecting at the start of the week."

Chapter Twenty-Two

2024 Amberfield, Natalie's home

Natalie stood at the window watching the street for Harriet's arrival. Her ex-wife and now best friend and colleague would be bringing breakfast, coffee and a bucket load of common sense.

Because Natalie Shultz was all out of that after this week's events. Sadie Swanson was coming to lunch tomorrow afternoon. They'd swapped numbers and Natalie had given her the address and then they'd shared an awkward moment on the station concourse where neither knew whether to hug, shake hands or just walk away.

In the end it had been a half hug/air kiss with both flushing a gentle crimson and a promise to see each other soon that had left Natalie feeling anxious. This was not an opportunity she could afford to fuck up.

The little silver Fiat slowed as Harriet looked for somewhere to park, and Natalie went to the door, unlocking and leaving it ajar for Harriet to let herself in when she finally found a space.

It didn't take as long as she thought it would before the cheerful voice made her smile.

"Cooee, anyone in?" Harriet called out, knowing full well that Natalie was indeed in.

"In the living room," Natalie called back but walked towards the door to greet her all the same. "Did you bring—"

"Coffee? What do you take me for?" She presented two cups in a cardboard carrier.

"A lifesaver." Natalie grinned, taking the cups from the carrier.

"That as well, maybe; however, I am here for all the tea, so, start pouring." Harriet flopped down onto the armchair. "Oh, pain au chocolat." She put the paper bag down onto the coffee table. "Not that you couldn't have made the coffee here."

"It's not the same," Natalie said.

"Fair. Okay, spill it. What happened?"

"It was surreal really," Natalie began. "The morning I arrived at the hotel." She stared out of the window remembering it all vividly now, "Just as the car pulled up. I noticed her." She turned back to Harry and smiled, "I mean, I thought it was her. I couldn't be sure, obviously it's been twenty-five years, but I was so convinced." She smiled.

"She can't have changed much then," Harriet said, glancing toward the framed photograph that had always sat on the sideboard for as long as Harriet had known Natalie.

Following her gaze, Natalie stared at the image. A photo her friend Alice had taken at the pub. Sadie had her arm slung around Natalie's shoulder, pulling her closer as she whispered something funny into her ear. They'd both laughed, and Alice had caught the unguarded moment perfectly.

"She's as gorgeous as she was, but maybe now there is an air of confidence about her that she hadn't quite fully grown into back then."

"You still fancy her then." Harriet chuckled.

"God, yes. She's…I don't think we ever stop finding someone physically attractive, do we?"

"I guess not. So, she's still hot. How did you reconnect?"

"She didn't see me that morning, but later, I saw her again. This time she was heading to the lift, and I called out to her. She turned but didn't stop and I assumed that was that. She either didn't recognise me or didn't want to speak to me."

"You don't look any different. She definitely would have recognised you."

"True, I've avoided the grey." She laughed, running her hand through her hair. "Anyway, after stewing in my room for over an hour, I decided I'd go and feel sorry for myself in the bar, and just as I was looking to order a late lunch, she was there."

"Just in the bar or specifically to see you?"

"To see me, I think." She couldn't hide the smile that stretched across her face. She reached for the pastry, "It was awkward but good to see her and to open the door to talking again."

"So, what was she doing there?"

"Oh, I don't know. I was so thrown by it that I didn't actually ask. She looked very much all business though. Sharp tailored suit and perfectly put together."

"Maybe she sells adult toys too." Harriet laughed. "Wouldn't that be crazy, if you'd both ended up in the same field?"

"Right now, I'm not discounting anything. It all feels very—"

"Universal," Harriet said knowingly. "Like it's all in the stars." She spread her fingers and moved her hands apart. "Fated lovers, bound to find one another again."

"Or just a happy coincidence." Natalie smiled at her friend. "Whatever it is, I'm just glad I'm getting the opportunity to maybe put things right."

Chapter Twenty-Three

1999 Amberfield, Aunt Lina's house

She closed the door behind her as quietly as she could, but of course, Lina heard. Natalie wondered sometimes if the woman had supersonic hearing like a bat. She looked like a bat, all pinched in the face, dark and brooding.

"Natalia," she called out, and Natalie sagged. "Come here."

Natalie took her shoes off and hung her coat on the hook before she shuffled into the kitchen. "Aunt Lina, everything okay?"

Her aunt sat at the small table with a glass of hot chocolate in front of her. She'd never understood why Lina had agreed to take her on and bring her to England. She didn't have a maternal bone in her body.

"Your father called. He wants you to know that it will be St Andrews. And you will be leaving on the 20th and start classes in September. It's all arranged, you will have a room, sharing with another girl who is a daughter of a friend of your mother."

Natalie felt the air leave her lungs.

Two weeks.

She'd tried not to think about it, burying her head in the sand, hoping that her father would change his mind, that she would eventually be able to convince him that staying with Lina was for the best, but even then, she didn't think she would have to worry until the start of September.

"I need to speak to him," Natalie said urgently, trying not to cry.

"That's not possible. He's terribly busy, you know this." Lina sipped at her drink without a care in the world, not understanding or caring about how much of Natalie's world was being ruined in this moment. "You are to have your things packed and ready. There will be no arguments about this, Natalia."

"I'm not going. I won't go," Natalie said defiantly.

"Then you will return home to Geneva tomorrow." Lina sneered at her. "You think you can make demands?"

"I won't go."

Lina shrugged. "Then you're on your own and you can leave right now. But remember, you take nothing with you. No clothes, no phone, no books. Nothing. Everything you have is provided for you by your parents, and your father has been clear, you will go to St Andrews, or go home."

"You can't do—"

"Yes, I can. This is my house; you are here as my guest. I have been paid by your father to provide you with the things you need, including your allowance, which will stop immediately. You will leave this house with the clothes you are wearing, only because I would not wish to embarrass my neighbours by stripping you bare."

Natalie's eyes went wide. "You wouldn't dare."

"Try me. My agreement to this ended when you turned eighteen, but I am forced to still have you here." She stood but leaned on the table with her palms. "My 14-year sentence is over."

"What are you talking about?"

Lina shook her head. "Oh, you think out of the goodness of my heart I wasted 14 years of my life here for you to be educated?" she scoffed. "I owed my brother, and he made me pay him back by dumping you on me."

"Owed him for what?"

"That's not your concern, but this is business, and my contract is over the minute you leave."

Natalie felt sick. The rush of adrenaline from being out earlier and spending time with Sadie, Alice and Tom was gone. Her entire being shook.

Without another word, she turned and ran up the stairs to her room. Flinging herself onto the bed, she cried like she hadn't cried ever. Fat tears streamed down her face, soaked up by the pillow she pushed her face into to muffle the sobs.

"I hate you," she said into the pillow over and over. The image of her parents and Lina swam in her head.

When there were no more tears left to shed, she sat up and wiped her face.

There was nothing she could do. Was there?

Chapter Twenty-Four

2024 Outskirts of Brighton, Sadie's flat

Sadie slipped off her coat and pulled her boots off with a sigh. What she needed now was a hot bath, a pair of baggy sweatpants and her favourite hoodie, and a night on the sofa with Blanca.

"That you, Darling?"

"Of course it is, who else would it be?" Sadie smiled to herself. Poking her head around the door, she found her laid out on the recliner, blanket over her lap and her cat, Muffy, on her lap. "You look comfy."

"We haven't moved for three hours, have we Muff?"

"I see you found the pastel de nata." Sadie grinned at the crumbs and the empty silver trays.

"A girl gotta eat."

"Yeah, yeah," Sadie said humorously, bending to kiss the top of her head. "I'll get us some dinner, shall I?"

"That would be nice. You did say you would order in."

"I did, didn't I? What do you fancy?" Sadie asked, pulling her phone out of her pocket.

"Is that burger place open?"

Sadie ruffled Muffy's head and said to the cat, "Mummy wants a burger, what do you think, Muffs?" Putting the phone to her ear and listening as it rang.

"Muffy thinks I can have anything I want, cos she knows she's going to get some."

"Oh, hello, yes." Sadie smiled at the recognition of her number in their system. "Yes, Blanca wants her usual. And I'll have the spicy bean—" She stopped to listen to him. "Uh huh, that's right. And how long will that be?" She let him answer. "Great, thank you."

Disconnecting the call, Sadie pushed her phone back into her pocket and looked around the room. It looked exactly how she'd left it. The puzzle she'd left out on the table for Blanca was untouched.

"Is it on its way?" Blanca asked.

Sadie smiled. "Yes. So, if you need the loo, now's the time to go while I sort out some plates."

"I'm okay." She fidgeted and Muffy glared at the disturbance but didn't move.

Narrowing her stare at the older woman, Sadie asked, "Did you remember to take your medication?"

Grey, watery eyes stared up at her. "I did."

"Okay then. I'm going to get changed into my comfies and then we can catch up. I have something I want your advice on."

"You know how much I love to do that." Blanca chuckled as Sadie left the room. "Hopefully she met someone who wasn't paying, eh, Muffy?"

Muffy didn't answer.

"Someone who might kickstart that frozen heart," she called out.

"I can hear you!" Sadie shouted from her room before she wandered back in. She was out of the business attire and into her favourite sweatpants and hoodie. Her hair was piled up in a messy bun and she had a handful of cotton pads, wiping at her make-up. She sat on the couch, crossed legged.

"We just want you to be happy. I'm not going to be around forever."

"You'll be around for a while yet." Sadie smiled, and then sighed, putting the small mirror and the wipes down into her lap. "You remember when we met?"

"How could I forget? I been stuck with you ever since." Blanca grinned at her with eyes that still held enough mischief in them. "It was a warm night; the beach was still busy, and you were sitting on the sand looking like the world had dropped out of your arse."

"You talk utter shit at times."

Blanca cackled. "I know, I get bored." She got serious and said, "It was Chino's bar, on the beach. The only lesbian hotspot for miles and you had spent almost the entire summer there, shagging your way through the tourists."

"Good memory." Sadie nodded and picked up her make-up removal again.

"And you were sad because you'd run out of money and once the summer season was over, you'd have no work at Chino's."

"Yes, and we all knew how you made a living."

"I took you under my wing." Blanca grinned. "And I was a hot chick back then."

"Stop fishing for compliments." Sadie laughed. For a woman in her late sixties, Blanca Alfonsa, aka Mae to those she mothered, was still a dashing woman. "Anyway, that's not what I want to talk about. Do you remember why I was sad when I arrived?"

"Some idiot had broken your heart."

Sadie nodded. "Yes, and that idiot was at one of the hotels I visited. We talked and I'm having lunch with her tomorrow."

"Well, now we have the beginnings of a story."

Chapter Twenty-Five

1999 Amberfield, Sadie's flat share

"What's the matter?" Sadie asked Natalie almost the moment she turned up on her doorstep. She looked like she'd booked a holiday in Spain, and it had rained the entire time.

"Nothing's the matter, why?" Natalie frowned and then quickly leaned in and began to kiss Sadie as though her life depended on it.

Sadie wasn't complaining; she'd never get tired of kissing Natalie. But on the doorstep, and within full view of any of her roommates should they wander past? She didn't care, but she thought Natalie would.

She usually would.

"Wow, that's a greeting." Sadie laughed and pulled her inside. "Come on, let's go to my room."

Natalie's nose scrunched as she glanced around the room at all the empty beer cans and pizza boxes. "How do you live like this?"

"By not being here." Sadie laughed as she tugged Natalie up the stairs and pushed open the door to her very tidy and clean room.

"Can we just stay here tonight and not go out. I want…I want to be with you," Natalie said once the door was closed.

Sadie shrugged. "Alright. We can do that. Let me call the guys and I'll order us a pizza, yeah?"

Natalie smiled. "I'd like that."

Sadie went downstairs and picked up the house phone. A mobile phone was too expensive on her budget right now, but one day she'd have one, she thought as she dialled the pub's number.

"Hey, it's Sadie. Can you let the gang know that I'll be stopping at home tonight, and I'll catch up with them later? Thanks."

She closed off the call and then dialled the pizza shop and ordered a mighty meat feast. Catching sight of one of her flatmates, she said,

"Hey Bony, I'm gonna be in all night, yeah, so no parties."

"Yeah, man," he said with a slow nod. "I'm just gonna be here with my spliff, alright."

"Okay cool," she said before grabbing two cans of Coke from the fridge and heading back upstairs. At the top of the stairs, she paused. Something was definitely up. She could feel it, and see it. She just hoped that Natalie would trust her with it.

The last thing she wanted to see was Natalie struggling with something. She opened the door and almost dropped the tins of Coke.

"Bloody hell," she said with a chuckle, not expecting to find her girlfriend with the strap-on round her naked hips.

"I wanted to see what it felt like," Natalie said before unclipping it and letting it drop to the floor. "You always wear it, and I was curious."

Sadie put the drinks down onto the dresser. "It's okay. I was just surprised, that's all." She picked it up. "I didn't think you'd want—"

"Oh, I don't," Natalie said quickly. "I just…I wanted to know what you felt like with it on."

"Okay. So—" She raised a brow. "You're naked and—" She bent down and picked up the belt with the dildo. "Did you want me to put—"

"No," Natalie said quickly. "No, I just want you." She moved toward Sadie and took the belt from her, dropping it back to the floor. "Your hands and mouth, on me, in me. I just – I want you," she said looking up into Sadie's dark eyes. "Is that alright?"

"Of course it is. I love you. Anything you want I'll give you," Sadie answered before kissing her. A soft, sensual kiss that pulled them closer to one another.

Natalie's eyes moistened with emotion. "I love you, so very much. Never forget that."

"How could I forget that? I'll have you here to remind me every day." Sadie grinned as she stripped off her clothes. "Are you going to tell me what's wrong?"

Natalie jumped onto the bed. "Just my parents, nothing important." She smiled and then squealed when Sadie launched onto the bed beside her and kissed her over and over until Natalie was laughing.

"I don't like you being sad," Sadie whispered.

"Then make me smile." Natalie grinned up at her. "Do that thing you do with your—" She gasped when Sadie's fingers teased her clit. "Or you can do that."

"How about I do it all?"

"That sounds indecent." Natalie giggled before she groaned at the featherlight touch of her lover's fingers. "Yeah, let's do that."

Staring down at her, Sadie slowed her movements.

"I love you."

Natalie's eyes closed. "I love you."

Chapter Twenty-Six

2024 Amberfield, Natalie's home

The kitchen windows steamed up when Natalie lifted the roasting tray from the oven, and the beef joint cooking in it sizzled and hissed. She stabbed it with the temperature prong, and satisfied it had reached the cooked stage, she lifted it onto a rack to rest.

The potatoes were already parboiled and shaken, covered in flour and ready to go into the hot oil.

She'd been unsure if cooking had been a wise idea, unsure further if Sadie would even want to eat at all by the time she was done explaining after all these years, but she had to admit, it had given her something productive to do to fill her time waiting.

Of course, Harriet had popped around earlier, wanting to make sure that Natalie was okay and not about to blow a gasket over the whole thing.

It was funny to Natalie, that her ex-wife was the one panicking for her, but then she remembered that the wife part really hadn't been a very thought-out thing. Another reaction to her life back then when she hadn't felt in control of anything. Harriet was her best friend, and nothing would change that, or the way Harriet was so protective of her.

She slid the potatoes into the oil and gave them a quick turn before putting the baking tray back into the oven and closing the door. Veg was prepared and just needed a few minutes to cook. She'd debated making Yorkshire puddings but decided it was a whole heap of mess that she didn't really need today.

With everything done, she untied her apron and left the kitchen. She caught herself in the hallway mirror, the full-length one she had salvaged from Lina's before the house had been emptied and sold by her father.

Thinking back to the day she'd taken it, and the days before that when she had nursed Lina, she wondered what the woman would think of her now.

Lina's illness had come on aggressively and quickly. She'd been surprised when Lina had called and asked to see her. Curiosity was the only reason she'd gone, but empathy had kept her there.

Aunt Lina was a miserable, mean-spirited woman, but she had had her reasons, most of which were unfathomable and cruel. She'd not had an easy life before taking on her brother's child.

Her own child, the product of a vicious assault that still traumatised her on her death bed, had been taken from her and given away. She would not bring shame to the family; her brother had seen to that and solved the problem and for that, she would be in his debt. It had felt incredibly cruel that she'd been forced to raise his child instead.

Running a hand through her hair and then straightening her dress, Natalie gave herself an approving nod just as the doorbell rang out.

As she walked towards the door, she could see the outline of her through the frosted glass. There was no mistaking her even now after all these years apart.

Reaching for the handle, she took a couple of seconds, composing herself. She was ready for this. She'd been ready for this for two decades.

When she opened the door and said, "Hi," it took everything in her not to gasp as Sadie spun around, obviously not expecting the door to be opened so quickly.

"Hey." She held up a bottle of sparking apple. "I didn't know if…" Her words trailed away, and she smiled. "Hi."

"Come on in," Natalie said, stepping back and making room for her guest to pass. She watched as Sadie took it all in while hovering in the hall, unsure where to go. "Can I take your coat?"

"Yes, good idea," Sadie said. Handing off the bottle, she dropped her bag to the floor and shrugged off her leather jacket to reveal a blue and white checked shirt that paired perfectly with the bleached jeans and stiletto-heeled cowboy boots.

Natalie took the coat and hung it before leading Sadie to the lounge.

They both stood there, looking somewhat awkward.

"Shall I open this?" Natalie eventually asked. She'd planned on wine with lunch, but this would work just as well.

"Sure, that would be nice," Sadie answered, still glancing around her.

Natalie tried to imagine what she would be like if this were the other way around and she was getting a first peek into Sadie's world. It would feel surreal, and she'd want to know everything, see everything, touch everything.

"I'll be right back. Please, make yourself at home."

Chapter Twenty-Seven

1999 Amberfield, Sadie's flat share

Making love, until Natalie appeared in her life, hadn't been something Sadie had done much of. It had always been sex. Raw, passionate, carnal even. But now, it was all she could think about.

Tenderness and pleasure, the way her lover's body responded to her, sent jolts of excitement through her own nervous system. Hearing Natalie's whimpering and mewling as she writhed and contorted to every touch of Sadie's fingers and mouth and tongue meant Sadie could almost come without anyone touching her.

She'd never understood the power of being able to give someone else that amount of enjoyment, but now she did. It was thrilling, but even more so because she loved this woman.

She loved her like nothing she had ever loved before. And she felt loved in return. Lying there in her arms, she felt the warmth of it all rush through her.

If they could get married, she was quite sure she'd be planning on asking Natalie to be her wife.

Twisting, she snuggled into Natalie's side and whispered, "I love you."

It was something she'd said many times, and yet, on this occasion, she felt something different. Natalie stiffened. It was minute, but it happened. Sadie lifted onto her elbow and looked down at Natalie. Her eyes squeezed shut.

Her mind went back to earlier when she'd arrived, and Sadie had felt it then too. Something was amiss.

"Nat, please tell me what's wrong," she said, keeping her voice gentle. She didn't want it to feel like Natalie couldn't tell her anything.

For a moment there was no response. And then Natalie sat up and threw the covers back. She started to pick up her clothes and pull them on.

Sadie watched, wondering what the hell was happening. And then her world fell out from under her.

"We can't see each other again," Natalie said.

"What?" Sadie scrambled to the edge of the bed and reached for her, but she backed away. "Nat, what are you talking about?"

"I said what I said, we can't…I have to go. I love you, but I have to go."

Nothing had ever impacted Sadie as much as those words had. Not when her parents chucked her out, not when she'd lost jobs or been dumped by other women. This was nuclear. This was something she'd never felt before.

Natalie looked at her, tears streaming down her face.

"I'm sorry," she choked out, and then she opened the door and left. "There's nothing I can do."

Sadie got up and grabbed her robe off the back of the door. She pulled it on and was out on the landing half-naked as she followed Natalie down the stairs, almost breaking her neck at the bottom when she lost her footing and had to jump the last two.

She barely caught up and just managed to hold the door shut before Natalie could open it and get out.

"Nat, what's happening? I don't understand." She knew she was crying, felt her facial muscles tense and hold as they crumpled and tried to squeeze her eyes closed.

"Sadie, you have to let me go," Natalie said, her voice now cool and calm. Her face was passive and unemotional.

"Fine," Sadie said, taking a step back. She was Sadie Swanson; she didn't cry over girls. And she didn't beg anyone for anything. "Go then."

She turned away and trudged back up the stairs, her heart pounding as it cracked and broke. She couldn't watch Natalie leave her. When the door opened and then closed again, Sadie bent and looked down at the door, hoping and praying Natalie would be standing there still. But she wasn't; she was gone.

Making it into her room, she fell back against the door, slid down to the floor, and sobbed until she had nothing left.

Chapter Twenty-Eight

2024 Amberfield, Natalie's home

Sadie watched Natalie leave the room. It felt strange to be here, to finally begin to find the answers to the many questions that had haunted her all these years. It was weird to suddenly be immersed in everything Natalie Shultz again. And yet, it felt all quite natural too, almost like she'd always been here.

When Natalie reappeared, holding two glasses, Sadie was still nosing at photographs, one of which had caught her eye. An image of them both at the Rainbow bar.

"That was a good night, wasn't it?" Natalie said, looking at the photo as she moved in beside her. She handed Sadie one of the glasses and then picked up the framed image. She smiled at it, like she always did, remembering back to the night.

"Yes, it was a lot of fun." Sadie smiled but looked away. She sipped her drink. "I'd forgotten about the photo," she said more as something to say to break the awkward silence.

Natalie placed the frame back down again and turned to Sadie.

"I know this is difficult and honestly, I've no idea where to start, so can we just say that no question or comment is off the table and that anything can be asked at any—"

"Why did you leave?" Sadie blurted instantly. It was the biggest question she had that needed an answer, the burning unknown that had haunted her. "One minute we were making love, the next you're telling me it's over and we won't see each other again, and then you were gone with no explanation. Why?"

Natalie nodded. "That's as good a place as any to start." She smiled and sighed all at once. "Okay, shall we sit?"

She waited until they were both settled, drinks placed on coasters on the table. One sat at either end of the sofa, legs crossed towards one another, but Sadie wrapped her arms tightly around herself. She knew she looked tense, and the way Natalie was looking at her said she noticed too.

But neither moved to comfort the other. That wouldn't be appropriate at all. She focused on Natalie's mouth and listened as the words began to spill out.

"I've gone over and over and over in my mind, how I would explain it, and now that it's come down to it, I don't quite know how to word it." Natalie fiddled with the ring on her finger again.

"Just start from somewhere," Sadie blurted. She wanted to scream at her *just tell me, I deserve to know*, but instead she kept calm and once more focused on Natalie's mouth and then her eyes.

"Yes. It's all so…the answer is that my father moved me to St Andrews. He'd hinted previously that I could stay with Lina and attend a local university, but despite my protestations he'd secured me a spot at St Andrews, and I was sent there with barely any notice. I thought I could persuade him to change his mind, and when he wouldn't, to my shame, I didn't know how to stand up to him. My choices where go to St Andrews and remain in the UK, getting the education I wanted, or go home and work for him. There was no way that I was going to go to Geneva and work for him; he terrified me."

"You could have stayed with me," Sadie interrupted. "I'd have—"

Natalie shook her head. "I wasn't bold like you. I didn't know how to be anyone other than who they said I could be, and I had no escape. Lina made it clear when I said I wouldn't go, that I would leave her house with the clothes on my back and nothing else. And I was only getting those because she didn't want to upset the neighbours with my nakedness."

Sadie raised her brows. She'd never liked that woman. There was always something cruel about her, so it was not really a surprise that that was how she would react, but still, they were just things. Material things they could have replaced.

"You could have stayed with me; we could have worked it out together," Sadie repeated, feeling the frustration begin to build.

"I couldn't just turn my hand to anything to support myself. I couldn't work in a bar, that wasn't me, and I didn't want that to be me. I wanted to go to university. I wanted to make something of my life."

Sadie huffed and stood up. "Because being with me would have meant living a shitty existence?"

Natalie stiffened. "No—"

"No?" Sadie said as the hurt from all of those years ago vomited out. "What was it -I just wasn't enough for you? Not good enough for your world?"

"That's not—" Natalie got up too and took a step towards Sadie, reaching for her, but she was shrugged off.

"You left me!" Sadie screamed each word. "Just walked away like I didn't matter. Can you even begin to imagine how that felt?" Her eyes bored into Natalie until she looked away.

"I—"

"Of course not. You never looked back, did you?"

Natalie's face turned red, the glare steely as she shouted, "I couldn't! Otherwise, he would have hurt you." She got up and paced quickly towards the window.

Sadie sat silently, watching as Natalie's shoulders rose and fell twice.

"He had a photo of you, and he made it very clear that if I didn't do as I was told…you would pay the price."

"And you believed him?"

Her hair whipped as Natalie swung around. "Of course I believed him. And I wasn't going to risk finding out for sure."

Natalie retreated into herself. Sadie watched as an air of coolness filled Natalie's being.

Stoic and passive.

"I would have given you everything," Sadie said in frustration, her shoulders sagging as a feeling of melancholy came over her. "I'd have done anything for you, to make things work for us, but you didn't even care enough to say a proper goodbye, to tell me where you were going." She pointed a finger at Natalie as the anger rose again. "You should have told me. I'd have gone with you."

For a moment, silence filled the room again.

"Are you just going to stand there and say nothing?"

"Are you finished screaming at me?" Natalie asked, still not moving.

Sadie nodded.

"I didn't know what that life might have been. And I wasn't ready, or capable of being brave enough to find out until it was too late."

"What do you mean?"

"I was naïve and pathetic; I know that now. And I had this ridiculous idea that if I could just get to my 21st birthday, everything would be okay. I'd have my degree, I'd have my grandmother's inheritance, and I'd find you again, and I wouldn't care about my father, and we'd—" She closed her eyes at the memory. "But I couldn't wait that long, and I came back, after Christmas. You weren't here."

"What do you mean you came back?" Sadie interjected. "Why didn't you just call me?"

"I did. I called the moment I didn't have someone watching me. I left a message with Bonehead, or whatever his name was. I called lots and it was either unanswered or one of the potheads said they'd tell you."

Sadie sagged. "I never got those messages."

"I assumed you just didn't want to talk to me, that you were still angry with me, and when I came back, you were gone."

"You really came back?"

Natalie nodded. "As soon as I could. I had to get through the first term and then I got a train—"

"You came looking?"

Natalie nodded. "Yes, but you weren't there. I had to go back and the following term, I was summoned home, and each term after that. I couldn't come back again until I finished university and got my grandmother's money.

"The minute the paperwork was signed, I didn't even wait for the money to hit my bank account. I got on a train, and I came here again, and I went to your old house, but there was a new set of students living there. And so, I went to the pub, but nobody there even knew you, and I thought that was odd, but then as I was leaving, I bumped into Tom, and he said you'd gone travelling years ago and nobody knew where."

"I went to Europe."

"Well, I had no idea where to look then, and I convinced myself you wouldn't want me to find you if you'd gone that far away."

They sat for a moment in silence, each with their own thoughts, before Sadie said quietly, "I gave you a week to come back to me and tell me you didn't mean it, but when you didn't come, I went to your aunt's house, and it was empty, just some furniture left. You were gone and I had nothing to stick around for."

It was Natalie's turn to listen. To hear the other half of their story play out.

"So, I packed a bag, withdrew my savings and got a flight to Spain." Sadie felt her throat tighten and the threat of tears prickle in her eyes.

"I never wanted to leave you." Natalie's eyes bore into Sadie. "I bought this house. I started my business here. I thought you'd come back at some point, and I'd bump into you somewhere and we'd work it out. But that never happened."

"I would never have come back here," Sadie answered. "And I never thought that you would have."

"My biggest regret was how I left things with you." Natalie stepped forward again, her voice finally cracking, and this time Sadie didn't move. "It was cowardly. I just…you were so lovely to me, and we'd just made love and I'd never felt so cherished…and then it hit me, I was leaving." The dam burst and the tears fell. "I felt like I had no choices, no control, because even if I stayed, I'd just be reliant on you rather than him. I wanted so much to be in control of my own life."

"I would never have controlled you."

Natalie smiled through her tears. "I know you wouldn't, but my life would still have felt out of control." She held Sadie's stare as she spoke. "We'd have lived in your tiny bedroom surrounded by your housemates' mess, with you working all hours to pay bills and buy me clothes because I'd have literally had nothing," she implored. "You couldn't afford a mobile phone. How was I going to ask you to buy me all the things I needed to go to university?"

"I would have found a way." Sadie felt herself becoming defensive again and breathed it out.

Natalie nodded, sniffed, and wiped her face. "Yes, you would have. And I didn't want that for you. I didn't want your life to become saving me." She sighed. "I needed to save myself."

"But you could save me?"

"That was different - that was an actual threat against you."

Chapter Twenty-Nine

1999 Scotland, St Andrews University

The car pulled up and for a moment, Natalie considered just staying put and refusing to move until she was taken back to Sussex, and more importantly, to Sadie.

The driver had already gotten out of the car and was unloading her bags. It was just herself, and her father in the back.

"I don't want to be here," she said quietly.

"What you want isn't in question, Natalia. This is what you need," he answered.

Reaching into his pocket, he pulled out an envelope. As he opened it, Natalie could see that it was a photograph. He slid it across to her.

Picking it up, she felt her heart race. It was a photo of Sadie.

"You will stop with this disgusting behaviour. You will stay here, and you will never contact her again, because if you do, Natalia, if you bring shame on my name," he poked Sadie's face in the photo, "it will be her that suffers. Do I make myself clear? This…" His face scrunched in disgust. "This filth ends now."

"I love her," she said desperately.

He scoffed. "Love? You have no understanding of love. This infatuation with someone like this…" He flicked the photo with his finger. "No daughter of mine will be a pussy-eating, vulgar—"

"I'm not vulgar," she finally snapped. "How dare you describe what Sadie and I have as though it's—" The sharp sting across her cheek shut her up instantly.

"Don't ever speak to me of this again. It's over, Natalia. You will find a boy, a handsome, rich boy with influential parents. Fuck him if you must, but you find the right boy to bring into the family. Someone with political leanings that align with—"

She stopped listening. There was no way she was sleeping with boys, for him or for herself. He could go fuck himself.

"...don't let me down. You study hard, fuck nice rich boys and then we will see what you are made of."

She opened the car door and began to step out when the photo of Sadie was snatched from her fingers. She turned back to him and watched with tears streaming her cheeks as he tore the image into pieces.

"Remember, I have eyes and ears everywhere," he said, opening his own door. "Let's go inside."

Natalie wiped her face and tried to hold it together. There was nothing more she could do other than protect Sadie from her father.

Opening the door to her room, she looked around with no real interest. It was like living in a castle, but she felt nothing like the fairy princess she'd always dreamed of becoming. Nothing like the queen she'd been when Sadie looked at her.

There were two single beds. Two desks, and places to store clothes and books. It all looked very nice and homely, but home wasn't here, was it? She'd thrown that away when she'd uttered those words and broken Sadie's heart.

She placed her bag down onto the bed on the left and then sat beside it.

"You'll be sharing with Lotte van Berg's stepdaughter, so behave, do as you've been told, and we'll have no more problems," her father said. He reached into his pocket and pulled out another envelope. "Credit card and phone. All the numbers you need are programmed in. I will receive the bill and know who you are calling." The inference that if she attempted to call Sadie, he would know. "There is £1000 in cash. You will receive £500 per month as an allowance."

"I hate you," she said, looking up at him with tears in her eyes.

He stared at her as though those words meant nothing to him, or that she hadn't even spoken. "Work hard, Natalia. Or return home to Geneva and I will find something for you to do to earn your keep."

With that, he took one more look around the room, waited for Hans to place her luggage down onto the floor beside the bed, and then he turned and left.

Less than a minute later, a blonde-haired head appeared around the door, a sad smile on the face of its owner.

"Alright?"

Natalie nodded. "Yes, thank you."

The head's body appeared, and it walked into the room. A hand reached out. "Harriet," she said. "Harriet Appleby. I'm next door."

"Natalie Shultz."

"So, I couldn't help but overhear…" Harriet screwed her mouth up awkwardly. "Your dad?"

"Legally that is who he is, yes."

"Yeah, I've got one of those." Harriet smiled kindly. "Thinks he knows everything, bossy as shite and a bully."

Natalie chuckled. "Yes, very much like that."

"Well, seeing as we're both new and have so much in common already, I decree that we are now best friends for the duration." She held her hand out again. "Deal?"

"Deal."

Chapter Thirty

1999 Amberfield

It had been six days since Natalie had dropped her bombshell.

Two of which Sadie had spent on her bed curled up in a ball, crying her eyes out, screaming into her pillow and wallowing.

Day three, she'd finally gotten up, showered and gone to work, where she was an absolute mess and told to sit out the back for most of her shift.

By day six, she'd given up hoping that Natalie would change her mind and come back. Instead, she'd decided to take things into her own hands and call her.

She waited until her housemates were out and then she slid down the wall in the hall with the phone in her lap and dialled the number to Natalie's mobile phone.

"The number you are trying to call is unavailable."

"No, this can't be happening." She hit redial.

"The number you are trying to call is unavailable."

She slammed the handset down and lifted it again, dialling the number for Lina's house. It just rang out. She redialled; it rang unanswered.

Getting up, Sadie squeezed her feet into her trainers without untying the laces. She grabbed her wallet and coat and headed out.

It was still sunny out, another balmy late summer's evening. She waited at the bus stop for what felt like an eternity and then had to endure the ride across town, sitting next to a man who clearly hadn't heard of deodorant.

By the time she got to the stop closest to Natalie's aunt's house, the sun was just starting to dip.

She jogged most of the way, until a stitch in her side put paid to that and she had to slow her pace or pass out. But eventually, she was there, standing on the street outside of the terraced house.

Nausea hit her instantly when she noticed the for sale sign that was now attached to the side of the gate. The bins overflowed with rubbish bags and household items like old lamps and pictures from the walls.

Slowly, she pushed the gate open and walked the short path to the door. She pressed the doorbell and waited. Hands in her pockets, shoulders hunched as she moved nervously from one foot to the other.

No answer.

She rang it again. Still no answer. Bending down, she opened the letter box and looked through. It looked empty. The telephone table that used to sit in the hallway was gone. No phone in the socket. No coats hanging on the hooks.

"You alright there, love?" a voice said from behind her. She turned and found an older woman staring at her over the fence.

"Yeah, was just looking for my friend."

The woman shrugged. "Well, they all moved out earlier in the week. Didn't leave a forwarding address."

"Right, that explains it then." Sadie took one last look at the house and wandered back down the path.

"Good friends, was ya?"

"Yeah. We were…" She glanced up at what had been Natalie's bedroom window.

"Aw, well good luck. I hope you find them again."

"Thanks," she mumbled as she forced herself to keep walking. At the end of the street, she stumbled into the alleyway where they'd shared their first kiss and crumbled, shattered, to the floor.

Her heart was broken as she sobbed and stuffed her fist into her mouth to stop the helpless cry that she screamed from being heard and drawing attention.

Chapter Thirty-One

2024 Amberfield, Natalie's home

"So, are you hungry? Do you still want to eat with me?" Natalie asked. She checked her watch; the potatoes should be perfect by now. "I just need to cook some vegetables."

"It smells delicious," Sadie replied, reaching for her glass again. She took a long swig.

"Alright, I'll just organise that then." Natalie stood up and headed for the kitchen. "Feel free to nose around some more," she called back.

Sadie chuckled, already half out of her seat to do exactly that. There was a unit with cupboard doors and drawers that was covered in framed photos. She perused them all, noticing the difference in age Natalie was in each of them and feeling another gut punch that she'd missed it all.

Birthdays, holidays, nights out with friends they'd have made as a couple. So much time gone.

The picture on the end had been taken not that long after they'd lost contact. She still had the same hairstyle, though slightly longer. With her was a blonde woman her own age and a couple of lads pulling faces in the background. Everyone was smiling or laughing, but it was obvious that Natalie was faking it. The smile wasn't how Sadie remembered it.

"That's Harriet," Natalie said from behind her. "She was the first friend I made at St Andrews. We're still friends, she works for me." Sadie watched as she looked away and fiddled with her hand. "Actually, she's my ex-wife, but it's not—" Natalie looked to the ceiling.

"Right," Sadie said, trying not to let the jealous reaction show. Someone else had been important enough to marry.

"It wasn't…we were stupid and did it on a whim," Natalie explained quickly. "We realised very fast that it wasn't what either of us wanted and we had the marriage annulled. And it's just something we laugh about now."

Sadie said nothing, still emotionally reeling from everything.

"Have you…I mean did you meet anyone, get married, meet someone?" Natalie stammered the words out.

Sadie placed the photo back down in its place.

"No, nobody special enough that I wanted to marry." She held Natalie's gaze as she said, "Only you."

She regretted it immediately, not because it wasn't true or needed to be said, but because of the reaction. Natalie's face flushed, her eyes watered and she took in several shuddery breaths.

"I'm sorry, I shouldn't have—" Sadie's hand reached for her like a magnet had just lifted it up and pulled it forward until it was inches away. She yanked it back. It wasn't appropriate now, not her place anymore.

"It's fine. I just…I wasn't expecting that." She turned and left the room again, leaving Sadie to rue the comment.

"Fuck," Sadie muttered. Turning on her heel, she followed Natalie out of the room and into the hallway. She listened for sounds and followed the clanking of pans and plates until she entered the large kitchen and found Natalie dishing up. It smelt delicious.

"I'm sorry. I don't know why I said that," Sadie said once she reached the other side of the island. "It was inappropriate."

Natalie looked up at her. "Did you mean it?"

"That you'd have been the only one I'd have considered marrying?" Sadie clarified. When Natalie nodded, she said, "Yes, I meant it. You were my world and if it had been legal and you hadn't left, and we'd still been together when it became legal, I'd have married you." She waited for Natalie to look at her again before she said, "Yes."

Natalie continued to dish up, silently piling roast potatoes into a porcelain pot. Several matching pots were already in use with enough broccoli and cabbage to feed half a dozen people.

"I married Harriet because I was lonely, and I didn't think I'd ever meet anyone like you again." She stopped doing what she was doing and looked at Sadie. "She was the closest person in my life. We'd been friends for years and never once crossed that line. Then she came to Paris with me, when I told my father that I wouldn't see him again. We got drunk on a riverboat on the Seine and ended up in bed together."

"Romantic at least." Sadie smiled and began to pick up some of the pots, following Natalie into a small dining room.

"When we woke up the following morning, both a little sheepish, we talked it through and decided why not give it a chance. We both loved each other, we were best friends, and we both had nobody else that we wanted. Three months later we thought getting married was the sensible thing to do. We both had shitty fathers and we both knew that if anything happened to either of us, potentially those idiots would have a say over us."

"Makes sense, I guess."

"No, not really. I discovered afterwards that actually I could just make her my power of attorney and vice versa. We weren't even intimate with each other during the marriage. It was all ridiculous, really."

"You must love each other very much, to want to protect each other like that."

They'd brought the last of the plates and pots through and took their seats.

"Yes, I suppose so." Natalie smiled. "She really has been the best friend that I needed."

"I'm glad you found someone like that," Sadie said, "I have a similar friend. She lives with me. Her and her pesky cat." Sadie grinned. "She took me under her wing when I needed it."

Chapter Thirty-Two

2001 Portugal, Chino's Bar

Spain had been fun, and Sadie had made her way around the coast, working bars and clubs for a bit of cash and then enjoying the opportunity to lose herself in the bustle of tourism. There was always a woman willing to occupy her and keep her mind off Natalie and the heartbreak she had caused.

She'd grown her hair out over the months she'd been away, and let a street hawker braid it, the beads rattling anytime she shook her head. Which was fun when she was dancing the night away and forgetting all about the reasons she was still here.

But Spain had been last summer, and then she'd gone to Italy for the winter season, lost the braids, and ended up in a small town not far from the Swiss border, though she'd never ventured across. That would be too much of a Natalie reminder. Up into the mountains where the skiers and snowboarders had arrived though, she could keep herself busy. She'd never been one for snow sports, but the tips had been good and when that season started to end, she was almost tempted to head home and use what she'd saved to find a room or a small flat.

The problem was, she still wasn't over it. The hurt, the longing, it was all still there. So, she'd got her bag packed and shared a car ride with a couple of others heading off elsewhere to Turin. From there it was trains and buses until she arrived in Lisbon.

"Where's the best place for work and gay bars by the sea?" she asked a woman reading a newspaper at the first gay bar by the sea she'd come across.

"What kind of work are you looking for?" the woman asked without looking up at her.

Sadie shrugged. "I'm skilled at bar work, but I've helped out at clubs and done some cleaning and stuff. Just looking for a way to pay for a room and some beers."

Finally looking up, the woman smiled. "If you work the bar well, the beers take care of themselves." She laughed. "Blanca. And you are?"

"Sadie, and yeah, you're right."

Blanca appraised her a little. "You know, you're pretty. If Luis took you on, you'd have half the lesbians of Lisbon buying you a drink."

Sadie blushed a little. "I dunno about that," she said, but the reality was, she knew how to let a woman buy her drinks all night, and she wasn't unhappy about the transaction that usually came with that.

"He's the tall man in the corner with the cigarette. Tell him Blanca said to talk to him, and he'll give you a job."

"Thanks." Sadie reached down and grabbed her bag.

"You'll be needing somewhere to sleep too. I have a room I rent. It's not much, but it's cheap and clean."

It was Sadie's turn now to check out the virtual stranger who was being so helpful. Much older, maybe in her forties, but still good for the years. She had dark hair and eyes, her skin tanned by the coastal sunshine.

There was something classy about her, an elegance that belied the bar they were in, which was far more set up for the younger crowd.

"You're wondering why an old woman like me is offering you a place to sleep."

Sadie smiled. "No, I was wondering whether I could trust a beautiful woman who was offering me somewhere to sleep."

"Oh, you come with the charm! Not many British have that around here." Blanca laughed and stood up. "Come, I introduce you to Luis and then you tell me why these eyes look so sad."

Chapter Thirty-Three

2024 Amberfield, Natalie's home

Natalie placed her knife and fork down gently on the plate and wiped her mouth on the napkin. Dinner had been a series of small talk and discovery and furtive glances at one another. It was sweet, and shy, and something she wanted to explore. If it had been a date, she'd have considered it a good one, one she'd want to repeat again.

"I think that might be the first time we've actually eaten together," Natalie said, studying Sadie now as she delicately cut into the last potato on her plate.

Sadie smiled as she glanced up. "Not counting crisps at the Rainbow, and pizza on my old bed, you might be right."

Blushing, Natalie said, "Or picnics in fields."

Natalie began to organise the bowls, emptying the leftovers all into one and stacking the others, ready to take to the kitchen.

Passing her plate across, Sadie said, "That was delicious, by the way."

"Thank you. Harriet taught me to cook. I'd never had to before, I was always a boarder and therefore meals were provided, or I was with Lina, and I ate what I was given. In Geneva, we had staff for that, so…university life was a bit of a life lesson."

"Can I help with washing up?" Sadie asked, reaching for a plate just as Natalie reached for the same one. Fingertips touched and Natalie snapped back her hand. "Sorry, I—"

"No, it's fine, I just—" Her eyes raised up until she was staring straight at Sadie. "Did you not – I mean…" She shook her head at herself and glanced at her hand, expecting to see flames. Was she being ridiculous? That feeling that felt like a bright ember had just ignited the moment their fingers met.

"I felt it," Sadie acknowledged, holding those eyes to her own. "I felt it when we touched, it was…" She swallowed. "I felt it."

Natalie pushed the plates to one side and sat back down again.

"I never stopped feeling it, Sadie, you must believe me. No matter what happened in my life, I never lost those feelings I had – have, for you."

Sadie flicked her fringe away, feeling irritated by it, or by the words, Natalie wasn't so sure, but she kept talking.

"I'm aware that a lot of water has passed under the bridge for us, and I am also aware that I'm the cause of that," Natalie continued. "But I have missed you every day of my life, and I have regretted every day of my life also, that I wasn't brave enough to hold on to you. I let my father and aunt bully me, and for that I will always kick myself."

Sadie considered Natalie's words before she spoke again.

"I can't pretend that what happened between us wasn't the happiest time of my life, but equally I can't pretend that how things ended didn't hurt me."

"I'm sor—"

Sadie held up her hand and cut her off.

"It didn't just hurt me, Natalie, it broke me. When you left like that, with no explanation, when you were just gone? I didn't think I'd ever get past it. And it took years. It took sleeping my way around Europe and changing my entire personality in order to come out the other side. I'm not even sure I am who you think you love anymore."

"No, I can see for myself how different you are now."

Sadie half smiled. "And if I'm honest, I think if you really knew the real me now, I'd probably not be someone you'd want to associate with."

Natalie looked confused. "What? Why?"

"We both made choices. The paths our lives have taken are similar, and yet, not the same. I'm not ashamed of anything I've done in my life, but my life isn't set up for romance and falling in love anymore." She stood up. "It was good to catch up, and thank you for the explanation—"

Natalie moved fast, up and out of her chair and around the table until they were face to face. "Don't go. Tell me you don't want to kiss me. That all these lingering looks between us over dinner meant nothing. That you're only here because you wanted an explanation and not because you're as curious as me about what might be."

When Sadie said nothing, but didn't move away, and her eyes flicked down to Natalie's mouth, Natalie knew nothing was stopping her from taking this chance.

She closed the space between them. Her hands wrapped gently around Sadie's neck, sliding up until her fingers cupped both cheeks. She held her in place, pressing her lips firmly against Sadie's, enjoying the feel of them again after such a long time apart. The spark ignited the fire that had lain smouldering all these years.

She'd barely had time to register it before she felt the movement of Sadie's hands around her waist, pulling her closer as their mouths opened and welcomed each other's tongues inside like old friends who'd missed one another. Each was instantly reminded of how the other liked to be kissed.

It was dreamlike, this moment she had thought about for years. The opportunity to once more be wrapped in Sadie's embrace, kissing her. Her hands slid upwards into Sadie's hair, holding on for dear life in case she made the foolish mistake of once more letting go of her.

Flushed and panting, Sadie pulled away. "I can't," she said quickly. "We can't do this again." She stepped backward and Natalie felt the icy cold slither over her once more.

"Sadie, please, let's talk—"

"No, I can't, I've got to – I have to go. I'm sorry; I can't."

Chapter Thirty-Four

2024 Outskirts of Brighton, Sadie's flat

"Back so soon?" Blanca called out when Sadie closed the front door.

"Yes, it was only lunch," she said, knowing full well that it was never going to just be lunch. She hung her coat and then entered the living room.

"Lunch turns into dinner, turns into bed, turns into—"

"I don't think that was on the table." She could lie with such ease when it meant keeping her heart safe.

"Oh please, you've loved this woman for almost three decades. It's always on the table."

Sadie said nothing, but there was no fooling her dear friend. Blanca's eyes, wrinkled and watery, narrowed at Sadie.

"Are you going to tell me, or shall we dance around it and pretend that whatever happened hasn't got you all troubled?"

Sadie lifted the crystal decanter on the sideboard and poured two glasses of Macieira and handed one to Blanca.

"We kissed," she admitted, knocking the brandy back and swallowing it down like it was a shot. Blanca said nothing, and she hated when she did that, because she knew the reason was to force her to say something more, which of course, she would now do. "We kissed, and it was – too much, so I left."

"You left?"

"Yes, I left," Sadie said defensively, heading back to the decanter to refill.

"Why did you leave?"

She put the glass down and pressed her palms against the top of the sideboard. "Because I couldn't handle it. I'm not used to…it isn't…it's too—"

"Emotional?" Blanca offered.

Sadie nodded. "Yes, I can't – it's easy with clients, I just switch that off and it's never emotional, it's never me giving anything of myself—"

"Except your body," Blanca said. "You can't lie to me, darling. I know, remember?"

Sadie turned to her. "It's different, it's not—" She huffed. "My body is just a physical pleasure. Nothing inside is involved, no love, no hate, no interest other than making it an experience worth their money and my enjoyment. It's an act, a performance, and I can't perform with her. I can't pretend it doesn't affect me being around her, and I can't give her, her money back and apologise for the inept response she's going to get if she pushes this."

"Pushes this? Did she force you to kiss her?"

"No."

"So, you had a nice lunch?"

Sadie nodded silently.

"And you talked?"

"Yes, we talked." She sipped the drink this time.

"And you got some answers?"

"I got answers, yes," Sadie confirmed. "Her father made her leave. She could either go away like he wanted, or go home with him, or leave with the clothes on her back. She had no choice but to go, and she regrets not standing up to him and fighting for us."

"And then you kissed." It wasn't a question. "Sounds to me like you had a nice time and maybe those same old feelings are still there."

Sadie downed what was left of the drink. "Of course they're still there, but I can't just let her back in like that, I can't." She slammed the glass down and wrapped her arms around herself. "And when she asks how I make my living, what do I tell her then?"

"You're a whore, so what?" Blanca shrugged. She spoke with no malice, no shame or disdain, just simple facts. "Every woman has sold herself in some way or another. Sex is always a transaction darling. I told you this many years ago." Blanca smiled at her. "And you just said yourself, she left you because she wanted something only her father could give her. She understands transactions and how they work."

"Not quite the same as fucking strangers for money."

"You feel ashamed?"

Sadie twisted around to face her. "No, I—" She looked away. "No, not ashamed, maybe just…the way she looks at me, like I'm still that twenty-year-old kid and now I'm not. And I'm not sure how, or if, she can put the two together and come away with…" Her words trailed off.

Blanca smirked. "There is still love there, I think. You want to impress her, to be the woman she wants. Don't deny yourself the chance to find some happiness with her." Blanca lifted her glass. "This was never a career for life, Sadie. Things can change. You can change."

"Maybe I don't want to change."

"The dream was always the cottage. You're almost there, and then what?"

"Then I'll think about retiring."

Blanca grinned. "My stubborn child."

Chapter Thirty-Five

2001 Portugal, Chino's Bar

Sadie yawned as she flopped down into the chair at Blanca's table. Her sunglasses were hiding the hangover and lack of sleep.

"Well don't you look like shit, Darling?" Blanca laughed and pushed a glass and the jug of iced water towards her.

"You know, I could go off you," Sadie said, but took the glass and filled it. She swallowed it down in one and poured another instantly.

Blanca smiled at her. "Burning the candle at both ends just leaves you in the dark." She indicated the sunglasses.

Sadie sighed. "It's true. I need to think about my options. Chino's pays well enough, and the tips are okay but it's long hours, and if I want to actually enjoy this part of my journey then I need to have a better balance of work and play."

"You always have options, Darling." Blanca sipped her coffee.

"What? Be like you?" Sadie scoffed. It was no secret what Blanca did to earn a living.

Blanca shrugged. "Tell me something," she said, leaning forward and putting her cup down. "You come to work, spend all day on your feet, cleaning, wiping, pouring drinks and then when that's all done and you've earned your money, you find a girl and you let her buy you drinks all night and then, you let her take you back to her hotel where you sleep with her, and you think what you're doing is any different to me?" She laughed and sat back in her chair. "Sex is always a transaction, Darling. I just know how much sex with me is worth, and it isn't a few cheap cocktails in a sleazy bar."

Sadie sat open-mouthed.

"I've never looked at it like that."

"Of course, because then you'd have to acknowledge that you're a whore, and a cheap one." Blanca grinned widely at her. "And you need to lay off the alcohol. You want to go home an alcoholic?"

Pushing her shades up onto the top of her head, Sadie stared at her. "I don't think I could do it."

"You're already doing it, Darling." Blanca laughed loudly.

"No, I mean I don't think I could ask them to pay, you know. It seems a little…impolite."

"You British and your manners. You want a drink, the bartender makes it, and you do what? You pay. You want food, you order it, and you pay. There's no difference. Look around you, everyone is here to have fun and get laid…that's easier for some than others, so you take advantage of that. You work out who are the women looking lonely. How many drinks on average does anyone buy you before you go back with them?"

Sadie shrugged. "I dunno, four or five."

"Two or three euros each, twelve or fifteen euros is what your body is worth?" Blanca shook her head. "You could earn two, three, five times that. You can be a whore and still love who you see in the mirror."

"Nah, I couldn't do it. It wouldn't feel right." She picked up the glass and sipped the water. "I could never ask someone to pay me."

Blanca shrugged. "Okay, then carry on whoring your ass for Cosmopolitans and cheap local beer."

Sadie laughed at her and pulled her sunglasses back down on her face. It was definitely food for thought.

"How do you…you know, what do you say when you—"

Blanca looked around the bar. "See that woman over there?"

"The one with a large-brimmed hat on?" Sadie asked, twisting in her seat in the direction Blanca pointed.

"Sim sim…look how she stops what she's doing every now and then and looks around her. She's by herself. She's not waiting for anyone, she's ordered her lunch, but she's checking around to see if there's anyone to talk to… She has a designer bag, so she's potentially wealthy enough."

"Alright, so, you'd say what to her?"

"What do you usually say to a pretty girl you want to sleep with? How do you get her to buy you drinks all night?"

Sadie shrugged. "I flirt a bit, I suppose."

"So, you do that. I would walk up to her, sit down opposite and smile. Introduce myself and tell her how pretty she looks in her hat. I already know she's into women or she wouldn't be here in this bar, so, we talk about the weather, her holiday, the small things…I make her feel a little desired. Then when she's looking at my mouth and wondering what I might do with it, I lean closer and say, 'we can take this somewhere more private.'"

Sadie listened intently.

"And then I say, 'I promise it will be a night you won't forget.' Her pupils will dilate, she'll lick her lips and you know she's interested, and then you say, 'if you can afford me.'"

"And then what?"

"Then there's this moment of confusion before recognition. It takes a moment for most. It's not a proposition they've considered before and so it's out of their – how you say? Comfort area?"

"Zone. Comfort zone."

"Sim, and that's when you say it's no problem, and you get up to leave…it forces the decision. Some will let you leave and that's okay. You move on, but many will stop you and once they do, you tell them the price."

"How much?"

Blanca shrugged. "Depends on what you're offering. You want to offer just a quickie, maybe its thirty for an hour. They want the night? Maybe it's a one-fifty. You decide; it's your business."

Sadie turned back towards the woman and watched her for a moment. It didn't take long for her to feel the eyes on her and glance over at Sadie, smiling shyly before turning back to her book, and then a quick furtive peek over the top of it, at which point she blushed when she found Sadie still looking at her.

"She's interested," Blanca said. "If you wanted her. Is she attractive enough for you?"

Sadie considered it. She usually went for women her own age. This woman was older, more Blanca's age, but she wasn't unattractive.

"What have you got to lose?" Blanca laughed. "You're gonna fuck someone tonight, why not her?"

"Alright," Sadie said, accepting the challenge. She stood up and swallowed down the last of the water in her glass. "I'm going to speak to her."

Chapter Thirty-Six

2024 Amberfield, Natalie's Home

"You kissed her?" Harriet said. Her face lit up and she clapped excitedly. "Was it as good as you remember?"

Natalie considered that. "I think it was, yes, but maybe because it's something I've wanted to do for such a long time that, quite frankly, it could have been awful, and I'd still have loved it."

"So, you kissed her and then…"

"She left." Natalie's smile slid from her face, replaced once more with the hint of sadness that had etched her features all these years.

"She left." Harriet frowned. "And you let her go?"

"What would you have me do? Tie her to the chair and hold her hostage?" Natalie scoffed. "This is me, Harry. Of course I let her leave."

"Yes, true. So, what now?"

Natalie shrugged. "I don't know. I guess I should give her some space."

"Fuck that, she's had twenty-five years of space." Harry laughed. "Seriously, Nat, you need to up your game. If you want the second chance, you're going to have to get out of your comfort zone and chase it."

"What if she doesn't want to be chased?"

"Ugh, sometimes I could throttle you." Harry pulled a face at her. "She came here for lunch. To eat with you."

Natalie frowned. "I don't understand what that means."

"If that Davina Gorman woman asked you to have dinner with her to discuss next season's Christmas dildo, would you?"

"Yes."

"Because it's work and something appropriate, right?" Harry waited till Natalie nodded. "But if she just wanted to have dinner with you to apologise for being the biggest jerk we know…"

"I would not have dinner with her." She threw her hands up. "What's the point here?"

"My point is that if all Sadie wanted was answers, she'd have just demanded them. She wouldn't have agreed to have lunch with you, and she definitely wouldn't have agreed to let you cook, at your house. She came because she wanted to spend time with you. To check you out. To see how you lived, blah blah."

Natalie was quiet as she took it all in.

"And she absolutely wouldn't have let you kiss her," Harry said enthusiastically. "You're going to have to do what you didn't do back then: fight for her."

"How do I do that?" Natalie stood up and crossed the room to the photo of them both. She picked it up and smiled. "I don't know where she lives, or where she works. All I have is her phone number."

Now it was Harry's turn to shrug. "Not thought that far."

Natalie blew out her cheeks and puffed. "You're right. I do need to fight for her. I need to prove to her that I'm not that cowardly little girl anymore and that no matter what life throws at us, I will be here."

"That's the spirit." Harry fist pumped the air. "In the meantime, I need to get some sleep for this big presentation of yours tomorrow."

Rolling her eyes, Natalie sat back down on the sofa. "Seriously, you are far too expectant. I do however have a box full of things for you all to play with."

Harriet rubbed her hands together gleefully. "Oh, I can't wait. It's the biggest perk of the job."

"What if she's right though?" Natalie asked.

Harry looked perplexed. "About what?"

"What if the person she is now, isn't the person I'm in love with? What if it's too late and who we were then isn't compatible with who we are now?"

"Find out." Harry reached for her hand. "You've nothing to lose, Nat. You haven't had her in your life for over two decades. If she's not who you hoped she was, then it's best to find out and then you'll be able to let it go with no what ifs."

Natalie nodded. "So sage, wise owl."

Harry chuckled. "I know, could have given Claire Raynor a run for her money back in the day."

"I'll give it a day or two and then I'll give her a call and see what's what."

"Now, that sounds like a plan."

Chapter Thirty-Seven

2024 Come Again HQ

Natalie walked into the office, pulling her small suitcase behind her as though she were walking down a catwalk runway about to board an actual plane.

She grinned and nodded as she passed the booths where her employees were hard at work marketing. Social media, magazines, everything that could push Come Again into the faces of potential customers.

Come Again was about to photograph and film an explosive late summer/early autumn ad campaign. An after the watershed, adult themed campaign that would suggest exactly why anyone should make it their priority to Come Again. They were exciting times in the office, and still nothing excited everyone more than a bag full of new toys to play with.

"Is that what I think it is?" James rushed over to take charge of the suitcase, twisting on his heel and flouncing away as though he were competing on *Strictly Come Dancing*. Natalie smiled at the antics of Harriet's personal assistant.

It was a yearly event now. She attended the expo and brought back many things of interest, and then they all had the morning to rummage through the case and decide on what they liked and didn't like, and which items would be sent to their special list of clients who would provide feedback that would ultimately decide if they were going to reach the stores or not.

"Can I stress that this year was remarkably low in anything new? Don't get overexcited," she called after him, but he was already gone, into the boardroom where he would lovingly lay them all out on the table beside the water glasses and jugs.

"Don't spoil it," Wendy said with a huge grin on her face, over Natalie's shoulder as she passed by to pour some coffee.

When all five of her trusted and most influential colleagues and employees were nestled around the table, Natalie looked around the room. As CEO of the company, she'd spent a lot of time gathering the executive team. They were not just people good at their jobs, but people she would work with and trust to operate the business cohesively and with imagination and tenacity.

Wendy was the Customer Experience manager. It was her job to make sure that all stores conveyed the perfect welcome to women looking to buy pleasure toys. It was her job to maintain training standards for the staff within store so that they could identify and sell a product with the utmost professionalism, no different to if someone were buying a pen or a watch.

Harriet's main job was marketing. As CMO, it was her ideas that were often seen on the posters and advertising boards. Snappy slogans and punchy sales pitches had seen Come Again through many sticky patches when the market looked to be losing out to cheap knockoffs from China. In any other company, it would also be assumed that Harriet was the COO, Chief Operating Officer, whenever Natalie was unavailable. Her perfect number two. Someone she trusted implicitly.

"So, new gadgets? Anything worth really getting into ahead of the game?" Harry asked as she took her seat and reached for a biscuit, and then the closest box to look over. "I am assuming that this is all the rage now?" She waved at the box. The words "remote control" were emblazoned on the packaging beside the words "programmable to your needs."

Natalie glanced at it and then nodded. "Absolutely. I didn't think there was much in the way of our stock sellers being outdated or in need of replacing. But I think it might be worthwhile looking into the technology available, that is only in its early days right now." She took her seat and leaned her elbows on the desk. "What fascinated me were the prototypes that are the next step up from those." She pointed at the box Harry had now placed onto the desk again. "Those require a simple app, and you can use on yourself or a partner, programming when they will vibrate, et cetera. All good fun, but innovation is taking huge steps. That's where I want to target. I want us on the precipice so that we are ahead of the game."

"Do we have any leads on that?" Mary Noble asked. Head of social media, it was her job to get the word out and excite the following every time they had something new to push, working side by side with Harriet regarding commercial activity. It was a good match.

"Actually, yes, and I'll email those contact details over," Natalie said before turning back to everyone. "There are complete body suits in the works, programmable to your body's reactions. In the future, I'm not even sure women will need to date." She chuckled.

Austin, the youngest member of the team, and the only straight male in the room, looked forlorn at that idea.

"Don't worry, Austin, they'll still want you for babies." Wendy laughed.

Harry shrugged. "Will they? Technically two women can create a child, albeit only female, but is that really going to be an issue moving forward?" She said it all with a straight face until Austin paled and then she laughed. "Oh, come on, Austin, who could deny a handsome devil such as yourself? There will always be women who want a man, and we are here to show them they're wrong."

James put his hand up. "Don't forget us gay boys will happily donate."

Austin sank into his seat. "You lot are mean." He grinned and sat up. "Anyway, back to business. I would like to set up some meetings this week with each of our departments to go over some HR changes and updates. Nothing too sinister."

"Perfect," Natalie answered. They all pulled out their diaries. "I can do tomorrow at ten."

Austin jotted that down. "Okay, everyone else?"

Chapter Thirty-Eight

2024 Hotel Mason

Sadie checked into her room with Blanca's words echoing in her ear.

"Don't ghost her. She's going to be confused and want to talk."

"I wanted to talk, and I had to wait twenty-five years," she'd replied petulantly. She didn't need to see the look on Blanca's face to know it was a ridiculous thing to say. "I know," she sighed in defeat. "I will message her as soon as I'm able to. I've already got five repeat clients scheduled. It's a busy week."

She unzipped her suitcase and unpacked her work clothes. Women who used her services didn't often request her outfits to fit any particular fantasy, but there was often a theme. She had them state that on the website so she could be prepared or decline.

Her spare room was filled with costumes and underwear, and toys. Things her clients over the years had requested. She smiled as she thought back to the Wonder Woman outfit she'd worn for one lady. In her fifties, she'd always had a thing for the character. Diagnosed with breast cancer, she'd wanted to enjoy the fictional desire in case it was too late. Thankfully, she'd recovered and had booked Sadie several times over the years for nothing more than company really. A nice dinner date, and a quick orgasm before bed. It was easy, and Sadie liked her life easy.

As she was hanging her high-end suit into the wardrobe, her phone rang. It didn't often ring. She'd get notifications of messages on her website, and she'd get texts from Blanca or other friends. Rarely did it ring, unless it was a cold caller. So, she let it ring out.

But when it rang again a moment later, she wondered if she should answer it.

She opened her bag and pulled it out, looking at the number calling. It wasn't one she recognised.

"Hello," she said confidently, ready to end and block if it was one more bloody phone company letting her know her contract was almost up, and did she want to hear what they were selling.

"Sadie, it's me, Natalie. I wondered if we could talk?"

"Natalie, oh, hi." She looked around the room for somewhere to sit. "Sure, what did you want to talk about?" she asked, knowing full well what she wanted to talk about. The kiss? The fact she ran like the wind?

She shifted her jacket from the chair in the corner and sat down. The sound of Natalie breathing in her ear unsettled her too easily.

"I just wanted to check in that everything was okay, that you…you're okay?"

"Yes, I'm fine. I just arrived at…my hotel, so unpacking."

"Oh, that's good. Work or play?" Natalie asked. Something about her tone sounded anxious about what the answer might be.

"Work. You know how it is, always something to attend," she said, trying to sound nonchalant about it.

"Yes, I suppose so. I didn't actually ask what you do. How rude of me."

Sadie tensed. She wasn't ready for that discussion quite yet. She said what she usually said when anyone asked via small talk. "I'm…in the entertainment industry."

"Oh, that sounds fabulous," Natalie said, and the tone changed to excitement. "I didn't quite imagine that at all. You looked all…well, business, I just assumed…"

"Well, yes, I guess I'm the business side of things mostly." *Please do not ask me any more questions,* she thought.

"So, singer? Acting? I'm so…well, flabbergasted really."

"No, nothing like that. I organise entertainment for my clients," she said, congratulating herself on not having to lie, just merely evading the finer details.

"Ah, I see. You book events and trips and things for people to do."

She decided not to answer that, instead changing the subject completely. "I wanted to say again, that dinner was lovely. I'm sorry I dashed off so quickly. I think the entire situation just threw me."

"Not a problem," Natalie said. "I was hoping maybe we could do it again. Dinner, not the kiss. I mean, obviously there was nothing wrong with the kiss, and I'm not adverse to it happening again, I just meant, that wasn't why was asking. I thought it would be nice, that's all." Natalie's ramble came to an end and Sadie had to admit, she found it endearing.

"I'd like that, so maybe we can do something at the weekend."

"Great, it's a date," Natalie said excitedly. "I mean, as in, you know—"

"I know." Sadie smiled. "I'll call on Friday."

"I just…I'm so glad we have this opportunity to say all the things that need to be said between us. And maybe have the chance to create something new now," Natalie said. "And this is my direct line at the office, if you wanted to speak to me or…anyway, I've rambled enough. You must think me quite the idiot."

"No, I don't think that." She noted the way her voice softened towards Natalie.

"Oh, well, that's good then." Natalie chuckled with just a hint of embarrassment to it. "I'd best let you get on with your day."

"Alright."

"And I'll see you Friday or speak to you Friday, whatever is easiest. I'll keep my weekend free."

"Okay, I'll be in touch."

"Great. I really would like to see you," Natalie said before adding, "Take care."

"Yes, you too." She closed off the call and placed the phone down onto the desk. When she looked up, it was her own reflection in the mirror that she noticed. The small smile on her lips. Was that all it took, a phone call from Natalie and the promise to meet soon, to make her happy?

Maybe so.

Chapter Thirty-Nine

2024 Come Again HQ

Wednesday morning, Natalie was in a good mood. It was hump day, the halfway point between Monday when she'd spoken to Sadie last, and the weekend, when she hoped that she would see Sadie again.

All she had to do was relax about it, which was easier said than done when she had absolutely no idea where, or when they would meet or even what they would do.

"Knock, knock."

Natalie glanced up at the open door to find Harriet poking her head around the frame.

"What's the frown for?" Harriet asked as she stepped inside and beelined for the chair.

Sighing, Natalie leaned back. "No reason really. I was just thinking about the weekend and potentially seeing Sadie again and wondering what we should do."

"Do?"

"Yes, I mean, I know it's not a date, and I know she will probably want to talk some more, but my house again? Or should I arrange a pub lunch, or—" She held her hands out wide, palms up. "Oh, I don't know. I'm overthinking, I know that much. How are you?"

"I'm alright, I just set up the studio equipment hire for the next commercial filming date. It's looking very exciting. I'm going to be meeting up with Lucia Sadler tomorrow."

"Good. I know she's only a minor reality star, but her platform online is huge. It will be a huge bonus to have her suggesting it would be wise to Come Again."

"Why don't you take her somewhere you used to go…that bar you met in?"

"A change of subject, okay. Well, yes, I suppose that could work. Would it not be a little bit…" Her nose scrunched as she thought for the word. "Crude?"

"Maybe."

"I want to make new memories, not constantly remind her of the time I broke her heart. And anyway, the pub is now a cocktail bar."

"Oh, well, that's true, I guess. But…" Harry held up a finger. "It was also a time when she loved you and wanted you."

"God, why did I have to be such an idiot back then?" Natalie said. She rubbed her hands over her face and pushed her hair back.

"Hey, if you hadn't been such an idiot, we wouldn't have met, and you wouldn't have the best marketing team about to catapult your company into the stratosphere."

"Fair enough, but I just kick myself that I didn't have a back-up plan."

"To do what? You said yourself, your dad threatened to hurt her. What was your eighteen-year-old self going to do?"

"I know." Natalie sighed. "You're right, no more feeling sorry for myself. What's done, is done. And now I have a chance to redeem myself."

The phone on her desk rang and she pressed a button to answer it on speaker. "Yes?"

"Ms Shultz, Davina Gorman is here to see you," Bina, her P.A. said confidently and with a brightness to her voice that always cheered Natalie up.

"Thank you, give me two minutes and then send her in."

"Of course."

The line went dead, and Natalie stared at Harriet.

"So, what should I do?"

Harriet stood up. "Buy some vibrators and stop worrying about Sadie. The universe will provide; it has so far."

"Not helping," Natalie said. She watched Harriet wave over her shoulder and exit the room. Pressing the button to speak to Bina again, she said, "Can you make sure that I am out of office on Friday afternoon? Book an appointment for me at my salon and please arrange coffee in the next ten minutes, otherwise I won't get through this meeting."

Bina chuckled. "No problem. Are you ready now?"

"Yes, send her in."

Within a minute, Davina Gorman was swishing into the office.

"Natalie, good to see you again," she said just as Natalie stood and moved around the desk to greet her. Air kisses and a half hug later, she was sitting in the chair Harriet had just vacated.

"Davina. Journey down okay?" Natalie asked, retaking her seat back behind her desk. There was a sense of safety there.

"Yes, came down last night actually." She gave a little wink. "Met up with that hook—escort, Evelyn, again. Enough notice and she's happy to travel. I mean, so she should be for £450 and dinner at a swanky restaurant."

Natalie smiled in a non-committal way. Some things really could remain private, she thought.

"I'm glad that worked out for you. So, about this autumn's collection. We're liking the look of the pastel range of the iVibe2000."

Davina nodded. "One of our most popular, yes. How many units are we talking?"

Natalie ran a finger over her notes. "There are five colours: Dusk Pink, Subtle Mauve, Sky Blue, Orchid Yellow and Leaf Green, correct?"

Davina smiled. "Yes, though we are considering the Gold Cream as a limited edition."

Unsure what exactly that would look like, Natalie just smiled and continued. "We'd be looking at an initial one hundred units per store. So, twenty of each colour. 2500 as a starting number."

"I would say we could certainly accommodate that. And if we were to bring in the limited edition?"

"I'd like to see it first, but I would imagine, if sales are good overall – and why wouldn't they be? – then we'd take another five hundred easily. We would be making these a focal point in the store, and therefore giving the iVibe2000 a huge promotion."

She was interrupted by Bina arriving with a tray of coffees and a plate of biscuits. She placed it all onto the desk and left without a word.

"My marketing team believe that if we can set up a introductory price for this promotion, then by Christmas we could have the number one seller on our hands, and obviously they'd be selling full price by then. If we can come to some arrangement regarding the first lot."

Davina reached for a cup. "I don't see why we couldn't. After all, it would benefit us both."

"As always. And we have Lucia Sadler lined up as our face of autumn. So, we expect to be doubling that order within a week of the ad going out. We'll be shooting that very soon."

"Then we should arrange a little promotional party, don't you think? See if we can't get a few more celebrities onboard, national magazines, et cetera. iVibe: Come Again, and again, and again." She laughed, and Natalie had to admit it had a certain ring to it.

"I'll pass that on to marketing."

Davina placed her cup down. "So, how are you? You seemed a little out of sorts at the expo. Usually much more engaged and social."

Natalie breathed in deeply, keeping control of herself and not blurting everything out. Because Davina Gorman was not a woman she wanted in on her private moments in life. "I'm good, I just need—"

"A good fuck? Honestly, I think it's the answer to everything." Davina laughed again.

"Maybe. It certainly has been a while. It's a good job I know where to go to relieve that issue though, isn't it?" Natalie joked.

"Seriously though, I know that I can sound a little crass about it, but we're busy women. We don't have time for romancing someone. Having the opportunity to pay for it occasionally is…it's freeing. You can be whoever you want to be, they're very accommodating, and it's not at all sleazy like you might imagine. It's a transaction, between two consenting adults. And Evelyn is…well, she's a very attractive woman." She stood up, readying to leave. "Think about it, and if you want the number, just give me a call. Like I said, very discreet."

"I'll think about it," Natalie said, reaching out and shaking hands, already knowing she had absolutely no intention of thinking about it. And she was sure it would be anything but discreet if Davina was involved in the process. "We'll talk again next week regarding the ad campaign and the promotional intricacies."

She sat back down again and closed her eyes. A few minutes to herself wouldn't hurt, especially if they were spent thinking about Sadie and their upcoming meeting.

Chapter Forty

1999 Amberfield, Aunt Lina's house

"What time is your aunt back?" Sadie asked as she pulled off her jumper and undid her jeans.

Natalie watched the show. "About an hour," she finally answered when Sadie knelt on the bed and pushed her backwards.

"Why are you always on top?" Sadie grinned, rolling and flipping Natalie with her.

"You like me being on top. Stop complaining," Natalie said, reaching behind herself and unclipping her bra. She fell forward and let her breasts sway above Sadie's waiting mouth. "Be nice and I'll let you—" She squealed when Sadie leaned up and captured her nipple between teeth. "Okay, you win." She laughed and flopped forward, enjoying the way teeth gave way and soft lips wrapped around and suckled gently.

Warm palms slid effortlessly up and down her thighs, teasing her skin and nerve endings. She felt them more firmly pulling her closer, urging her forward.

"What do you want me to do?" she asked when Sadie let her nipple escape.

Sadie grinned. "Sit on my face?"

"Won't you suffocate?"

Pulling the pillow under her head, Sadie laughed. "No, come on."

"Okay." She was about to move. "Oh, wait." Natalie jumped up and off the bed, slipping her underwear off. "Easier?"

"Yeah, now turn around and get back up here," Sadie instructed.

"Turn around? But then my bum will—" Natalie frowned.

"Will you please just trust me and do what I ask?" Sadie said.

Too turned on to argue, Natalie did what Sadie said and straddled her waist again, but this time, facing her feet. "Okay."

She felt her hips being pulled backwards and shuffled on her knees until she could feel Sadie's breath against her skin.

"Don't stop there," Sadie said, hands on her hips urging her to sink down and feel the warmth and wetness of her waiting tongue.

"Oh, god," she cried out as Sadie swiped through her folds for the first time. "So…good." She laughed, more at herself for ever doubting Sadie.

When she relaxed and was getting used to the different movements, she felt the pressure of Sadie's hands again, once wrapped around the join of her thighs and hips, the other pressed against her torso, firmly pushing her forward.

"Lick me," she mumbled before thrusting her tongue inside of Natalie, the movement causing her lover's hips to thrust backwards.

Natalie looked down and comprehended the situation. This was what Alice had waffled on about one afternoon, a sixty-nine. An apprehension came over her. She wanted to get it right, but focusing was difficult when Sadie was doing magical things with her own tongue.

Sadie's hips bucked up at her, her legs spread wide and open. An invitation to stop thinking and start doing.

It's just angles, Natalie told herself as she lowered towards her own prize.

Chapter Forty-One

2024 Hotel Mason

"So, good night?" Blanca asked when she called to check in. It was the golden rule: Blanca always knew where Natalie was, and how long she would be, and to call the police if she hadn't checked in. "I was expecting you home tonight."

"Yes, well, can't turn down a good offer last minute. £900 banked." She smiled. "Breakfast and dinner thrown in."

"And several orgasms. I would say life is treating you well, darling." Blanca chuckled.

"Does it get any better?"

"Hm, that does sound pretty good." Blanca groaned a little and Sadie imagined her settling into her chair. "And with Natalie still in the picture…have you heard from the delightful Ms Shultz?"

"She called me yesterday. We have tentative plans for the weekend."

"I see. Sounds promising."

"Does it?"

"Yes. You don't think so?"

Sadie stared at herself in the mirror and watched as she barefaced lied. "Not really."

Blanca laughed. "Okay, you tell yourself that. Are you fixed for the week?"

"I have several offers."

She logged into her bank account and checked the balance. In all honesty, she could buy the cottage by the sea now if she really could find the one she wanted, and maybe she would. If she sold the flat, she wouldn't even need a mortgage.

She could move Blanca in there to see out her last years and get a nurse to stay when she was away working. A thought of Natalie came into her head. What would she think? The put-together, elegant businesswoman.

She shrugged; it didn't matter. Natalie had no rights to her life, or to have any input on any aspect of it. They were reacquainted and working on a friendship of sorts.

Falling back onto the bed, she said, "Who are you kidding?"

She heard Blanca's voice in her head, *"There's still love there."*

"Sadie?"

"Huh, what?"

Blanca chuckled. "Lost in thought?"

"No, I—" She pushed the image of Natalie from her mind. "What did you say?"

"I said, I'll let you get on with your day, and make sure you text me later when you've confirmed details and times."

"Yes, of course. And you have a good day. Try and get outside for a bit, huh? It's lovely weather; the sun will do you good. It's why we have a garden flat."

"So bossy, but okay, okay, I'll take Muffy out and sit in the sunshine every day."

"Good, and don't forget your pills."

"I won't, I have an alarm set."

"Alright, I'll speak to you later then." She closed the call and put the phone down, then picked it up again and scrolled through her messages until she found Natalie.

"And say what?" she said to herself as she contemplated sending a text. *You could just be honest and say you wanted to speak to her,* her inner voice answered back. *You shut that off years ago. You're a fool for opening the door again.*

"Oh, shut up," she told herself and flung the phone onto the bed. Natalie Shultz would have to wait.

Chapter Forty-Two

1999 Amberfield Riverbank

"Sadie, wait…what's the hurry?" Natalie called after her as they both ran along the riverbank.

"Come on," Sadie said, laughing and grabbing her hand. "We'll miss it."

"Miss what?"

The sound of muted music and singing wafted out from the pub, getting louder when the door opened, and Sadie dragged Natalie inside.

Pushing their way to the bar, she waved a hand and got the bar staff's attention. "Two pints," she said, indicating with her fingers.

"What's going on?" Natalie asked, still catching her breath.

"It's drag night," Sadie answered with a huge grin.

"What on earth is drag night?" Natalie laughed, just as a large cheer erupted and the crowd clapped when a tall man with a huge Dolly Parton-style wig on his head appeared on the stage. He wore over-the-top make-up and a huge grin as he sang out the first line to "Jolene."

"That's drag night." Sadie laughed and paid for their drinks. She nudged Natalie's arm and pointed towards a table where two people were getting up and pulling their coats on. "Grab that table."

Finally settled, Sadie pulled her chair around closer to Natalie and slung an arm around the back of her, watching Natalie's face light up as the drag act started telling rude jokes and making fun of some of the people nearer the front.

"Oh God, she's hilarious." Natalie laughed.

Sadie lifted her pint to her lips and took a swig. "I knew you'd like it."

"Thank you," Natalie said. "You always seem to know what I like and need."

"I just pay attention, and honestly, you're easy to please."

"Am I?"

Sadie shrugged. "Yeah, you're not demanding like some girls can be. What you see is what you get and…" She leaned closer. "I like what I see."

"And what you get?" Natalie smirked at her over the top of her glass.

"Yeah, can't deny it."

"I should hope not." Natalie grinned after she sipped her pint. "I feel so…at ease with you. Like nothing is too much, and what I want matters."

"It does. *You matter.*" Sadie emphasised that point.

A loud roar went up when a new drag artist appeared and began to fake a striptease, singing "Big Spender" and cavorting around a makeshift pole.

"People are dancing," Natalie said enthusiastically. Her eyes lit up as she turned towards Sadie. "Can we?"

"Dance? Alright." They stood up. Sadie whipped off her jacket and placed it around the back of the chair to hold the table.

For a moment, she just watched as Natalie's hips swayed left and right as she made her way through the crowd to the dance floor.

These were the moments she knew she would remember forever.

Chapter Forty-Three

2024 Outskirts of Brighton, Sadie's flat

Sadie climbed wearily from her car and reached into the back seat for her bag. Heaving it out, she locked the door behind her and headed for her flat.

The moment she turned the key in the lock and pushed the door open, she smiled as the sound of afternoon quiz shows and Blanca shouting answers hit her ears.

"What is the capital of Indonesia?"

"Jakarta!" Blanca shouted, gleefully clapping. "Is that you?"

"No, it's the honey monster," Sadie called back, smiling at their little joke. She dropped her bag and poked her head around the living room door. "All good?"

Blanca pulled a face that said she was indifferent, but then smiled. "I am now you're home and we can open that bottle of Tinta Barroca."

"Like you needed me here for that." Sadie wandered over, bending to kiss the top of her head. "Cuppa?"

"Okay, seeing as you're making it."

Sadie picked up the empty cup, still warm from its last endeavour to the kitchen. "If there is one thing I am good at—"

"It's keeping your clients happy. Your tea-making isn't that good." Blanca smirked and held up the empty plate. "Biscuits would be nice."

"You are intolerable." Sadie grinned but took the plate and left the room.

"Did you speak with Natalie again?" Blanca called after her.

Sighing, she filled the kettle and flicked it on.

"No," she called back and waited a moment for a response that didn't come.

With the tea made and plate of biscuits, Sadie carried the tray back through into the lounge. Big eyes stared at her until she put the tray down and handed over the biscuits.

"Why not?" Blanca asked.

Sadie shrugged and sat down on the sofa.

Mimicking the shrug, Blanca mumbled in Portuguese before she twisted slightly in her chair and glared.

"You spend half a lifetime missing this one woman. And now, when you have opportunity, you shrug? *Meu bem-querer*, you love her, no?"

"That's not the point, B."

"It's the only point, amor."

Sadie placed her cup down gently, her eyes closed as she considered things with Natalie. "I don't know that I can be who she wants."

"And who does she want? You've asked her?"

"It's not that simple," Sadie said, feeling defensive.

"It could be...instead you're choosing this." Blanca raised her hands in defeat. "You rather just sit here and be emu."

"Ostrich," Sadie corrected.

"Same thing. Beautiful bird, long neck, head in sand."

"Emus don't bury; in fact, neither do ostriches. It's a myth. And I'm not burying my head in the sand, I'm fully avoiding and aware of it."

"I thought you'd agreed to meet her this weekend."

Picking her cup up, Sadie said, "No, I said I might..."

"Hm, so you've told her you won't?"

Without taking a sip, Sadie put the mug down again. "Not yet, but as soon as I finish my drink, I shall do that."

Blanca nodded slowly. "Soon you will realise that life is too short. When you love like you love her, you cannot ignore it."

"Well, right now, I can. And I will."

Chapter Forty-Four

1999 Amberfield

Sadie threw down her jacket before pulling the blanket from the bag and laying it out flat so that Natalie could flop down on it.

Joining her, she stretched out her legs, smiling when Natalie used her thigh as a pillow. Leaning back on her hands, Sadie watched with interest as Natalie twisted a dandelion in her hand and looked up at it.

"What are you thinking about?" Sadie asked, pushing her sunglasses further up her nose and staring up at the sky too.

"Us," Natalie answered, as though that were the simplest and most obvious answer she could have given. "I was thinking about what kind of house we will live in."

"Oh yeah? What kind did you imagine?"

"I dunno. Something nice and big, but not too big, and it needs to have a garden with lots of flowers and maybe a pond."

"A pond, okay." Sadie considered it. She'd never lived in a house with a garden, let alone something as fancy as a pond.

"You don't like the idea of a pond?" Natalie asked, twisting onto her side. Her head still rested on Sadie's thigh. "We don't have to have a pond; we can have whatever we want."

"No way," Sadie said, running her fingers down Natalie's cheek. "If you want a pond, we're having a pond. I want you to have everything you ever dreamed about."

Natalie frowned and sat up, her mouth moving left and right as she thought about something. "Some of my dreams have been quite out there. And I never even dreamed about you, so I think we can make new dreams together."

"Alright, well, I am all for making new dreams."

"Good. So, what house do you want us to live in?" Natalie dropped back down again and began picking daisies from the grass.

For a moment, Sadie was stumped. She didn't have dreams. Dreams were for people like Natalie, with money and standing, not for people like her whose parents split when she was born. She had never really known her dad. Knowing her mum had been difficult enough.

Sadie's dreams at best had been hope. They had been to get away, find any job, do whatever it took to make sure she never had to go home again. Her stepfather was a jerk.

Natalie made everything feel different though. She could finally look forward to a future with someone who loved her.

"I don't care about the house. I just want a bed we can sleep together in, and a couch we can curl up on, and a TV. If I have you, that's all I need. Everything else would just be a bonus."

"Aw, well, if it meant I could be with you, I'd live anywhere."

Sadie laughed. "No you wouldn't."

Natalie sat up again, smiling widely. "True, I'm not living in that room of yours." She leaned in and pressed her lips against Sadie's. "I want a house where you don't have to put your hand over my mouth every time you make me come."

"I'm seeing the attraction of a large house." Sadie nodded, smiling with her.

"I knew you'd come around to my way of thinking," Natalie said, settling back down and using Sadie for a pillow again.

Chapter Forty-Five

2024 Amberfield, Natalie's home

Natalie checked her phone for the umpteenth time and sighed once more when the screen remained the same. No messages from Sadie.

She felt the depths of disappointment fill the void. All week, she'd told herself not to get her hopes up, but it was impossible not to. Not after that kiss, and the way Sadie still looked at her.

Her stomach tightened when the phone buzzed into life and the screen lit up, and for just a moment, Natalie was excited. Until she saw Harry's face smiling at her.

"Hello?" she said sadly once she'd answered it.

"That sounds cheery," Harry replied. "What's the matter? Has she cancelled?"

"No, I mean…I don't know. I've not heard from her at all, and I thought by now…" She glanced at her watch. Just gone seven P.M. "I guess I assumed she'd have called today to arrange something."

"That's shitty. After all the effort you've gone to. Shall I come over?"

"No, I'll be fine, I'll…" The buzz of a message came through. "Hold on, just got a message."

Pulling the phone from her ear, she tapped the screen until the message's icon was visible and the name Sadie appeared on the screen.

Sadie: Sorry I haven't been in touch, had a hectic week. I don't think I'm going to be able to make it this weekend. Xx.

"Nat?" Harry's voice came through the fog. "You alright? Is it her?"

"Yes," Natalie said, putting the phone to her ear again. "She can't make this weekend."

"Right, I'm coming over. I'll pick up Chinese and a bottle of wine."

She didn't give Natalie any option to say no before the call was closed and Natalie was left sitting alone in the silence of her living room, with the TV flickering on mute.

Picking up her phone, she re-read the message several times before she realised she had tears in her eyes.

Natalie: Oh, hey, that's alright. I guess you're busy with life and maybe a nice quiet chilled weekend is what you need.

She was about to press send when she added.

Natalie: I hope to hear from you soon.

Then she deleted it; she didn't want to sound needy.

Natalie: That's a shame, I was looking forward to seeing you, but I guess

She deleted that too. Too much like she was a victim.

Natalie: Okay, no problem. Catch up with you another time. X

Did that sound cold and uncaring? She went to delete it but stopped herself.

"Stop overthinking," she said to herself.

She pressed send.

Chapter Forty-Six

2024 Outskirts of Brighton, Sadie's flat

Sadie pursed her lips as she watched the screen. Natalie was typing. Natalie stopped typing. Natalie was typing again.

"For god's sake, just say it," she said to the phone as Natalie deleted whatever it was she was going to say and started again.

Blanca arched a brow. "What are you hoping she says?"

"Honestly? That she tells me to get lost."

The eye roll was spectacular as Blanca breathed in and out slowly. "Sometimes I wish I'd just slapped you hard and sent you back to England to find her twenty years ago."

Sadie made a face at her and watched the screen again.

She felt nauseous when it finally beeped that a message had come through. Dragging the screen down, she read it without letting Natalie see she had.

"Dammit, why does she have to be so nice all the time?"

"Maybe she just is nice, and maybe you are just a fool."

"Whose side are you on?" Sadie said to her.

"I am on the side of love, and of finding someone to take you on and look after you. So I can get old and die without worrying about you."

Sadie huffed and threw the phone down onto the seat. "I wish you wouldn't talk like that."

Blanca shrugged slowly. "Because being emu means it won't happen?"

"Ostrich," Sadie said in frustration.

"Whatever. I won't be around forever, and I need to know that you will be taken care of—"

"I can take care of myself," Sadie interrupted. "And you are not going anywhere for a long time, so shut up and drink your wine."

"I am aware that you can take care of yourself. That doesn't mean you should. You need love. You need someone else in your life."

"I've got you and that bloody cat of yours."

Blanca gasped dramatically. "Muffy, you don't listen to her, she loves you."

"I don't, bloody thing scratched me again the other day," Sadie said, looking down at the healed mark on her hand.

"Don't change the subject," Blanca said. "What you going to be, the oldest whore in town? This life comes to an end, and it's coming to that place for you."

Now it was Sadie who gasped. "Are you saying I'm past it?"

"No, I'm saying that even whores deserve to retire and enjoy the fruits of their labour before their world becomes so…" She pulled a face. "Miserable and lonely."

"I am not miserable, or lonely," Sadie said defensively, her arms wrapping around her to make that point.

"No? tell me, when was the last time you went out for fun? With friends."

Sadie didn't need to think too hard about that because it hadn't been for months, maybe longer.

"Yes, see, this is my point. You have nobody but me and Miss Muffy, so, stop being a dick."

Chapter Forty-Seven

2024 Amberfield, Natalie's home

"This isn't Chinese," Natalie said when the aroma of curry wafted up from the two bags Harry carried into the hallway.

"I know, but the good Chinese was closed, so I figured a decent Indian instead would suffice. And it would go better with these." She held up a carrier that clinked.

"Beer?"

"You like beer," Harry said, pushing past to take everything to the kitchen. She plonked the bags down onto the island and realised that Natalie hadn't followed. "Hey…" she said, walking back out and into the hallway, where she found a visibly upset Natalie.

Her shoulders shook as she sniffed and tried to hold it all in.

"Okay, come here," Harry demanded, but she reached her before she had the chance to move.

Natalie found herself swept up into a bear hug and gripped at the sleeves of Harry's shirt.

"I'm sorry, I just…I was expecting Sadie and then she cancelled and then I was expecting Chinese and wine and now it's beer and curry." She spoke without taking a breath. "And I love curry, and I do like beer, you're right, so I don't know why I'm so upset and—"

"Alright, let's breathe, shall we?" Harry led her through to the kitchen and pulled a stool from under the counter. "Sit."

Natalie did as she was told and watched as Harry reached into the bag and pulled a bottle covered in condensation from it, twisted the cap, poured a glass and then pushed it on the counter towards Natalie.

"Drink that. I'll plate up while you talk."

Natalie downed half the glass and then wiped her mouth on the back of her hand as she suppressed the urge to burp.

Harry stared at her.

"Ladylike."

"Sorry, I'm just…" Natalie huffed and then blew out her cheeks. "Frustrated."

"I gathered that." Harry opened one of the containers and the waft of cumin and curry filled the air.

"I guess I just got my hopes up and now…" She shrugged, her shoulders sagging. "I realise that it's not that big of a deal for her as it was for me, maybe?"

"Or maybe…" Harry stopped spooning the curry onto plates and looked at Natalie. "Maybe she's just nervous, or busy, or feeling awkward…twenty-five years is a long time."

"I know. So many missed opportunities. If only her housemate had been less stoned and given her my messages, all of this would be a moot point."

"Would it? You can't know that. Things happened this way because that's what was meant to be." She scooped up a spoonful of the rice. "I keep telling you, the universe knows what it's doing."

"Well, I wish the universe would let me in on the secret, because I just…I just want to—" She blew out a long, slow breath. "I just want to find Sadie again, and to see if this time, we can make it work."

"And if that's what is meant to be, you will." Harry pushed the plate across the island. "Now, I suggest, we eat this and then get drunk?"

Chapter Forty-Eight

2024 Amberfield, Natalie's home

A week had passed in silence, so hearing from Sadie that morning had been unexpected, but exciting.

Natalie looked in the mirror. She'd had her hair done again, and Manuel had persuaded her to try something new, a shorter style than she was used to. Her curls bounced more with less weight to them.

Cut just above her shoulders with a few layers chopped in, she had to admit she liked it. The added highlights softened her face.

She'd been in such a good mood when she'd received Sadie's text asking to meet later, that she'd taken herself shopping afterwards and found the perfect summer dress to wear.

Stepping back, she spun around and admired the new look. If this didn't grab Sadie's attention, then she'd just have to work harder, but she was pretty sure she was on the right track at least.

She slipped the dress off, and in her underwear, moved around the room, retrieving a more casual outfit to wear while she waited to hear from Sadie.

The text message she'd sent a couple of hours ago confirming 7 P.M. still hadn't been read, but she didn't let that worry her, not just yet. Sadie was most likely busy and would reply when she had the chance. After all, an entire week had gone by without talking. She just needed to be patient.

"Just got to keep busy till then," she said to herself. Which was easier said than done when she was as excited as a kid at Christmas.

By seven o'clock however, she was feeling like a coiled spring. Her text message, now sent almost eight hours ago, was still unread.

She called Harry.

"Harry, talk me off the ledge," she said hurriedly.

"Okay, good evening to you too. What's the matter?"

Natalie sighed. "Sadie texted earlier wanting to come over, and I replied back to confirm that it was a yes from me, and she still hasn't replied, hasn't even read the message and so now I'm working myself up with ridiculous notions of her ghosting me in revenge."

"Revenge, huh? I mean, you know her best. Does she strike you as the vengeful sort?"

"No, of course not, but I don't know…maybe she's changed, maybe now she's so angry with me that revenge is—"

"Natalie, will you listen to yourself?" Harry chuckled. "You and her have history. She's not ghosting you. She's probably just gotten bogged down with work, or lost her phone, or dropped it accidently down the loo. We've all done that."

"I haven't."

"Ok, most of us have done that. My point is, there are a lot of reasons why she may not have read your message yet. If she reached out about coming over, I highly doubt she's just going to ghost you."

"You're right, thank you. I just needed to hear someone say it. I guess I'm still jaded from last time. I was hoping we'd have gone to dinner or something this evening. I need to stop letting my imagination run away with itself."

"Well, get yourself some dinner, and if she calls later, arrange to do something tomorrow. There's no rush, Nat. One more day isn't going to hurt."

Sighing again, Natalie got up. "I'll go and make a sandwich. Not really feeling hungry now."

"She'll be in touch, Nat. Don't stress about it," Harry said. "And if she doesn't…well, then I'll come over again and we'll do something fun like getting off our faces on fancy cocktails."

Natalie laughed at her friend. "Okay, that's a deal."

At ten p.m., she'd given up and gone to bed. Sitting up against fluffy pillows, she read her book and tried to put thoughts of why Sadie had ignored her out of her mind.

She was doing an okay job of it as she turned page after page. The swashbuckling hero was fighting off a marauding band of pirates and she was engaged with the plot.

The doorbell ringing wasn't something she was expecting, or the urgent banging on the door that followed and made her jump out of her skin.

She put the book down and tossed the covers back. Getting up quickly, she grabbed her robe, still pulling it on as she made her way onto the landing.

"Hold on, I'm coming!" she bellowed as she made her way step by step down the stairs. At the bottom, she could see a figure behind the stained glass, illuminated by the outside security light.

"Sadie?" she whispered to herself. Moving with more speed to the door, she flung it open. "Hey, I wasn't—" She stopped talking the moment Sadie turned around to face her.

She had red-rimmed eyes and make-up smeared down her cheeks. She tried to speak, but the words wouldn't sound more than a strangled cry, and she staggered forward and fell into Natalie's arms.

Chapter Forty-Nine

2024 Amberfield, Natalie's home

Sadie trembled as Natalie led her inside and into the living room. Her voice shook as she tried to speak, but the words wouldn't come out coherently.

"Sit down, I'll get some tea," Natalie said.

"Vodka." Sadie finally managed to halt the sobs just enough to be understood.

"I think I have some brandy. That will have to do."

Pouring a glass, two fingers deep, Natalie tried to imagine what on earth had happened to make Sadie so upset and bring her here for what she assumed and hoped was comfort.

"Here, sip this and—"

Sadie put the glass to her lips and swallowed the contents in one.

"Or neck it," Natalie said, taking the glass from her. She put it down on the coffee table and kept her attention on Sadie. "Better?"

Two stuttering deep breaths later, Sadie nodded. "Sorry, I – I didn't know where else to go and—"

"It's quite alright, you know you're always welcome here." She slid down to her knees in front of Sadie. "Can you tell me what's going on?"

Sadie sniffed and Natalie reached for a box of tissues and passed them to her.

"Thank you," she said, wiping her nose and then blowing delicately. "I got home and—" Her line of sight began to stare off into the distance. "I found her in the garden. I thought—" She shuddered out a breath and squeezed her eyes shut. "I thought she was asleep. The back door was open and there was a half-finished cup of coffee on the table. Muffy was laying on her lap still."

"Muffy?"

"Blanca's cat. She rescued her as a kitten on her last trip home to Portugal." Sadie looked at Natalie's face and tried to smile. "She was barely breathing. I called an ambulance, and they said it looked like a suspected heart attack, which makes sense because her heart isn't…she has tablets for it." She pressed her lips together and let the tears fall again. "I stayed by her bed all day, all evening, but she didn't wake up."

"Oh, Sweetheart, that must have been so upsetting," Natalie said, her arms already moving to embrace her. Sadie clung to her and shook again as the sobs racked her entire being. "It's okay, I'm here. Let it out."

"I just…I – I knew something wasn't right. We always message when I finish—when I get done, I just assumed she was having a lie in. I'm just glad that I cancelled my last – something said go home, you know?" Sadie pulled away, tugged more tissues from the box and wiped her face again. For the first time she seemed to notice where she was. "I'm sorry, I didn't know who else to turn to and—"

"It's fine. I'm glad you came," Natalie said, meaning every word. "I've a spare room, will you stay?"

"Oh, I didn't think about that, I don't have—"

Natalie cupped her cheek. "You don't need anything, except to let yourself grieve and let me be there for you."

"Okay," Sadie said in barely a whisper.

"What do you need right now?" Natalie asked, her fingertips absently moving against Sadie's thigh.

"I don't know." Sadie smiled sadly. "I must look an absolute state."

"Well, I don't think that matters." Natalie returned the smile. "I'll tell you what. I'll go up and organise some pyjamas and make-up remover. Do you want to take a shower?"

"Would you mind?"

"Of course not. Come on, I'll show you where everything is and then, have you eaten?"

"No, I'm not sure I—"

Natalie placed a finger against her lips. "I'll make something light, an omelette. Nothing fancy or too difficult."

Sadie nodded. "Alright, thank you."

Chapter Fifty

2024 Amberfield, Natalie's home

Under the safety of the water, Sadie let her tears run free. She couldn't quite take it all in. Blanca was gone. Twenty years or more of friendship had come to an end as easily as it had started.

She'd just slipped away without a proper goodbye, and it hurt.

Stepping out of the cubicle, she wrapped the towel around her hair and wiped the mirror clear of steam with her palm. Her face was make-up free with red-rimmed eyes. She could count on one finger how many people had seen her looking like that.

And that person was gone.

Only Blanca had witnessed the state of her when she'd been travelling. The way she'd fallen apart over Natalie leaving. How she'd found herself entering a world she knew nothing about and would have scoffed at anyone who'd ever suggest she could sell herself. Only Blanca had been there on the few occasions her client had been a little too rough, or a little too abusive.

The mother her own mother had never been. She pressed her face into her hands. How was she going to do this now without Blanca by her side?

"Everything okay?" Natalie asked following a quiet knock on the door. "I've left some things on the end of the bed and placed a tray on the—"

Sadie opened the door.

"Oh, sorry, I didn't mean to rush you, I just thought—"

"Thank you. I'm okay, I was just thinking about Blanca." Sadie smiled sadly. "You've been really kind, I don't—"

She felt a warm palm wrap around her bicep. "I've been who and what you need, and I'll continue to do that, for as long as you want me to," Natalie said.

Their eyes locked on one another as Sadie studied her face. She meant what she'd just said; Sadie could see that just looking at the determination on Natalie's face.

"I know it's hard for you to trust me. I understand that. But I'm not going anywhere," Natalie insisted when Sadie didn't speak. "I'm here, with you, in whatever capacity you need."

"Right now, I think I just need to sleep and—" She clasped a hand over her mouth. "Shit, I need to go."

"What's wrong?" Natalie asked, her eyes widening at the sudden change in demeanour Sadie was exhibiting.

"Muffy," Sadie said quickly. "I forgot about Muffy. She'll be hungry and looking for Blanca."

"Okay, the cat?" Natalie asserted. "Alright, how about you get dressed, eat the omelette and then I'll drive you over and we can collect Muffy and bring you both back here."

"How could I have forgotten?" Sadie scolded herself.

"You didn't. You've remembered now. We'll go and collect Muffy, and everything will be alright."

The minute Natalie was parked, Sadie opened the car door and raced for the front door to her flat, pushing her key into the lock and going inside before Natalie had switched the engine off.

"Muffy," she called out, looking in each room for the fluffy grey cat who would not be impressed at being left by herself for so long. "Muffy, where are you?"

Calmly, Natalie followed slowly into the home Sadie shared with Blanca, and hovered before she closed the front door and decided she needed to be decisive right now.

She wandered inside and turned into the first room on her left, a large airy lounge with suitable furniture. It was in darkness, so she flicked the light switch on and moved inside.

One area of the room looked very lived in. A reclining armchair was worn, the cushion dipping where it was used regularly. Books were piled up on the small table next to it, along with a glass tumbler with the remnants of a dark liquid at the bottom.

There were photos of a life somewhere warm. Sunshine and palm trees. Smiles and colourful drinks.

She could hear Sadie moving from room to room still, calling for the cat, but as she turned to look around, she heard the small squeaky meow.

"Muffy, is that you?" she asked gently, poking her head behind the armchair and finding two big eyes staring up at her. "Hello." She held out her fingers and encouraged the cat to sniff her. "Come on, you've got an adventure ahead of you. I know you must be very scared right now, but it's all going to be okay." She inched forward and kept talking.

Muffy must have considered that she was tolerable because she got up and came out of hiding, rubbing her face against Natalie's fingers.

"There you go. See, I'm a nice person." When Muffy was within reach, she swooped down and scooped her up. Turning to go and find Sadie, she almost dropped the cat. Sadie was in the doorway, watching her. "I found Muffy," she said, as though that wasn't obvious.

"She let you pick her up?"

"Yes, quite easily. She's a literal pussycat."

Sadie raised a brow. "She's a feral little monster with anyone other than Blanca."

Natalie looked at the cat, all snuggled against her. "Well, clearly Muffy has a keen sense of who's to be trusted."

There was silence for a moment, and Natalie wondered if Sadie was internally digesting that as fact or arguing it as bullshit.

She went with the latter when Sadie said, "I was thinking it's probably easier if I just stay here with her."

"Oh, right, I mean if that's what you want," Natalie said, still holding the cat. "Do you want to be alone?"

"I'm not sure," Sadie answered with a sigh. "I just don't want to put you—"

Natalie stepped forward. "I meant what I said. I'm here for you, in whatever capacity. If you want me to go, I'll go, but if you're just saying that because you think it's the right thing to say then I'm going to argue the point. I'm happy to take you both back to mine, or I can stay here with you."

Sadie's eyes swept the room and landed on the empty chair. Blinking away the tears, she said, "I don't think I want to stay here yet."

"Okay then. So, shall we find Muffy's carry box and get some things together for you both and then go home?" She said 'home' without thinking, but if it had fazed Sadie, she hadn't shown it.

"Alright. Let's do that."

Chapter Fifty-One

2024 Amberfield, Natalie's home

Muffy crept out of the box and looked around her new surroundings. She meowed and hissed and then like lightning, she ran for cover under the dresser.

"I guess she's going to need a moment to settle and adjust, and we'll need to make sure she doesn't go outside yet," Natalie said. "I'll leave her box out so she has something that smells of her. Should make her feel safer."

"Have you had a cat before?"

Natalie half smiled. "No, is that the wrong thing to do?"

Sadie shook her head. "No, it's the perfect thing to do. I just – I assumed you must have had knowledge of a cat."

"Had a child once," Natalie said easily and almost laughed at the look of panic that hit Sadie's face. "For about three days before her mother came back from a weekend away. That felt like a very long trip."

"Yeah, I can imagine." Sadie let her bag slide down her arm and fall to the ground. "You didn't want kids?"

"I suppose at some point I questioned it. I dated several women who had them, but those relationships never lasted, and I think it was always down to the fact that we'd get to the point where I'd have to be all in and that meant parenting, and I'd always pull away."

"So, you don't like kids much." Sadie smiled.

"I love kids, I just – I didn't have the best experience growing up. And I suppose I thought I'd be a terrible parent because of that."

"They really did a number on you, didn't they?" Sadie said.

"Hm." Natalie took a deep breath and smiled as she breathed out and noticed the time. "Shall we get you set up? You must be exhausted."

At the mention of sleep, Sadie yawned. "Yes, I think that's probably a good idea." She gathered up her things and followed Natalie upstairs.

The light was still on, the pyjamas on the bed where they'd been left. Not that Sadie needed those now she had her own, but neither of them mentioned that as she dumped her bags and stood awkwardly for a moment. The last time they'd been in a bedroom together had been the night Natalie had disappeared from her life.

"I'll go and organise everything for Muffy and then go to bed. I'll see you in the morning," Natalie said, her fingers gripping the door handle.

"Oh, I don't want to keep you up. I can deal with Muffy, Blanca would—" Just saying her name brought tears again and Sadie visibly sagged. "Sorry, I just can't get used to it."

"Do you need a hug?" Natalie asked, aware that infringing too much in Sadie's personal space might not be something that was wanted.

"I don't know what I need." Sadie laughed it off between sobs. "But yes, maybe a hug would be nice."

There was nothing more to think about as Natalie stepped forward, releasing the door handle to reach for Sadie and pull her in against her chest. Her arms wrapped around her so naturally, it was as though they found an old imprint and settled easily into it. How she had missed this, longed for it.

"It's okay to feel sad," Natalie offered quietly, rubbing her palm up and down Sadie's back in as soothing a manner as she could. "It's alright to cry and even rant if you need to."

"That's what she would say," Sadie said before turning and nuzzling into Natalie's neck. Wet tears soaked into Natalie's skin and clothing. She didn't care. It was blissful, in a way.

"Then she was a wise woman."

Sadie pulled back, wiping her eyes with the back of her hand. She looked a little embarrassed.

"She really was. We've been friends for over twenty years. She gave me a room when I needed somewhere to live in Portugal, and then when I came home, a year or so after, I got a call. She'd been in some trouble and needed to get away, so of course I offered my couch." She sat down on the edge of the bed and brought her hands to her lap, fidgeting with a ring that she wore on her thumb.

Despite being tired, Natalie allowed her to talk.

"I think she stayed for a couple of months and then she thought it was okay to go back home, but within the year, she phoned again. She was bored with life in Portugal, she wanted to start over somewhere else…so she came to live with me. Every few years she'd go back and visit friends and on one trip, Muffy returned with her," she said, repeating the story she'd told previously.

She looked up at Natalie through wet lashes.

"I don't know how to live on my own. She's always been at home. Always on the end of a phone."

"You don't have to worry about that for now. You can stay here for as long as you need," Natalie reassured and meant every word. Sadie could stay forever.

"Thank you, Natalie. I mean that, thank you."

The awkwardness returned, and Natalie had a sudden urge to remove herself from the situation, feeling her own emotions beginning to grow and settle into something that she wasn't sure would ever be returned.

"Why don't we get some sleep and then in the morning, we can see how you feel, maybe get some fresh air with a walk."

Sadie nodded. "Okay, I'm sorry. Go to bed, you look exhausted."

Natalie looked at her watch. It was almost three in the morning. She hadn't been up this late in years.

"I'll live. You have nothing to be sorry about." And she meant that in every sense. "Good night, Sadie."

She closed the door and stood silently outside for just a moment. It was all so surreal, wasn't it? The love of her life was on the other side of the door, in her home again.

This time, she wouldn't fuck it up.

Chapter Fifty-Two

2024 Amberfield, Natalie's home.

Natalie sat up and bashed at the pillow with her fist, infuriated that sleep wouldn't come. But how could it, when in the very next room was the love of her life? Sadie was heartbroken and sad, and there was nothing Natalie could do to comfort her any more than she already had.

Her head swam with a hundred and one questions and thoughts. On one hand, she was selfishly glad that Sadie had turned to her. That after all these years, and a chance meeting last week, when her world fell apart, Sadie's first thought had been to go to her.

And then, aware of her selfish thoughts, she felt guilty that in Sadie's hour of need, she was lying here imagining a knock on the door and Sadie standing there, asking to come in.

"For god's sake, just go to sleep," she castigated herself. Flopping back down and squidging the pillow up under her cheek, she reached out and tapped the clock, waking the display from its snooze.

Almost four.

She huffed again and was about to batter the defenceless pillow once more when she heard a noise in the hallway. Lifting her head, she listened intently.

There it was again.

A shuffling noise outside of her door.

Her heart rate sped up. Was it Sadie, wanting – no – needing her?

"I'm awake," she said quietly but loudly enough that anyone outside could hear. Nothing happened. The door remained shut, no voice replied, but the sound continued. It moved away and then back again as though someone were pacing back and forth maybe.

Curiosity got the better of her and she threw the covers off and tiptoed to the door, opening it slowly. She popped her head out and investigated the dark hallway.

There was nobody there.

About to turn around and head back to bed, she heard it again and swung around, this time looking down and into the ray of light from her bedroom lamp, to find Muffy playing with something that she was batting back and forth along the hallway. Upon closer inspection, Natalie saw what it was: a spider. A big, black, hairy, long-legged spider.

She screamed.

Muffy meowed loudly and ran. The spider was already half-dead and making no attempt at a getaway.

Bright light bathed her as the spare room door opened, and Sadie stood there holding a large vase in her hands, her face concerned but ready for action.

"What the hell?" she asked when finally realising that it was just Natalie standing in the hallway looking terrified, but happily no burglar in sight.

Stepping out of the room, she did a quick sweep of the area to double-check, and when she found nobody else lurking, she dropped her hands and lowered the vase.

"Are you alright?"

"Yes, sorry…I heard a noise and went to investigate. I didn't know if you'd got up or…anyway, it was Muffy. She must have come out of hiding and decided to explore the house, and clearly, she was having an adventure, because she was playing with this." Natalie pointed to the carpet and the spider all tangled up. "I think it's dead."

Sadie's line of vision followed where the finger pointed.

"Oh, that's…sorry, she isn't usually so murderous with things that aren't human hands."

Natalie's eyes bugged. "I don't mind the murder; I just don't want to witness the crime or deal with the body."

Sadie chuckled. "You're still scared of spiders?"

"It's the fourth most common fear. After failure, death and disease," Natalie said defensively. "Not that I've…" She stopped trying to explain herself. "So, anyway… can you…"

"Remove the corpse?" Sadie said seriously, but she couldn't hide her amusement. "Sure." She bent down and reached for it.

"Jesus Christ, with your fingers?" Natalie exclaimed.

"It's just a spider," Sadie said, gazing up at her. "And a dead one, literally nothing about it is going to hurt me."

Natalie shuddered and backed away. "I believe you, I do, but—" She felt the doorframe to her room hit her back as she watched Sadie stand up, carrying the tiny creature in the palm of her hand. "I'm going to have to…" Natalie stepped sideways, into her room and quickly closed the door, peeking through the gap, before firmly closing it and running to the bed.

The sound of Sadie giggling did nothing to ease her sense of dread as she moved away and climbed back into bed. She heard the toilet flush and then there was a gentle tap on her door.

"Come in."

Sadie's head poked around the opening, and in the half-light of the lamp, she smiled. "I'm sorry, I shouldn't make fun of you. It was mean. The spider is gone."

"Thank you," Natalie said, subconsciously tugging the duvet up to her neck.

"Are you alright?" Sadie asked, rubbing her sore eyes. She'd been crying again. Maybe she hadn't stopped, and Natalie just hadn't noticed in the darkness of the hallway, but she noticed now.

Natalie nodded. "Yes, sorry, I know it's an overreaction. I wasn't expecting it."

Sadie's eyes softened. "Well, I'm sorry Muffy woke you up. I can put her in with me if it's an issue."

"It's fine, I wasn't asleep," Natalie said quickly. Muffy hadn't done anything wrong, apart from having murderous mitts.

"You must be exhausted too."

Natalie relaxed a little. "Yes, sometimes I can't get my brain to switch off."

"Yes, I understand that feeling right now." Sadie smiled slowly. She went to speak and stopped herself.

"What is it?" Natalie asked. She wanted to know every thought Sadie had. Every curiosity, every mindlessly numbing pointless thought.

All of it.

Sadie looked away quickly. When she looked back, her lips were pressed together, her expression full of thought.

"Do you want some company?" Sadie asked slowly. "I don't think I want to be alone right now."

If Natalie was supposed to think about that for more than a second, then she read it completely wrong. Her hand was up and out of the covers, instantly grasping the corner of the duvet and throwing it back to reveal the pale yellow sheet beneath.

"Hop in. No point being cold."

Chapter Fifty-Three

2024 Amberfield, Natalie's home

The times that Sadie had woken up with someone else in the bed with her in recent years, she could count on one hand. Occasionally, a client would request it and pay for her time, but generally it was a smash and grab for them both and she would go home alone or to her own bed at a hotel. In her private life, it was even rarer.

But as she felt consciousness nudge her awake, she had the sudden awareness of the warm back she found herself pressed up against.

Even when they were together all those years ago, they'd never spent an entire night together. Not with Aunt Lina always lurking; there was no way she'd allow Natalie to have a sleepover, or even worse, to stay out all night.

So, this was a first.

It hadn't been planned. In fact, she barely remembered how it had happened. They'd just been talking and then…here she was, and clearly, she – or to be more specific, they – had both fallen asleep.

And gravitated towards each other, she thought.

Her instincts told her to roll away quickly, to get up and leave the room before Natalie woke up and everything would become weird.

That would solve any awkwardness, wouldn't it?

But the reality was, she liked it, didn't she? If she were honest, there had been many nights over the years when she'd thought about what this would be like. Her senses overwhelmed her as the soft scent of a sleepy body, shampoo and perfume all lingered just enough to make her feel heady and a little excited, nervous even.

Waking up with Natalie Shultz in her bed, in her arms, wasn't that what she'd always wanted?

She forced her body to relax, to let the tension leave so she could allow herself to enjoy it, just for a few minutes. Natalie was still asleep. It wouldn't hurt, would it? Not when she was in so much emotional pain.

It was what she needed.

Blanca would see the funny side of it. She'd say she was the cause of it and enjoy taking the credit, even if it didn't mean anything in the grand scheme of things. They'd fallen asleep, that was all.

Her thoughts and plans were ruined in the next moment when a sleeping Natalie turned and burrowed against her. Natalie's knee pushed between Sadie's as she mumbled something incoherent and squeezed her balled fists into the space between them. Her fingers slowly unclenched to rest easily against Sadie's chest.

Sadie closed her eyes and let her senses take over again, absorbing Natalie's scent once more.

Sound followed, a soft snuffling where her nose was squashed, bent against Sadie's collarbone. Sadie smiled to herself about that.

But it was the fingertips that were pressed against her chest with only the flimsy material of her pyjamas stopping flesh touching flesh that really caught her by surprise.

Just a simple touch.

"There's love there still." Blanca's voice echoed in her head again.

That was the last thought she had before sleep took her again and she drifted back into the world of dreams.

Natalie tried to stretch and for the first few seconds was confused as to why her limbs couldn't move. Then her eyes shot open and refocused on the small mole right in front of her, a blemish that she recognised instantly as the same one Sadie had on the little dip at the base of her throat.

A long, thin arm wrapped snuggly around her and held her close to the warmth of Sadie's body. Like lovers entwined, somehow, they'd been drawn together.

She couldn't deny that she liked it. If she were honest, when other people had graced her bedsheets, she'd closed her eyes and often imagined it was Sadie pressed against her.

She'd been hoping and wishing for Sadie with every birthday candle she blew out, every wishbone she pulled.

But this wasn't real, was it?

This was just happenstance.

Two people coming together to comfort one another in different ways, accidently falling asleep and naturally gravitating towards one another because that was human nature. That was all, wasn't it?

Sadie was sad and in mourning, and Natalie had just been kind and responsive without overstepping. She had to keep reminding herself of that.

The bigger problem she had was how to extricate herself without waking Sadie.

After the shock of losing Blanca just the day before, sleep would be the best thing for Sadie. But Natalie had a feeling that the moment she moved, Sadie would be awake too, aware and on the front foot to get out of here.

There didn't need to be any awkwardness, if she could just slide out from under Sadie's grip.

"You've been there for the best part of two hours. I don't know why you're wriggling free now," Sadie's sleepy voice said, her eyes still closed.

Natalie couldn't keep the nervous chuckle from escaping.

"Sorry, I didn't…I thought I'd save us both the awkward agony of…but you seem to have been aware so…"

She'd been aware. The thought hit Natalie like a lightning bolt. Sadie had been aware, and she hadn't moved away. That had to mean something, didn't it?

"There are worse things to wake up to," Sadie said as she arched her back into a stretch and finally pulled her arm free, rolling onto her back and in the process, releasing Natalie's leg from between her warm thighs. "Like Muffy licking your face. Seriously, not how one wishes to be woken."

Natalie chuckled again, but this time, she sat up. "I will remember that and keep the door firmly shut."

She glanced back over her shoulder at Sadie, now sitting up against the pillows, and studied her for a moment. Swollen eyelids were the only real tell-tale sign that she'd been crying most of the day before, but it was obvious to Natalie that lurking beneath the surface would still be an unimaginable sadness.

"I was thinking we could get breakfast down by the river, if you fancied it?" When Sadie didn't instantly agree, she added, "Or we could stay here, and I can rustle something up."

She looked past Sadie at the clock. It was almost ten, and then she remembered.

"Oh, of course, you don't eat before two."

Sadie gave a small smile, her eyes misty again. "I think under the circumstances it's not an issue. Breakfast by the river would be lovely."

"Okay then," Natalie said brightly enough but not too enthusiastically. Someone had died, she reminded herself. "Why don't I go and sort out Muffy, make sure she's all fed and watered for the day, while you grab a shower?"

"Honestly, one night in bed together and you're already bossing me—" She threw the covers back and jumped out of bed quickly.

"Oh, I didn't mean that at all," Natalie said, the words causing a spark within her that meant she became flustered until she noticed the smile widening on Sadie's face. "You were joking with me." She laughed at herself.

"Still taking everything literally," Sadie said. She stopped in the doorway, one hand wrapped around the frame as she stared back at Natalie. "It's nice knowing you haven't changed too much."

Chapter Fifty-Four

2024 Amberfield Riverbank

The riverbank development was a fairly new addition to this side of the river. The opposite bank had been revitalised some time ago, with several popular restaurants and bars serving Bath Street, the nearest town, just across the thin stretch of water.

Several bridges crossed the river. Here the river wasn't as wide and a footbridge had been put in years ago to allow access to Bath Street, but now the Amberfield side was catching up and the entire area was a beautiful spot to enjoy with friends, or as Natalie had done many times, by yourself.

"This takes me back," Sadie said as they strolled together along the footpath. "We used to walk down here to cut through to the bridge and go to the pub."

"I know. It's all changed now though, lots of cafes and boutiques popping up. It's quite the place to be." Natalie smiled up at her and tried not to get ahead of herself with ideas that Sadie might want to spend more time here, with her.

"Is the pub even there?"

"The building is. But it's been turned into a fancy cocktail bar," Natalie answered.

"Oh, that's a shame," Sadie said, before adding, "Might be nice to pop in and see the old place one day."

"Feeling nostalgic?" Natalie hoped so.

"I guess." They moved aside to let a cyclist pass. "Meeting you again has…exorcised a few ghosts?"

"I hope so. I really want to draw a line under all these wasted years and—" Natalie caught herself before she said too much. "Ah, here we are." She pointed to a small café, Aston's. Square tables, each with four matching chairs, marked out the space at the front of the building, with wooden planters creating a border between the restaurant and bar on either side.

Sadie glanced up at the clear blue sky. "Outside?"

"Yes, I think so." Natalie grinned.

They took their seats, and not for the first time did Natalie admire the woman sitting opposite her. No longer the girl she once knew but a woman. Confident, charming, witty, and beautiful.

Out of work attire, Sadie looked relaxed and comfortable in casual blue jeans, a white blouse and heeled boots that gave her at least two inches over Natalie's snazzy sneakered feet.

"Be right out, just got to clear this table, okay?" A striking woman with short dark hair smiled at them. "Menus on the table there." She highlighted with her eyes rather than pointing with her fingers. Her hands were full, already laden with a tray filled with used crockery.

Sadie leaned in. "Family?"

Just as easily, Natalie leaned forward and whispered, "That's Georgia, and yes, family, if you're asking if she's gay." She felt a twinge of jealousy. "Your type now?"

Pursing her lips, Sadie said nothing, and Natalie looked away down the river at a small boat.

"Is Amberfield the place to be for the gays now?" Sadie asked.

"No, I don't think so. Georgia only came back because her sister was killed in that awful plane crash a couple of years ago." She pointed up at the name scrawled across the boarding above the entrance. "Aston, that's her sister."

"Oh." Sadie pulled a sad face. "So, not an ex then?"

"Not an ex, no. She's married if you must know. Her wife helps out at the weekend with the kids. Georgia took the three of them on after…" Natalie explained, the jealousy building as she considered a thought that was creeping in. What if she wasn't Sadie's dream girl any longer? When she realised that she hadn't finished her sentence and Sadie was looking at her expectantly, she added, "Everyone knows everyone in Amberfield. That hasn't changed."

"Do you know all the gossip?" Sadie narrowed her eyes and grinned playfully.

Natalie was about to respond when she caught onto the playfulness and pursed her lips. She picked up the menus. "Don't be mean." And without looking up, she added, "I know that footballer from Bath Street Harriers is dating the sister of someone who teaches at the primary school."

"Oh, that footballer?" Sadie smirked. "You'll have to enlighten me. I'm not up on my sports."

Natalie put the menu down. "It was all over the local papers. The women's football team in Bath Street…Nora Brady. Another player tried to ruin her career."

"I see. Well, that does sound fascinating," Sadie said with another playful smile. "Thank you for taking my mind off of things." She placed her menu down. "And no, she isn't my type."

"Right, what can I get you?" the woman, Georgia, interrupted before Natalie could respond. Notepad in hand, she looked back and forth between the two of them and waited.

"I'll take a black coffee, and the avocado smash with a poached egg on sourdough," Sadie said, glancing up and adding, "Thank you."

"And I'll have a white coffee, latte, cappuccino…I don't mind so long as it has milk." Natalie smiled. "And can I get the—" She drew her finger down the menu as she decided, enjoying the fact that Sadie was watching her intently. "Can I get the smoked salmon on rye with a fried egg, and a side of avocado?"

"Sure can."

"Thank you," Natalie said, placing her menu back in the stand.

"Drinks will be right out. Food will be about ten minutes. That okay?"

"Sounds perfect," Sadie answered for them.

Georgia repeated back the order and then left them to continue their conversation.

"I want you to know that I am not ignoring what happened for you yesterday, and if you want to talk about it, about Blanca, at any point, you should…I'm just aware that you might not want to, or be ready to, or want me to be the one you speak with about it," Natalie said.

Sadie slid her sunglasses back onto her face and sighed. "I'm not avoiding talking about her. I just don't know what to say yet. It doesn't feel real." She looked away and watched as a couple walked past pushing bicycles. "My entire life was so ordered, so structured, and now I feel like – I feel like everything has come off the rails all at once again and I don't know how to manage any of the emotions it's bringing up."

Natalie bobbed her head. "I think that's perfectly understandable, under the circumstances. Your friend has died."

"I was talking about—"

"One black coffee and one latte?" A different woman carried the tray out and put it down on the edge of the table as both women reached for their drinks. "Anything else I can get for you?"

"No, thank you," Natalie said quickly, wanting the woman to leave so that Sadie could continue. "You were saying?"

Sadie shook her head. "It doesn't matter."

"It matters to me," Natalie threw back, her hand instantly reaching out to cover the back of Sadie's. "*You* matter to me."

"That's just it - that's what I'm talking about, all these emotions when you say things like that. You left me, Nat. You walked away and for years I mourned that loss, and now here I am, mourning again, and you are here and it's all creeping back in again, and I don't know how to manage that alongside losing B."

For a moment, the silence built between them and hung like fog on a misty morning. They stared at one another through it, each with their own thoughts until finally, Natalie blurted out what she'd been wanting to say all along.

"I love you. I always have, it's always been you. You're still the one, and I can't keep denying it, not now I've found you again."

"I know, and maybe I feel the same way but…I'm not the same person that I was back then."

"Neither am I. I would expect we're both very different in lots of ways, but not those core reasons why we fell in love with each other."

Sadie chewed her lip before she said, "There are parts of my life I'm not sure you'd understand."

"Try me." Natalie stared intently. "We're going to enjoy breakfast and make small talk, and then we'll go home, and you can tell me what you think I won't understand."

Chapter Fifty-Five

2003 Portugal

Justine arrived on a flight in May and was still there in August. And for the first time since leaving England, Sadie thought she might have met someone she liked more than just a one-night shag or seducing into being a client.

They had fun together.

Lying on the beach all day, topping up their tans and relaxing in the water. Justine was exciting, but calm. She was someone Sadie felt comfortable with, and those people were rare in Sadie's opinion.

"I was thinking we could go get some coffee and then spend the day at the beach again," Sadie said, climbing out of bed and pulling last night's underwear back on. "After I've been home and changed, obviously." She grinned over her shoulder at the prone body still in bed.

"Hm, sure, we can do that. You know how much I like seeing you in that bikini."

"Hm, I know how much you like seeing me out of that bikini," Sadie said slowly and seductively, mounting the bed again and kissing her way up the bare leg that had kicked off the sheet.

"True. I can get onboard with a day at the beach, and then later you'll come back here, right?" Justine giggled when Sadie's lips touched a ticklish spot on the back of her thigh.

"Sure, once I get done with work." Her lips nibbled the flesh, her tongue snaking out and casually sliding around the curve of Justine's buttock.

"At the bar?"

"No, my other job," Sadie said quickly before biting the plump cheek and causing Justine to giggle. "You know I love it when you laugh like that."

"You just love me," Justine said confidently, twisting around so Sadie could straddle her waist.

Sadie stared down at her, enjoying the way her hair fanned out around the pillow, and her pupils dilated at the sight of Sadie hovering over her.

"Maybe I do."

Justine grinned. "So, why are you so elusive about this other job?"

"I'm not elusive. It just doesn't matter." Sadie grabbed her wrists and pulled them up above Justine's head and pinned them there. "All that matters is here and now."

"I think it matters, Sadie. I'm falling in love with you. I want this to work between us. We shouldn't have secrets." Justine wriggled free and sat up, Sadie still straddling her thighs. "Why won't you tell me?"

Sadie went to move off, but Justine was faster and held on. "Tell me where you work. Is it another bar and you don't want Luis to find out, is that it?"

"No, that's not—" She felt herself backed into a corner. This woman could be someone special, someone who would share this life of hers with her, but she was right, they couldn't have secrets, especially not one like this.

"Sadie, please. You can trust me." She reached up and cupped Sadie's cheek. "Just tell me."

"Okay," Sadie finally said. Composing herself, she considered how to word it, but the reality was, there was no easy way to tell someone you sold sex for a living. "I work as an escort."

Justine's eyes narrowed as she tried to process what that meant. "Like taking people places and showing them around?"

"No, an escort as in—"

Justine's eyes bugged.

"A hooker? You're a fucking hooker?" She let go of Sadie and tried to get up, but this time it was Sadie who held firm.

"It's not like that—"

"You fuck people for money, Sadie, it's exactly like that." Justine scoffed. "Jesus, no wonder you're so fucking good in bed, had plenty of practice."

Sadie felt the sting of those words and when Justine pushed her off this time, she fell to the side and let her escape.

"You're a whore and you didn't think you should tell me first? How many people have you fucked and then come to me? What filthy diseases could you have, huh?"

"I don't, it's not – I take precautions, for fuck's sake."

"Oh, well that makes it all alright then, does it?" Justine grabbed her clothes and began throwing them at her. "You need to go."

"Justine, we can talk about this," Sadie tried.

"No, get out, and don't ever come back here." She picked up the pair of jeans she'd worn the night before and reached into the pocket. Pulling out a twenty euro note, she threw it at Sadie. "That should cover last night, right?"

Sadie watched her storm off to the bathroom. Tears welled in her eyes, shame surfacing. She felt the same abandonment she'd felt when Natalie had just disappeared, only this was worse. This felt personal.

Pulling her clothes on faster than she'd ever dressed before and with tears streaming down her cheeks, she ran. Out the door, down the stairs and out into the street. She didn't stop running until she was home.

By the time she'd got back to Blanca's she was exhausted and crashed through the door, almost knocking over a pile of clean washing Blanca had folded.

"*O que ne terra?*" Blanca said as she caught hold of the distraught girl she'd come to love like her own daughter. "What is happening?"

"Nothing, I need to—"

"Sadie, you stop right there. You tell Blanca what the hell is going on."

The stern words filled with love made Sadie stop in her tracks.

"I broke up with Justine," she said before more tears spilled down her cheeks.

"*Por que?* Why?"

Shoulders sagged as she grew heavy and ready to just fall apart.

"Because she asked what my other job was. She said she loved me, and we shouldn't have secrets, that I could trust her." She said everything so fast that Blanca was having trouble keeping up. "So, I told her, and she went crazy, and she threw twenty euros at me, and I've never felt more like a whore than I did in that moment."

"Oh, sweet child, come here." Blanca reached out and pulled her close. "I'm going to kill her."

Chapter Fifty-Six

2024 Amberfield, Natalie's home

Natalie flicked the kettle on and moved around the kitchen collecting mugs and teabags, while Sadie sat quietly on the stool contemplating how much of her life she needed to share, if anything at all.

She didn't owe Natalie any explanations of her life choices, and maybe now wasn't the right time, not in her emotional state regarding Blanca.

She had a weird sense of not understanding when Natalie turned, took one look at her and then moved quickly to smother her in a hug she wasn't expecting. It took several moments to realise that she was crying.

"It's okay, let it all out," Natalie encouraged, running her hand repeatedly over the back of Sadie's head in a soothing motion.

The urge to apologise began spouting before she could stop herself. "I'm so sorry," she repeated, but she wasn't sure what she was sorry for or who she was sorry to. Her fingers reacted, gripping tightly and clinging onto Natalie as though her life depended on it.

Natalie just shushed and soothed, no requirement for words that would have no meaning. She hadn't known Blanca, and she barely knew Sadie now, so Sadie was grateful for the silence.

"Oh, goodness," Sadie said, finally detaching herself from Natalie's embrace. She smiled through wet lashes when Natalie passed her a tissue, and she looked sheepish when the nose blowing sounded like a foghorn at sea.

"Why don't we have that cup of tea in the lounge, and you can tell me about Blanca?"

Sadie nodded. "Yes, okay."

"You go through. I'll finish off and be in shortly."

When Sadie stepped down off the stool, she was greeted by Muffy floating around her ankles. She reached down and picked her up. "Oh, Muffy, I know, I miss her too," she said as she carried the cat out of the kitchen.

In the lounge, Muffy wriggled to be put down on the floor. Cat-free, Sadie sat on the sofa, only to be pounced on by Muffy again, instantly kneading her paws and claws on Sadie's lap.

It wasn't long before Natalie reappeared and placed the mug down beside Sadie on the side table. She pulled the curtains, closing the last of the daylight out, and then she switched on some lamps before taking the other end of the couch.

"So, what was she like?" Natalie smiled, kicking off the conversation.

"Wild." Sadie laughed. "Not so much now, but back then, Blanca was the life of any room she entered. She had this acerbic tongue that would lash out at anyone stepping out of line, but if she liked you…then you had a friend for life."

"And she certainly liked you," Natalie said.

"She took me under her wing. I think I became a surrogate daughter. She was a mother figure to me, that's for sure."

"I'm glad you finally found someone to be that person for you. I know your own parents were…difficult."

Sadie laughed loudly. "Yeah, understatement of the century."

Natalie smiled at that. "I was trying to be diplomatic, and anyway, you might have worked things out with them for all I know."

"Like you worked things out with yours?"

"Touché."

"Blanca was like having a pit bull by your side. Nobody dared mess with me, and if they did…they never came back, and I never asked what happened to them." Sadie held her hands up. "I'm sure it was all legal."

"Maybe I'm glad I didn't meet her. I might have discovered if it were legal."

"She liked you, well not in the beginning. Back then she might have ripped you a new one." Sadie smiled. "Recently though, when she found out we'd met again, she was encouraging me to—"

"To?" Natalie tilted her head curiously.

"To see where it might go. She said there was love there still, and that shouldn't be ignored."

Half-hidden behind her mug, from their conversation earlier, and again now, Natalie dared not hope as she asked, "And what do you think about that?"

Sadie stared directly at her and thought for a moment. Just when Natalie had thought there would be no answer, Sadie spoke.

"I think I might want to find out."

Chapter Fifty-Seven

2024 Amberfield, Natalie's home

Natalie felt her insides flip and roll all at once. Looking across at Sadie, she realised she'd been unprepared for the declaration.

There was a unique, painful moment when you realised your dreams could come true, but the reality was, not now.

"I want that," Natalie said. "I do. I really want that."

"I sense a but…" Sadie arched a brow at her.

With a gentle smile, Natalie fidgeted until she was able to scramble across the couch and almost sit in Sadie's lap.

"Right now, I think that it's pertinent that we, you, process everything around losing Blanca, and what that means for you, and for us."

"Okay."

"And wherever that leads, whatever that means for us, I will be here. There's no need to rush, I'm not going anywhere, but I need to know that if we do this, it's with our eyes wide open and not because we're somehow—"

"Filling a void?"

"I suppose so, yes. I've loved you for over half my life; that's not going to change if we take a little pause while you mourn your friend."

Sadie remained silent for a moment, eyes locked on Natalie, who didn't look away.

"What if what I need is you? What if what I've always needed was you?"

Natalie smiled, reached up and touched Sadie's face gently. "I'm here. I've always been here."

Muffy reached out a paw and with one eye on Natalie, extended her claws until they stabbed through the denim.

"I think Muffy is making a point," Natalie said, gently dislodging the paw and receiving a hiss for her trouble.

Sadie smiled. "I liked it, you know."

With a cute tilt of her head, Natalie asked, "Liked what?"

"When you kissed me, before, when I ran like the wind. I ran because I liked it," Sadie admitted.

"Oh." Natalie grinned. "So, taking it slowly, do you think maybe it would be okay if I did that again?"

"Get to know each other again?"

Natalie leaned in. "Yes, I'd like that."

The kiss began hesitantly.

It was unlike the frantic one they'd shared recently. This was different. Reverent.

An underlying need was beneath it that may well be fuelled with grief and loss, but none of that mattered in the moment. Nothing else mattered to Natalie other than trying to convey every feeling she had for this woman in this one kiss.

It would never be enough.

Pulling back, she bit her lip. "I'm going to take some time off of work—"

"You don't have to do that," Sadie protested.

"I know, but I want to. I wouldn't be able to focus anyway." She laughed. "Let's use this time to talk, and just be."

Chapter Fifty-Eight

2024 Amberfield, Natalie's home

"Bina just informed me that you're not coming in. Is everything alright?" Harry's voice sounded worried through the handset.

Pressing the button on her coffee machine, Natalie waited for it to whir into action before replying.

"Everything is fine. I'm just taking a few days off to be with Sadie."

"Sadie?" Harry exclaimed. "What's gone on?" There was excitement in her voice now, and Natalie had to stifle the chuckle that threatened.

"It's not like that—well, it is but—" She turned to make sure Sadie was out of earshot. "Sadie turned up here Friday night, distraught. Her friend has died and—"

"She turned to you for comfort and support." Not a question, very much a statement.

"Yes, something like that. Obviously, it has given us some time to talk and—" She pulled a stool out from under the island and sat down where she had clear view of the hallway. "We've both acknowledged that we want to see where this second chance might take us."

"Nat, that's amazing. Alright, look, I can keep things plodding along here, but I do need you to be available for anything important."

"Okay, I can do that."

"And anything that requires dealing with Gorman. She irritates me."

Now, Natalie did chuckle. "Fine, I will deal with her should the matter arise."

"Great. Well, I guess I should get off the phone so you can get on with comforting Sadie."

Natalie was about to reply with details of exactly how she would love to be comforting Sadie one day when the woman in question rounded the corner and stepped into view.

"Yes. And that would be lovely. I must go."

"She's there, isn't she? How red have you gone?"

"Oh, shut up." Natalie flustered but laughed, nervous and a little embarrassed. "I'll speak to you later."

Sadie smiled at her as she pulled the stool opposite out and slid onto it. "Everything alright?"

"Yes. All good," Natalie said quickly. Standing up, she turned her back on Sadie and focused on finding mugs for the coffee that was brewed. "I was just speaking to my—to Harriet. She's in charge while I'm away from the office." She turned back and held up a cup. "Coffee?"

"Please," Sadie answered.

"Did you sleep alright?" Natalie asked, changing the subject. Although it was a sore subject, personally. She had hoped Sadie would continue to sleep with her, but they'd talked and agreed it was too soon to be making that a habit.

"Somewhat. It was difficult to drift off, and I had some strange dreams. But I guess I got enough hours that I'm not exhausted."

"That's good." She poured two mugs and placed one in front of Sadie, sipping her own with intermittent blowing to cool the hot liquid. "So, did you want to do anything today?"

"Hadn't actually thought about it."

"Okay, well I'm available if you decide—"

"What do you want to do?" Sadie asked her. Their eyes met and held across the island. They'd been lingering on each other longer and longer each time they found themselves locked in one another's gaze.

"I—" Natalie swallowed down the urge to suggest something very inappropriate. "It's a beautiful day—"

"Do you remember when we used to go and lay on a blanket in that field?"

Natalie blushed, remembering. "How could I ever forget the place I lost my virginity?"

Sadie chuckled at the memory. "I did offer a bed, but you were so insistent."

Standing up again, Natalie rounded the island. Sadie twisted on the stool to meet her, her thighs parting just enough that Natalie could step between them.

"I was in love and horny, what did you expect?" She smiled when Sadie's palms slid up her thighs and rested on her hips. "You were such a gentle lover."

"I'm still a gentle lover," Sadie whispered against the lips that were now so close.

Natalie closed her eyes and pulled back. "And I intend to find out, when the time is appropriate."

She moved to step away but found herself held firmly in place.

"It's appropriate."

Chapter Fifty-Nine

2024 Amberfield, Natalie's home

"Are you sure?" Natalie asked before things went too far. The exploration that had found a gap between her blouse and trousers stilled against her skin.

"Yes," Sadie said firmly, those fingertips now gripping to pull her closer again. "Take this off."

They'd moved from the kitchen to the lounge. The intention had been to talk some more, but it was clear to them both that things were moving too fast for that, both women succumbing to the carnal needs that would soothe each other's souls in different ways.

Natalie smiled, straddled across Sadie's lap. She was reminded of the days before, long ago, when Sadie would instruct and cajole her. She sat up and watched as Sadie's stare focused on her face before slowly lowering to watch nimble fingers undo each button.

"You know, I always liked this part," Natalie admitted.

"Getting undressed?"

"No, you watching me get undressed." With the last button worked free, she shimmied the material free from her shoulders. "I always felt so…I don't know, desirable?"

"You've always been that; don't stop there." Sadie smirked up at her.

Reaching behind her back, Natalie stopped for a moment, very aware that twenty-five years had changed her body. Her breasts were no longer quite as pert. Although she often jogged, she wasn't a gym bunny with firm abs anymore either.

"Is something wrong?" Sadie asked her.

Natalie swallowed and shook her head with a small smile. "No, I was just…it's been a while since I've been naked with anyone and…"

"You're nervous?"

"I guess so."

Sadie sat up, reached around her and unclasped the bra. When it was loose, she dropped back again.

"You're as beautiful now as you were then. I want to see you."

Natalie leaned forward until her mouth was a whisper away from Sadie's and the bra that had fallen down her arms had landed across Sadie's neck and chest.

"I always wondered if you'd still be so commanding," Natalie said before tugging Sadie's bottom lip between her own.

"Oh, I can be anything you want me to be." Sadie's voice dropped into seductive the moment her mouth was free to speak again. "Now." She slapped Natalie's backside. "Be a good girl and take it all off for me."

Something in those words, or the way Sadie said it, or just the way she was looking at her, made Natalie's innards whirl. Any doubt or nerves dissipated, and she knew in an instant that she was wet and turned on.

Climbing from her lap, Natalie stood beside the couch, topless and more confident than she'd ever been in her life, looking down at Sadie sprawled out along the sofa.

"Sit up," she said, directing Sadie.

"That's new." Sadie smiled, but she did as she was told, not asked. Her legs swung around to plant her feet on either side of where Natalie stood.

"I'm not the innocent little virgin you corrupted anymore," Natalie replied, holding eye contact.

Sadie scoffed playfully. "Corrupted?" She smiled like a triumphant woman. "I like that. But you were so easily corruptible."

"I wanted so much to be like you."

"And what was I like?"

Closing her eyes, Natalie let her hands roam her torso, cupping her own breasts and then moving up into her hair, before they fell and hung loosely by her side.

"You were so...confident. Adventurous. You had a kind of joie de vivre about you that just fascinated me from the moment you glanced down the bar at me, and then stalked your way towards me like a lioness about to catch her prey."

"And you were my prey?"

"God no, your demeanour changed and suddenly you looked at me like nobody else ever had." Her fingers moved to fidget with the cotton belt around her waist.

With Sadie transfixed on her, she pulled the knot free. "You looked at me like I was the only person on the planet you'd look at again." Once loose, they instantly fell to puddle around her feet, revealing white lacy knickers and a small tattoo.

"And how do I look at you now?"

Natalie smiled slowly and stepped forward, putting herself in between Sadie's knees. "The same." Her hand reached out to cup Sadie's chin. "When you found me in the bar at the hotel, and I turned around, I could see it...the way you look at me."

Sadie nodded. "Because it's always been you."

"I know," Natalie whispered.

Leaning forward, Sadie's head rested against Natalie's stomach, the hot air of her breath tickling enough to cover Natalie's skin in goosebumps.

"Interesting choice." Sadie's voice husked as her finger ghosted across the skin. Just above Natalie's right hip bone was a pair of red lips. Feminine lips, like a kiss.

"Other than my actual lips, this was the last place I remembered you kissed me before..."

Sadie looked up and said almost in disbelief, "Was it?"

Natalie nodded silently and watched wordlessly when Sadie kissed the spot again, her lips moving slowly across Natalie's stomach to the other hip.

"Now you can make a chain." Sadie smirked, her palms sliding up the sides of Natalie's thighs, stopping when material hindered her path. She hooked her forefingers and pulled slowly until the underwear was no longer an issue.

"Just how I remember," Sadie said, breathing her in. "I want to taste you again." Her tongue flicked out, pressing between folds.

Natalie gasped. "Wait. I want—"

"Tell me," Sadie said, staring up her with dark hooded eyes that said so much more than Natalie could put into words.

"Take me to bed," Natalie said, holding her hands out for Sadie to take. When their fingers interlocked, she heaved her lover up. Face to face, excitement flowing through her being, she said, "I've wanted this for so long…to be in your arms again, to feel your hands on my skin, touching me…I can't quite believe you're here."

"I've felt the same way. All these years have felt so empty."

"Yes, they have. And I know that right now your emotions are—"

Sadie placed a finger against her lips. "My emotions regarding Blanca don't change. I can acknowledge that a distraction is kind of nice, but my emotions around you haven't changed either—"

"I just don't want to wake up tomorrow and hear you say this was a mistake."

"Never." Sadie shook her head. "I've wanted you my entire life. You're still the one."

Natalie nodded slowly and smiled. "I'm suddenly nervous." She laughed. "Which is ridiculous when I'm standing here naked in front of you."

Sadie laughed. "Okay."

"When I used to think about what it would be like if we ever had this chance again, I always thought it would be romantic, and slow, and an exploration, but—"

"But?" Sadie's brow raised playfully.

"I feel like there's an urgency. I feel like if we start, it's going to be on the couch, against the wall, halfway up the stairs and finally falling into bed. So, not that nervous." She chuckled.

"Well…" Sadie said, running a fingertip down Natalie's neck, tracing along the bump of her clavicle and down between her breasts. "There's no reason we can't have both, is there?"

"No, I guess not." Natalie gasped when the fingertip became a palm pressed against her breast. Her feet moved as she was reversed and her back hit the coolness of the wall.

Her mouth was smothered, tongue engaged in an instant battle for dominance in her own mouth. All thought went out of her mind as her leg was raised and hooked around Sadie's waist, those fingers pulling and pinching at her nipples before dipping lower and finding her wet and wanting.

"Oh, Jesus," Natalie managed, adjusting her hand on Sadie to support her weight. "Fuck, yes, like that."

Encouragement seemed to spur Sadie on. The more Natalie moaned, the more Sadie upped her speed. Harder, faster thrusts. The photo frame on the sideboard fell as Natalie's hip nudged the unit with every movement.

She was going to have a mark, but she didn't care as her arms wrapped around Sadie's neck and her head fell back to hit the wall, crying out as the first waves of pleasure began to erupt and surge through her body.

There was something carnal about it, something animalistic in the way Sadie didn't hold back. For the first time in far too long, Natalie allowed herself to be immersed in the sensations and not give a flying fuck what she looked or sounded like.

Inhibitions gone, she used all her strength to lift her other leg and clamp herself between Sadie and the wall.

"Take me to bed," she pleaded just before Sadie's palm was forced against her clit, almost all movement halted by the closeness of their bodies. "And take these clothes off," Natalie demanded as she pulsed her hips and rubbed against the flat of Sadie's hand.

She felt her body begin to contract. Her muscles tightened and released. The mewling turning to a muffled cry with her mouth now pressed against the crease of Sadie's shoulder and neck.

Her body shuddered and shook until finally, she calmed enough to loosen her grip around Sadie, still pressed up against the wall.

"So, bed?" Sadie asked.

"Hm-hm, but…clothes off now, and then I'll reciprocate…halfway up the stairs."

"That's an offer." Sadie smiled. "You gonna unwrap those legs and let me undress?"

Natalie shook her head, smiling. "No. I'm quite comfy."

"Oh, in that case then." Sadie wriggled her hand free and placed both hands underneath Natalie, squeezing her buttocks before stepping back, laughing when Natalie squealed. "I'll just have to carry you." She lurched towards the door and out into the hallway.

"Okay, okay, put me down." Natalie slapped her shoulder playfully.

Sadie staggered another step before letting her down onto the first step of the stairs. An inch taller now, she stared down at Sadie.

"This is it, right? A second chance?"

"Yes."

"Okay then," Natalie said. Feeling the confidence flood back again, she turned and began to climb each step, slowly, glancing over her shoulder at Sadie undressing. "I don't need you to tell me what you like. I remember everything…but if there's something new, maybe you can let me know and I'll add it to my—" She stopped halfway, and took it all in. Sadie naked back then was something she adored; Sadie naked now was something else. "I think I'll work it out."

Chapter Sixty

2024 Amberfield, Natalie's home

Still naked, Sadie lay flat out on the bed. Natalie curled behind her with one leg draped across the back of her thighs.

It was intimate.

An intimacy she had to admit she had missed over the years. Sex was fun. Sex was easy. This was something else, something very different and something she now realised she wanted more than anything.

But the guilt ate at her.

She hadn't been honest with Natalie when she'd made unspoken promises of a second chance. And her friend was dead, lying cold in a morgue somewhere, and here she was fucking her grief away.

She scolded herself.

It wasn't fucking.

They hadn't done that. They'd never done that. You couldn't, could you, not when emotions and feelings and love like they had were involved. The very essence of everything they did together would always be enveloped in that. It would never, could never, be just sex and fucking.

The room was dark, furniture casting shadows in the corners, and with tired eyes, she was sure she saw Blanca sitting in an imaginary armchair. Blinking, she raised her head and stared intently. Nothing there, just a chair Natalie had in the corner of the room, but Muffy sauntered over and jumped up to sit on what would have been Blanca's lap.

Had the cat felt it too?

She shook her head and closed her eyes again, shivering in the summer evening chill.

Natalie moved.

The soft swell of her breast pressed against Sadie's naked back, her skin warmed by the presence. She smiled to herself when Natalie subconsciously pressed her pelvis forward. Damp curls tickled against Sadie's hip, encouraging another bout of want and need before fear eclipsed it all.

She was seized with memories of Justine throwing twenty euros at her, her face contorted into disgust when she understood who she'd been sleeping with.

That one moment in time had been what had stopped dead in its tracks any potential new relationship. Dating anyone had become a painful experience whenever she reached the point of potentially making it more serious.

Natalie was different though, wasn't she? It wouldn't be like that when she told Natalie, would it?

Her thoughts quieted with the soft palm that stroked down her back.

"That's nice," she mumbled into the pillow.

Lips pressed against her shoulder. "I didn't realise you were awake," Natalie whispered.

"I'm not."

"Oh, is that so? Are you dreaming?" Natalie said playfully, her leg tightening its grip across Sadie's thighs.

"I must be," Sadie returned, all thoughts of Justine gone for now.

"It must be a very…good…dream," Natalie said between kisses that made their way across Sadie's shoulders, culminating in a gentle tug of an ear lobe as her body followed and she lifted herself and pressed her front completely against Sadie's back. One leg knelt on the mattress, putting her at a slight angle.

"What are you doing?" Sadie tried to lift but couldn't, not with the way Natalie had pushed her pelvis down against her buttock, wriggling until she opened, and her clit pressed against the flesh.

"I'm enjoying you." Natalie giggled just as her hips thrust forward, retreating and thrusting forward again.

"I see. Because you didn't get enough the first time round?"

Sadie shivered when Natalie's mouth vibrated against her ear. "I will never get enough."

Sadie lifted her butt to meet the movement. "Challenge accepted."

Chapter Sixty-One

2024 Amberfield, Natalie's home

Sadie woke the next morning to two things that were very different from her usual lifestyle. One, the soft, warm and very naked body pressed up against her, and two, the large ball of fluff that was sleeping soundly on the pillow with its furry tail across her face.

"Uh, Muffy, I do not think—" The cat lifted its head just enough and opened one eye to glare at her before promptly ignoring the prod and slapping her tail down to make the point.

Natalie mirrored the cat and looked up through one eye at Muffy ensconced quite comfortably.

"Oh." Natalie's voice was sleepy, but humoured.

"Yes, oh. This is not the kind of pussy I'm prepared to share my bed with." Sadie pushed the covers back, stood up abruptly, and reached down to pluck Muffy from the pillow. "You might have got away with that with your Blanca, but not with me, Fluffy McMuffy."

A short fight began as the cat dug its claws into the soft material and virtually lifted the pillow with it. With one hand securely holding Muffy around the waist, and the other unhooking each claw, it was somewhat comical as Natalie now sat up to be entertained.

The door to the bedroom was ajar, an explanation at least as to how the mischievous furball had gotten in, and Sadie couldn't really complain when it was she, in her haste to drag Natalie into bed the previous night, who had forgotten about the cat and not made sure the door was firmly shut.

"Out you go, Fluff Muff." The cat wriggled free and jumped from her arms, darting back into the room before she had the chance to stop it. "Muffy!" Sadie shouted. "Get out from under there."

Natalie bent over the edge of the mattress and peered under, unable to stop herself from laughing at the scene as Sadie moved, still naked, around the room, crouching low to try and see under the bed and find where Muffy was hiding.

"Oh, let her stay." Natalie chuckled. Rolling back, she patted the mattress. "Come back to bed."

"You know we can't keep doing this," Sadie said, reaching under for Muffy and getting swiped for her trouble. "Ow, Muffy." She pulled her hand out and sucked the welt.

"Doing what?" Natalie leaned on her elbow and sat up to peer over the edge of the bed.

"Keep sleeping together, waking up like this. It's too much, too soon, don't you think?" Sadie responded, still on her knees. She didn't know why she'd said that.

"I think we've wasted enough time, but I realise that this is an emotional time for you. So, if you need to slow it down then I'm okay with that."

Sadie stood up and huffed. Her eyes misted over instantly as her chin wobbled.

"Sadie?" Natalie pushed back the covers and moved to her side.

Sadie shook her head. "I just – it hit me again, she's gone and – here I am frolicking naked and sleeping with you, and—" She covered her face with her hands and wept.

"Oh, sweetheart, I don't think she'd be unhappy about you—" Gently she pulled the hands away from Sadie's face and stared into the watery pools as lashes blinked furiously to stem the flow. "Being happy."

"No, she'd fucking love it." Sadie chuckled through the tears. "I'm going to miss her. I do miss her." Her face fell again, unable to stop the grief from pouring out.

"Of course you do," Natalie said, wrapping her arms around her. "She was a huge part of your life, and she still is."

She felt the nodding head against her shoulder and tightened her hold on Sadie as she shuddered and sobbed into Natalie's neck.

After a minute or so, Natalie led her back to the bed and climbed in beside her, wrapping them in a duvet cocoon.

"Whatever you need, we will do," Natalie said. "You just say it and I'll be right there with you."

Sadie silently nodded.

When Muffy jumped up and found the comfortable spot on the pillow again, neither said anything, but Sadie's hand stretched up and stroked the cat's back gently. A signal that she understood: Muffy missed Blanca too.

Chapter Sixty-Two

2024 Amberfield, Natalie's home

"We need to talk," Sadie said to Natalie's back.

The aroma of bacon filled the kitchen as Natalie moved around organising a late breakfast for them both. Avocado slices were on a plate, along with tomatoes.

"Okay," Natalie said slowly. She didn't turn around. There was something in the tone of Sadie's words that said this wasn't going to be a comfortable conversation. Three days had passed and though Natalie had sensed there was something holding Sadie back, she hadn't pushed for it, knowing she would share when she was ready.

She continued buttering slices of bread and then loaded them with slices of greasy, thick bacon, avocado and tomato, cutting them into two halves before she finally turned.

"Have you had second thoughts?" she asked Sadie. "I know these past few days have been—"

"No," Sadie said deliberately, "but you might. There's something I need to explain to you."

Sadie's response startled her somewhat, but keeping her cool was something Natalie was good at, wasn't it? Years of dealing with her father and Lina had taught her to stay calm. Don't speak before you understand everything.

"Why would I do that?" She placed a plate down in front of Sadie and indicated the stool. "Sit."

Natalie took the stool on the opposite side of the island, hands clasped in her lap as she watched the expression on Sadie's face move from confident to unsure and finally fixing somewhere in between the two.

"I'm ready to hear it, so say whatever it is you need to say and then give me a minute to process it," Natalie instructed.

Sadie nodded. "If you're serious about doing this with me—"

"I am," Natalie interjected. "Was I not clear enough the other night? That is what I want."

Sadie nodded again. "Me too. But there's something I need you to know about me, about my life and my job…"

"Alright," Natalie said slowly. "I can manage you having to travel—"

"That's not it," Sadie said. She pushed the plate a little further away. "I told you I work in the entertainment business."

"Yes."

"And that's not technically a lie, but it's not entirely true either," she said, twisting the ring on her thumb back and forth nervously.

"Sadie, nothing you say is going to change how I feel about you, not after all these years. Just tell me what it is."

The silence seemed to permeate everything. And for a long moment, Natalie was convinced that Sadie would just get up and walk away.

But just as suddenly, Sadie sucked in a deep breath, her chin raised up, and she said almost defiantly, "I'm an escort."

"What does that mean?" Natalie asked, because she thought she knew what that meant, but she needed to clarify just in case she'd somehow gotten the wrong end of the stick, and it was a job title for something completely different.

"It means I go on…dates, with women." Sadie waited a beat before adding, "For money."

The answer confirmed that Natalie did indeed know what that meant. The devil, however, was always in the details, wasn't it? It would be too easy to react to the initial feelings of…what? What did she feel about it?

"On dates? Clarify that for me." Her eyes searched Sadie's face, reading every minute movement. Right now, she looked uneasy.

"I sleep with women for money," Sadie finally answered. "I don't know how else to say it." She kept her eyes firmly on Natalie's face.

"You have sex with women, and get paid for it?" Natalie asked, feeling her stomach churn.

"I don't always have sex with them, but if that's what they want me to do, then yes, I'll have sex with them."

Natalie raised up off her seat to lean closer, a concerned look spreading across her face. "Are you in trouble? Do you need money?"

Sadie shook her head. "That's not why I do it," she said, her tone a little aggrieved at the suggestion. "And I'm not an addict either. There's no nefarious reason I need saving from. I'm not looking for a hero to sweep in and save me."

"Why do you do it then?" Natalie asked. It seemed like a pertinent question under the circumstances.

Sadie pulled her shoulders back. Whether the confidence was real or not, Natalie was instantly put on the back foot.

"Several reasons, really. The first being I'm good at it."

Natalie couldn't disagree with that, but the idea of being that good with *other* women didn't sit quite so easily.

"And?" Natalie pushed for more.

Sadie shrugged. "I like it. It's flexible. I work when I want to. I decide who my clients will be. It's a transaction of resources and finances. No different to any other profession. I provide a service and—"

"They pay to have sex with you, yes, I got that part," Natalie interjected, trying to keep the jealousy out of her voice. She thought about the way Sadie dressed, the car she drove and how she held herself. "It pays well I assume?"

The question wasn't about the money. It was a way of distracting herself from the idea of anyone else in Sadie's arms.

"That is the bonus, yes." Sadie half smiled at the question, but her eyes narrowed as though she'd heard something in there that she didn't like. "It's not all about money."

Natalie nodded. "I didn't mean to imply that it was." She picked at something non-existent on her jumper. She felt uncomfortable as they stared at one another. A million questions running through her head all kept coming back to one.

"And it's safe? You're safe, I mean physically and…it's clean?"

Sadie chuckled. "Yes, as safe as any interaction with another person can be."

Natalie breathed deeply. "I'm not sure I'm ready to find the humour in it, Sadie."

"Of course, I'm sorry," Sadie acquiesced.

"So, someone just calls you up and—"

"They make an appointment, via my website. They must create a profile and I vet them and then decide if I wish to take them up on the offer. If I do, then I set out my terms and fees and arrange to meet them."

"For sex?" Natalie reiterated, unable to get past the idea of anyone pawing at Sadie that way.

"Often yes, not always," Sadie reiterated. "I have several long-term clients who just want someone on their arm for a party or company to have dinner with. I am purely a date for those people. But yes, with others, if they want a more intimate connection."

"And how does this work within the realms of a relationship between us?"

"Honestly? I've no idea. Relationships and my life haven't quite gone hand in hand much over the years."

"I can't say that I'm not surprised by that," Natalie answered fairly.

Sadie looked out of the window. "No, I suppose not." Her attention turned back at the sound of the plate scraping on the counter. "So, what do you think?"

"I think that this wasn't how I expected today to go," Natalie said. Picking up her bacon sandwich, she took a bite and chewed slowly.

Sadie's eyes narrowed at her again.

"This wasn't the reaction I was expecting either."

Natalie shrugged.

"Who am I to judge you?" She reached forward and pushed Sadie's sandwich back towards her. "I'm not saying it's going to be easy, or not a problem. I don't know yet. I need to process this properly and I'll have a lot more questions, I imagine."

"Okay, that seems fair," Sadie said.

Natalie took another bite and then asked, "So, how did you get into this line of work?"

Sadie plucked half of the sandwich up and bit into it.

"I just fell into it, really." She smiled. "I met Blanca in Portugal, as you know. And I was enjoying myself…a lot. New people arrived every week and I…" She shrugged. "You can imagine…at some point Blanca said, 'you know the only difference between me and you, is that I get paid for it.'"

"So, Blanca was—"

"A hooker, yeah. Anyway, it got me thinking. I was exhausted working all hours in bars for a wage that barely got me through the week, and Blanca was right, I was meeting women, charming them into buying me drinks, and sleeping with them anyway…why not get paid?"

"And I suppose you're telling me because it's not something you have any intention of stopping any time soon?"

"I don't know what my future holds, but right now, I have to pay bills like the rest of the world. So, no, I have no plans to stop yet.

Also, because I don't want us to be starting this again based on a lie or secrets."

Natalie nodded. Her mind was awash with questions she wasn't sure she wanted to know the answers to, but it would eat at her if she didn't ask them.

"Do you have to find them attractive?"

Sadie shook her head. "I don't think it's about that for me."

Natalie watched as Sadie's cheeks reddened.

"So, what is it about?"

"Pleasure, I suppose, at least that's what it used to be about. A wall to hide behind and still get my needs met. I need to enjoy the act of giving them something they can't get elsewhere for whatever reason."

"You've always been that way in bed," Natalie said, chomping the last piece of bread.

"Before you, I wasn't," Sadie admitted. "Before you I was very much all about the thrill. Meeting you changed me."

"Why?"

Sadie grinned at her. "You were so…oh I dunno, naïve and sweet, but also curious and intrigued and so excited to try everything. I wanted to give you that. And I guess when I went travelling and I was sleeping around, I think a part of me was always looking for you again and when I couldn't find that in anyone else, I reverted back to my old self and became very switched off around intimacy."

"I'm sorry." Natalie's hand reached out and Sadie met her halfway.

"Don't be, I don't regret a single thing in my life."

"But if I hadn't left—"

"I wouldn't be a whore?" She went to pull her hand away, but Natalie gripped more tightly.

"That isn't what I meant."

"If you hadn't left, we'd have been sleeping in my shitty room. I'd still be working bars, and you'd have given up the dream of university."

Natalie shuddered theatrically. "I'd have insisted we move out to our own place."

Sadie nodded and smiled. "Yeah, they were pigs. But still, we wouldn't be here."

"We might have been. I'd have still inherited my grandmother's money. My university days would just have been delayed."

"Maybe."

Natalie paused to think, sipping the last of her tea.

"So, how are we going to make this work? Would it be like an open relationship?"

Sadie's eyes widened. "No. I'm not in a relationship with anyone else. You and I would be together. And work would be work."

"Can we negotiate rules?"

"Like what?"

"Do you kiss them?"

Sadie thought about it. "Occasionally. Not often."

"What if I didn't want you to kiss them?"

"Then I'd ask why."

"I don't know, it just feels too…intimate, like there should be things that are only for us."

"Alright, what else?"

Natalie stood up and took the plates to the sink. "I don't really know, if I'm honest, Sadie. As much as I would never judge you and your choices, I still have no idea how this will feel to be involved with. Or how I will feel when you go to meet one of these clients and I'm at home by myself." She turned back to face Sadie.

"I get that."

"I'm not a jealous person on the whole, but then I've never been in the position of knowing other hands are touching what's mine." She felt her cheeks heat as she spoke and shook her head quickly. "I didn't mean that how it sounded."

"I quite liked how it sounded," Sadie admitted. Standing from her perch on the stool, she crossed the room. "I like being yours," she said as she moved in and trapped Natalie against the counter. "I always have been."

Natalie's palms slid up and over Sadie's shoulders, her fingers interlinking behind Sadie's neck.

"We're not much different really," Natalie said, half smiling at her.

"How so?" Sadie asked, her lips ghosting across Natalie's mouth.

"I sell sex too." She smiled into the kiss that followed.

Chapter Sixty-Three

2024 Going to Sadie's flat.

"Are you sure that you're ready for this?" Natalie asked. "It's barely been a week." She watched while Sadie searched her bag for keys and became frustrated when she couldn't find them.

Sadie dropped the bag in anger and mumbled an expletive under her breath.

"I'm never going to be ready for this, but it needs to be done."

Natalie sidled around the table until she was close enough that she could touch Sadie's arm.

"I know. It doesn't have to be done right now though, that's all I'm saying. Maybe another couple of days—"

"You've already taken enough time off, and I haven't worked for days," Sadie said.

"Maybe we shouldn't worry about work right now." Natalie's palm stroked gently. "You can stay here as long as you want to. Muffy seems at home."

Sadie smiled. "I'm not in any rush to leave. I just – I feel like I've abandoned her."

"Blanca?"

Sadie nodded. "Yes, like I just packed my bag and ran."

"Okay." Natalie glanced down at the table and her handbag, dipped her fingers into the gaping front pocket and pulled out a set of keys that she hung off her finger. "Shall I drive?"

"Please." Sadie leaned in and kissed her cheek. "And then I'll take you to lunch."

"You've got a deal."

The flat felt cool and eerie when Sadie pushed the door open and stepped inside for the first time in days. That wasn't out of the ordinary – she was often away from home for days, sometimes weeks, at a time – but the flat had never been empty before. There had always been a heart beating somewhere within the walls. Now it was just silence. No TV playing quietly in the background with Blanca chuckling away at the entertainment.

She shuddered out a breath and composed herself.

"Okay?" Natalie asked. Her warm palm landing deftly in the small of Sadie's back felt comforting and urged her forward.

"Yes, I guess it just feels so empty. I half expected to hear *Tipping Point* and Blanca shouting out the answers. She loves a quiz show."

They walked into the lounge, both stopping to stare at the empty chair and the TV's blank screen.

"Do you have a plan on what you want to do first?" Natalie asked.

Sadie glanced at her, so close and yet never encroaching too much. Natalie was just there, at hand, waiting and willing to be of service. Exactly how Blanca had been in her life. Dependable but unobtrusive. Although Blanca had never done the things Natalie did with her.

"I think maybe find all her personal paperwork and go through anything that needs dealing with. I know she had a will made. And I'll need her address book and phone so that I can contact anyone relevant. Not that there will be many." Sadie frowned. "She distanced herself from family years ago, or I should say, they distanced from her."

"Because of what she did for a living?"

"Surprising, huh?" Sadie said with a sarcastic edge. "Most people don't want a whore in the family."

Natalie grimaced. "I wish you wouldn't use that word."

"Why not? It's what she was. It's what I am," she said defiantly.

"I don't know, it just sounds so…"

Sadie turned to her. "I sell my body for money, that makes me—"

"A businesswoman," Natalie said confidently.

Sadie grinned. "Fine, I can accept that." She sighed and took Natalie by the shoulders. "Are you sure you can?"

"Accept that you're a businesswoman?" Natalie stared at her hard.

"Yes." Sadie chuckled.

The tension eased.

"Yes, I think so, but like I said, it might take some adjustment. We'll work through it." She stepped in close. "I'm not losing you again."

"I hope not."

"Hey," Natalie said. Reaching up and cupping Sadie's cheek. "We'll work it out."

Sadie covered her hand. "Okay." She smiled before taking a deep breath. "And you need to go back to work."

"I'm the boss. I can take as much time off as I want," Natalie said. "I want to be here for you."

"I know." Sadie kissed her palm. "I need to organise her funeral, and you have this huge campaign about to be filmed and—"

"And my team can manage that."

"I know—"

"Are you trying to get rid of me?" Natalie smiled.

"Yes, you're such a distraction." Sadie grinned back. "Thank you, I don't know how I'd have gotten through this without you. But I think…I'm a distraction for you too."

Chapter Sixty-Four

Come Again Headquarters, Monday Morning

Natalie picked up the phone and rang the number she'd now memorised. When Sadie answered, she smiled into the handset.

"Just checking in. Everything okay?"

"Yes," Sadie answered. Natalie could hear the kettle hissing into life in the background. "Just making a cup of tea and then I'm going to organise my diary. I have an appointment with the funeral directors later too."

"Do you need me to come with you?" Natalie pulled her planner across the desk and ran a finger down the page, grimacing when she noticed the end-of-day appointment with Harry and Davina. They were going through rehearsals for the ad this morning, and she'd promised to be there for the actual filming later in the day. "I know it's taking a toll waiting for the coroner to release the body."

"No, I'll be fine. It's just a chat about what she might like and—" Sadie breathed deeply. "I'll be fine, honestly, and if I'm not then I'll call you."

"Okay, I can live with that. I'll possibly be home later than usual; apparently, I must attend filming later and meet our star."

Sadie laughed. "I'm sure that will be such a hardship." She laughed again and then a thought occurred to her. "Why don't I meet you after and we can get some dinner? I doubt either of us will feel up to cooking anything."

"That sounds perfect. I'll make some reservations and send you the details."

"Alright, have a good day," Sadie said, disconnecting the call.

Natalie looked at her watch. It was barely eleven and she'd gotten absolutely nothing done.

Picking up the phone again, she buzzed through to her P.A.

"Bina, could you book a table for this evening at Joie for me, for two?"

"Of course. Just a heads up, Lucia Sadler is in the building and some of the staff have gone a little haywire." Bina giggled. "And when I say some, I mostly mean James…apparently, he just adores her."

"Why am I not surprised about that." Natalie smiled. "I'll pop down later and say hello."

"I'll hold your calls when you do," Bina said. "Ms Gorman called, she said she would be here around four thirty to watch the filming with you."

"Great," Natalie said between gritted teeth. "Hopefully, they will get it done in one take."

She heard Bina giggle as she placed the phone down.

Harry was in her element when Natalie stepped quietly into the room for the second time that day.

Unnoticed, she leaned back against the wall and watched. The space had been emptied of its usual desks and technical equipment, and then dressed as a boudoir. The bed was layered in red and black satin. She wasn't sure why they hadn't just hired a studio, but the director and Harry had insisted that using the Come Again vibe would bring something extra to the entire thing. Who was she to argue with artists?

Cameras angled in several positions and directions, with an almost all-female crew operating them. Huge lights lit it all up and Harry stood beside one of the cameras watching on the screen as the director gave Lucia Sadler her instructions.

The blonde twenty-something reality star listened intently, nodding and smiling, having fun. Maybe all the hype around her wasn't quite as true as Natalie had assumed. She'd certainly been polite enough when Natalie had popped up earlier and said hello.

Harry turned and made eye contact.

"Hey," she mouthed silently. A minute later and she was walking quickly towards where Natalie leaned. "What do you think?"

Natalie pushed off from the wall. "It looks exactly how the mood board said it would. I'm impressed." She smiled and glanced quickly at her watch. It was gone five.

"Don't worry, we don't need Davina's say-so on this. She's invited out of politeness, that's all," Harry said, reading Natalie's expression.

"Yes. You're right, I just abhor tardiness. And I have a date, so I'll be leaving no later than six, regardless of whether Davina deigns to honour us with her presence."

Harry grinned. The mutual dislike of Davina Gorman was already acknowledged.

"How's everything going with Sadie?"

Natalie couldn't avoid the broad smile that spread across her face. "I know it's a little macabre…I never met Blanca, and I'm sad for Sadie, but I can't help but feel grateful that it was me she turned to and for how it's allowed us the opportunity to spend this time together."

Harry nodded. "Nothing you could do about her friend dying. It's not like you had anything to do with it or wished it on the woman. You've done nothing to feel guilty about. Enjoy it."

"I am. Whatever it is and for however long it lasts, I am making the most of it."

"Is she okay?"

"Yes, I think so. She's grieving and that's normal under the circumstances. I am just there for her in any way she needs."

"Oh, I bet." Harry smirked, turning slowly when the director shouted.

"Okay, silence on set."

There was a hushed quiet for less than a minute before the doors opened and Davina all but crashed through them, dragging a suitcase behind her while speaking loudly into the phone.

"Yeah, sure I get it, that's disappointing, but you know...okay, well another time then," she said, stopping right in front of Natalie. "Yes, you absolutely will. Okay, ciao."

The entire room had turned towards her and stared.

"Are we done?" the photographer asked, her cheeks flushed and her eyes a steely grey. She was not a woman used to being held up.

Davina closed off the call and squeezed her phone back into her pocket.

"Sorry, did I interrupt something?"

Chapter Sixty-Five

Funeral Directors, Brighton

Sadie put the phone back in her pocket. "Sorry about that," she said to the funeral director who'd stopped mid-coffin pitch when Sadie's phone had continued to buzz.

"That's quite alright. Urgency comes at any time." He smiled and without missing another beat, continued with his sales pitch. "Clearly the range is extensive. Would you have any idea what you think Blanca would have liked?"

"Honestly, we never had that conversation. I didn't think it would be something I'd have to consider for years, you know?"

He nodded. "Of course." He cleared his throat. "There's a lot to consider, and still time, but it is advisable to book a time slot as soon as possible."

Sadie nodded silently as she flicked through the brochure again. "I think maybe the pine." She turned the page. "Or the oak." She huffed. "Oh, I don't know. It's all so—"

"Would you like to take a day or two to think it through? Maybe you have a friend who would be of help."

Her thoughts instantly found Natalie's smiling face.

"Yes, I guess it wouldn't hurt."

He smiled kindly at her.

"And do you have any idea about an internment or cremation? There's quite a difference in cost, obviously."

"Cremation. I'd like to take her ashes back to Portugal at some point. There's nobody there who would care for a grave, but I think she'd like to go home."

"That sounds like a good plan." He jotted the information down before looking up at her again. "Can I maybe make a small suggestion?"

"Yes, please do, I'm open to any help with this."

"Cremations are…to be blunt, I would encourage anyone to spend the least amount on the coffin. Funerals are expensive enough, and for something that is only going to be turned to ash—"

"I understand." Sadie nodded. "Blanca was someone who loved to look good, but she was also someone who didn't waste hard-earned money." She smiled and picked up the brochure again. "Maybe the bamboo wicker?"

"It's an excellent choice. And looks very nice. Of course, the added bonus of being ecofriendly, always a good reason to choose this style."

"Let's go with that then."

"Okay. I'll speak with the crematorium and get some dates together. And we will arrange for Blanca to be brought here where we will look after her."

"I am grateful. I do hate the idea of her being alone in the morgue."

"You don't have to worry about a thing. We're here to help with everything you need, and you may visit any time you want to."

They both stood, and Sadie caught the time on the clock. It was gone five.

"Thank you," she said, shaking his hand.

She was already pulling her phone from her pocket again as she left the shop and stepped out onto the street, feeling herself calm when the voice in her ear said a quiet, "Hello?"

"Hey, can you talk?"

"Yes. Give me one second," Natalie said before the phone was muffled and the sound of a door opening and closing filled the silence. "Hey, are you okay?"

"I guess so. I was just thinking that I'm in town and it's quicker to pick you up than go home and wait for you? Maybe we can get drinks somewhere before dinner?"

"That would be ideal. Do you know where the office is? We're just finishing up. I'll be free in about twenty minutes."

"I can Google the address." Sadie smiled.

"Okay. I'll let reception know to expect you and let you in," Natalie said.

"No frisk by a burly security guard?"

Natalie chuckled. "I can arrange that if you'd like."

"Hm, I think I'll wait till later and let you do it."

"Oh, well, in that case consider me hired." There was noise in the background again. "I need to get back, but I'll see you soon."

"Alright, I'm on my way now."

Chapter Sixty-Six

Come Again HQ

Lucia Sadler writhed wantonly on the bed for what felt like the 20th time as the director encouraged and cajoled her to find her inner sexy. Natalie considered if the poor girl had any inner sexy left. She couldn't imagine having to perform like this in a room full of strangers.

The photographer stood on the end of the bed; camera pointed downwards, capturing hundreds of still images.

"Perfect," she said. "Just like that. Remember what it is you're wanting."

Lucia purred, "Come again." Her hand disappearing under the perfectly draped sheet.

"And that's a wrap." The director grinned. The photographer was checking the screen on the back of the camera as several people moved in to help Lucia get up and into a robe.

Lucia smiled as Natalie shook her hand and gushed, "That was amazing."

"Oh, you're so kind. I just did what was asked."

"Well, I for one am really glad we have you onboard for this campaign."

Lucia's face lit up. "Honestly, I'm the one who is grateful. It's nice to be asked to do something grown up and sexy…" She giggled. "…that isn't porn. I'm forever being invited to those kinds of events. I love the Come Again range, and the way it empowers women sexually. I'm all for it."

"I'm glad to hear that," Natalie said. "It's pushing the boundaries. Having to keep everything just on the right side of the law and watershed, but I think it's perfect."

"I think it's daring," Lucia said. "Women especially need to know that sex is fun and for them to enjoy."

"I agree."

"Did someone say sex is fun? Champagne?" Davina asked with a grin, sidling up beside Lucia, carrying a tray of amber-filled crystal flutes. "This was great. We should collaborate more, don't you think?"

"I'm always open to business with the right products," Natalie answered like a political mastermind. "Have you met our star? Lucia Sadler, this is Davina Gorman. She's behind the company that makes the iVibe2000."

"Oh, well, I do hope I can snag one for myself." Lucia giggled.

"I'll deliver it personally," Davina flirted.

Natalie rolled her eyes but was soon smiling again when, over Davina's shoulder, she caught sight of Sadie coming into the room.

"If you'll excuse me, my date is here."

"A date. Good for—" Davina turned and grinned before leaning in. "And now I know why my date was unavailable tonight. You took my advice, huh?"

Natalie frowned, and then noticed the look of sheer panic that came across Sadie's face. She watched in horror herself as Davina moved towards her lover.

"Evelyn, how are you?" Davina said loudly. She leaned in. "You didn't tell me you had another client I was in competition with."

"That's because I don't." Sadie spoke quietly but firmly.

Natalie held eye contact with her. A multitude of thoughts and images rushed through her mind. The passive look on Sadie's passive face told a story all by itself.

Her body tensed up, as Davina continued to talk at her.

"Oh, so we can hook up later. I'm really in need having just watched this," Davina continued, oblivious to reading the room and the unspoken conversation taking place between Natalie and Sadie.

"I'm sorry, that's not going to happen," Sadie said more firmly. Natalie could just about read her lips, but she could definitely read her body language. It shouted to be anywhere but here.

Davina laughed and nudged her shoulder into Sadie's arm, whispering loudly enough for Natalie to hear, "Come on, you can do two of us surely. I don't mind waiting my turn. I can make it worth your while."

Sadie didn't respond other than to back away as Natalie began to move towards them, her memory firing information at her as she watched Sadie react to Davina.

An image of Sadie walking towards the lifts, Davina a few steps in front heading off to meet Evelyn. She'd thought it at the time but brushed it off because Sadie wasn't called Evelyn. But now, she knew differently. Now it was obvious. Sadie was Evelyn and it was Sadie that Davina had been gushing over every time they'd met up recently. How had she not put it together?

She felt jealousy rise, and then anger, and then worse, nausea. Feelings she wasn't used to, and didn't want, but they were there, nonetheless, and she had nowhere to go with them except to keep moving towards Sadie.

When Natalie was close enough, Davina said, "You don't mind sharing her tonight, do you?"

Natalie's eyes closed slowly as she got a grip of herself, a well-learned practice when dealing with her father and his despicable behaviour. Opening them just as slowly, she turned to Davina and said, "I do mind, actually."

"Oh, I just thought, we could negotiate a deal." Davina winked and then shoulder-nudged Natalie. "Or a little ménage à trois?"

"Don't you ever do that again," Natalie said vehemently to Davina. "Don't you dare treat her like she's a sex toy you can play with."

Davina shrugged. "She's a hooker, we're the clients. That literally means she's a sex—"

Before Natalie could say another word, Sadie turned and moved quickly towards the door. Pushing through them, she was out of sight before Natalie had a chance to stop her.

"How dare you treat another human being like that?" Natalie stepped forwards, the anger now finding a target. "You should leave before I say, or do, something that I won't regret."

Harry leapt in. "Natalie? Shall we go for a walk?"

Natalie shrugged the hand on her arm off. "No, thank you, but if you could show Davina out, I'd be grateful."

Chapter Sixty-Seven

2024 Come Again HQ

Natalie ran out of the room and into the corridor. Sadie was nowhere to be seen. She kicked off her heels and picked them up before she ran the length of the hallway and pushed open the door to the stairwell, taking them almost two at a time until she reached the bottom and flung the door open.

She caught sight of the back of Sadie's head leaving through the revolving doors.

"Sadie, wait!" Natalie called out, but it fell on deaf ears.

"Everything alright, Ms Shultz?" The burly security guard stepped forward, ready to jump into action.

"Yes, thank you Kelvin, I just need to catch my friend."

He hit a button and the doors stopped revolving and opened to make it easier for her to pass through.

"Dark hair, Claudia Winkleman-like?" he asked.

"Yes."

"She went that way." He pointed to the right and waved at her as she ran into the evening sunlight, shouting a "thank you" in her wake.

Sadie was up ahead, already in the car park, hurriedly heading towards her car.

"Sadie, please. Wait," Natalie tried again.

For a moment, she thought Sadie still hadn't heard her, until she stopped walking and stood impassively with her back to Natalie.

Putting a spurt on, Natalie ran as fast as she could with bare feet on gritty tarmac. She winced and pushed the pain aside as tiny stones dug into her soles.

Coming to a halt as she reached Sadie, Natalie pressed her hands to her hips and half bent over.

"Why did you leave?" she asked, gasping to catch her breath.

Sadie wiped her face, wet tears leaving a trail of mascara down both cheeks.

"Okay, that was a stupid question," Natalie answered. "But—"

"I saw it in your eyes, Nat. The disdain."

Natalie stared at her.

"The way you looked at me, when you understood what was happening."

"Yes, I was shocked, I can admit that. I never assumed I'd be face to face with what you do," Natalie said. "I never thought…" She sighed. "I didn't consider that I'd bloody know any of your clients."

Sadie nodded. "I should have considered that…" She looked away.

"When you came in and she beelined for you, I remembered back at the hotel. Before we talked, I saw you and called out. Davina was ahead of you and I'd…for a split second I thought you were together, but I knew that couldn't be because she was meeting someone called Evelyn."

"You didn't think I'd use my real name?"

"Honestly, Sadie, I haven't actually spent much time thinking about other women and you, so no, I didn't think—"

"Sorry, I guess I feel a little…" Sadie stared intently at Natalie. "Are you going to leave me again?" she asked urgently.

"What? No, why would—"

"I wouldn't blame you, but I need to know. I need to be prepared this time."

"Sadie, no." Natalie reached out, thankful that Sadie allowed the touch. "I'm not leaving. Why would I do that?" She pulled her closer, wrapping both arms tightly around her. "I love you," she whispered against Sadie's ear. "Do you hear me? I love you."

A car horn blared, a woman waving furiously at them to get out of the way. Natalie raised a hand and gave her the finger as they both stepped to the side.

Chuckling, Sadie pulled her hand down but kept hold of it, interlocking their fingers as the woman drove past, silently mouthing off in the security of her car.

"I'm sorry," Sadie said when the moment passed, and all was quiet again between them.

"What for?"

"Everything. Running off. Your friend being my client."

"Davina Gorman is not my friend. Let me be clear about that. She's crass, and uncouth, and I don't care who she is, she had no right to treat you like that."

"I've never had that happen before," Sadie said. "Not the rudeness, that's – I can deal with that, but a client turning up in my private life, that's…I didn't know how to deal with it and then I saw your face and realised you'd put two and two together and I just – I panicked."

Natalie squeezed their fingers. "I can understand. I admit when it hit me, I – I felt jealous. And then I felt angry with her for the way she was treating you, and us."

"I'm sorry."

Natalie put a finger to Sadie's lips. "Shush, apologies are not needed, but conversations are…if this is to work, then we need to be prepared for things like this or have a plan in place to make sure that it doesn't reoccur."

Sadie looked into her eyes. "You're really okay with this?"

"Love is not transactional. I either accept you as you are, or I don't. That's all there is to it. Would I prefer things were different? Probably, yes, if I'm honest. The idea of someone like Davina putting her mucky paws all over you doesn't sit well—"

"She doesn't put her paws all over me. She only gets Evelyn; she never meets me."

"Isn't that just semantics? It's your body in bed with her, your skin she—" Natalie shuddered. "Can we talk about this at home?"

"Yes, of course. Do you want to skip dinner?"

"No, I don't. I booked us a table at Joie. So…" She ran a hand through her hair and looked around, aware now that they were still stood in the car park. "We're going to go and enjoy a nice meal."

Chapter Sixty-Eight

Joie Restaurant

Sadie took a moment to just look at Natalie. The girl of their youth had grown up and become a woman of conviction, empathy and courage.

"Thank you," she said, catching Natalie off guard.

"For what?"

Smiling, Sadie said, "For what you said to Davina. For telling her off and defending my honour."

Natalie breathed deeply. "Well, she deserved it. How bloody rude for a start, but no, I will not stand idly by and have my…have you treated like you can be bought in one of my stores."

"Even though I can?"

The comment rankled Natalie for all of a moment before she picked up her glass and took a sip.

"You may charge women for your time, that doesn't mean they have the right to talk to you as though you are less than…I'll not stand for it."

"I love you," Sadie said, reaching her hand across the table and laying it flat so Natalie could take it.

"I love you too," Natalie answered, slipping her fingers between Sadie's.

The food arrived and they released each other's grips and proceeded to eat in relative silence, until a burning need to understand something erupted from Natalie.

"Tell me the difference between you and Evelyn."

They sat opposite one another in a quiet corner. There was a view of the river through the window on one side, an empty table for now on the other.

"I want to know Evelyn," Natalie added before Sadie had the chance to speak.

"No, you don't." Sadie smiled as she sipped her Merlot. "Evelyn is...detached, cold, unemotional. She's the part of me that is purely hedonistic. She's engaged enough to make her client's experience a good one, and for herself to find something that does it for her, but she's not me. Nobody else gets any part of me."

"Except your body, the physical."

"Yes, that can't really be avoided, but it is limited," Sadie said.

"How so?" Natalie asked, pushing her pasta around to cover it in sauce.

"Do you really want to know all of this?" Sadie asked, putting her glass down and dropping her hands to her lap. "Because I'm happy to tell you anything you want to know, but I can't take it back if it's something you can't hear."

Natalie nodded and stopped twirling her fork in the spaghetti. "I understand that, but I think it's something that I need to try and grasp." She reached one hand back across the table and waited for Sadie to take it again. Squeezing her fingers, she said, "We need to know if I can deal with it before things get any—"

"I could stop," Sadie said, shocking herself with the idea too. "If it became too much and risked us, I could stop."

Still holding hands, Natalie smiled. "If that's your choice, I will support it, obviously, but I'm not expecting or asking for this between us to be transactional."

"Everything is transactional, babe. That's how life works," Sadie said with an air of dismissiveness.

"Maybe that's how it is for most people, and even for us in the past, but right now, all I want is to be with you, to be loved by you and for us to be able to accept each other for who we are."

"And if I worked in one of your stores selling strap-ons and vibrators, I might agree, but I don't. I sell my body...I sell parts of me that most people want only for themselves."

"So, tell me. Explain to me who and what a client gets when you take their money."

Sadie put down her fork and stared across the table at Natalie. "There are two kinds of client: the ones who know exactly what they want, and those who are nervous. The first kind are explicit. They say what they need, and I decide if Evelyn wants that. If she does, then it will generally go one of two ways. They'll want Evelyn to dominate them, take charge and give them a good seeing-to. Which is easily orchestrated."

She watched as Natalie fidgeted in her seat and ran her hand around the back of her neck, spine straightening. Not in a disgusted way, but just reacting to the idea of it. "You like that idea?" Sadie smirked.

"Go on," Natalie encouraged, without answering the question, but she returned the smirk.

"The other kind want to do the dominating. They want to put Evelyn into their fantasy positions and give her the time of her life. On those occasions, I mostly decline, but now and then…it's been what I've needed."

"So, there are times when you are involved and not Evelyn?"

"Those times are very few and far between and have often come during a period of emotional turbulence," Sadie explained. "I know it sounds so—"

"I guess the difficulty for me is putting aside your body from your mind, and that water muddies when you're saying that you needed something from those interactions."

"I understand how that could read that way. I like sex and I've been unattached emotionally for a long time in the sense of a relationship, so have there been times when I have enjoyed a session with a client? Yes, I can't deny that. Have there been times when I've needed something from the interaction? Yes, again I'm not denying that. But I was single and didn't have an emotional and intimate support. So, I used them just as much as they used me."

"And now, what you're saying is that you have me for your emotional and intimate needs, so clients will no longer be used that way?"

"Yes, that's what I am saying."

"Unless I'm the cause of your emotional upset."

"What do you mean?"

Natalie sipped her drink. "I mean, if we argue or fall out over something, are you going to—"

"Sex isn't a weapon, Natalie. I'm not going to use my clients to take revenge over a personal issue we might have."

"Of course, sorry, that was a horrible thing to suggest." Natalie swigged her next mouthful.

"It was yes, but not surprising when I think of Lina and your father's influence on your life."

"They certainly didn't help, nor did the several short-lived romances that filled my twenties and thirties. I'll work on that." Natalie smiled sadly, before putting the subject back on course. "And what about the other type, the nervous ones?"

Sadie smiled warmly. "Well, generally they're women who are curious about women. There are many reasons why a woman might choose another woman to provide her sexual pleasures and fantasies. They have the idea that it's not cheating. Or they've never acknowledged that side of themselves and want to find out in a safe and easy way. Mostly they're the 'lie back and enjoy it' kind of client. Occasionally one will be braver and want to reciprocate."

"They'll touch you, taste you…be inside of you?"

"Yes."

Natalie picked up her fork and began twirling again.

"In those instances, it feels like I'm a teacher. Allowing them to explore a world they'd never considered."

"When are you planning to return to work?" Natalie asked, not looking up.

"I hadn't thought about it. I suppose after the funeral," Sadie answered.

Natalie dropped her fork and looked up with wide eyes. "Oh, god, I completely forgot…how did it go with the funeral people?"

"As expected. There's a lot to consider. I need to go through Blanca's paperwork and see if there's anything in it that would shed any light on things she might want."

"Okay. We could do that after dinner?"

Sadie nodded. "Are we okay?"

"For now. I think it's going to be a day-by-day, client-by-client kind of thing, don't you?"

"Alright, I just – I want to be all in with you, not holding anything back, and yet, I feel like I need to resist in case you decide you can't handle things and—"

"I told you - I'm not going anywhere. We will work this out, somehow, someway."

Chapter Sixty-Nine

Riverbank, Amberfield

It was still light and warm as they left the restaurant. A shared dessert had probably been a little more than both needed, but it had been delicious.

"Shall we take a walk?" Natalie asked, slipping her arm through Sadie's.

"Sure, why not?" She smiled as they set off towards the bridge.

It wasn't that long before they were standing outside of the old Rainbow Pub, now a wine and cocktail bar called Ringo's. A neon light spelled out the name in the window.

"Doesn't look very busy," Natalie said. "Shall we go in?"

"On a school night?" Sadie grinned but took her hand and pulled her towards the door, just like she'd have done all those years ago.

Natalie giggled as Sadie yanked the door open and they walked in to find a half-empty bar area with round tables. The lighting was low, and the décor left them both glancing at one another and grimacing.

"God, it's changed, hasn't it?" Natalie said, her natural curiosity taking it all in.

"Well, we should probably order a drink," Sadie said when someone stood up from a seat behind the bar and smiled at them.

"Alright, but we had wine and you're driving," Natalie warned.

Sadie shrugged. "So, we'll walk home." She turned the barman. "What do you recommend?"

He looked startled. "Uh, I literally started work today."

"Right, okay." Sadie looked around for another member of staff. "So, what can you do?"

He picked up a wad of paper and smiled nervously. "I have instructions, so I can give it all a go."

Natalie's eyes widened, her back to the poor guy.

"We could get a bottle of wine and take it home," she suggested.

"What? No, we need to celebrate your day." Sadie grinned. She turned back to the barman. "What's your name?"

"Ben," he said quickly.

"Okay, Ben, I tell you what. How about I tell you how to make a cocktail?"

"Uh, okay. My manager will be back after eight, though."

Sadie glanced at her watch. "I don't fancy waiting for thirty minutes, so…" She clapped her hands together. "Let's make a couple of Cosmopolitans, yes?"

He seemed to get a little bit of confidence from her excitement. "Alright."

Sadie leaned over the bar and pointed at the glasses. "Two of those."

He lined them up. Natalie stood back and watched the pair of them as Sadie rattled off the ingredients and showed Ben how to use the cocktail shaker like Tom Cruise in the film *Cocktail*.

When he poured the liquid into the glasses and stood back to admire his work, he looked like a new man.

"Wow, that was pretty easy," he said, pushing them across the bar. "Thank you."

"No problem." Sadie held up her card to pay, but he waved her off.

"On me."

"You sure you won't get in trouble?"

He shook his head. "No, my dad's the owner. I'm only working here because he's stuck."

"Hard to run a bar these days I suppose." Sadie looked around. "I used to work here when I was your age, and it was a gay bar."

His face lit up. "If you ask me, it would probably have been better to have that kind of bar around here. Cocktails are a bit expensive when you've got a lot of students heading into town for spoons."

"Maybe you should sell the idea to him."

"Nah." Ben wiped the counter down. "He's planning to sell up and move to Benidorm. He's had enough of the rain and the late nights."

"Ah, well." She held up the drinks. "Thank you."

Turning around, she found Natalie sitting at the table where their old booth would have been.

"Our spot, huh?" She grinned.

"It felt appropriate. You don't look out of place." Natalie said, taking the drink from her. "Just as commanding of the bar as you ever were."

Sadie laughed. "I guess you can take the girl out of the bar, but never take the bar out of the girl." She held the glass up. "Cheers."

"Well, seeing as we've started, maybe we should get drunk for old times' sake."

Leaning in, Sadie said, "And then go back to my sleazy bedsit and fuck till dawn?"

Natalie's eyes lit up and she swigged down the cocktail. "I could be persuaded."

Chapter Seventy

2024 Amberfield, Natalie's home

The ornate box sat open on top of the table in the kitchen. Both women stared into it. Alcohol took the edge off, but they weren't quite as drunk as the four cocktails and two glasses of wine might have led anyone to believe.

"Jesus, your sex box makes mine look like a virgin's," Sadie said as she reached in and plucked a sex toy out and examined it, before putting it to one side and choosing another.

"Perks of the business. I've never used any of them, not even sure I want to with some of them." Natalie slurred a little, lifting the footlong double-ended dildo out and running a cursory finger along it. Her face scrunched and she placed it down onto the table. "Not sure I'll ever use this."

"So, what do you like, now you're all grown up and experienced?" Sadie winked and flashed her a grin when she twirled the furry handcuffs.

Natalie snatched them from her and laughed. "These are fun. They can stay." She grinned as she quickly clipped one cuff to Sadie's wrist. "I prefer a slightly more dominant partner, but one who actually cares if I'm enjoying it. I guess I always looked for you too."

"Dominant, huh? I always thought you were quite confident without me being dominant." Sadie twisted her arm and unclipped the cuff. "Later, I'll put these on you."

A shuddery breath left Natalie.

"You dominate in ways that are quite subtle," Natalie said, lifting the strap-on belt. "Put this on."

"Now who's being dominant?" Sade chuckled but took it from her.

Leaning in closely, her mouth brushing Sadie's ear, Natalie whispered, "I didn't say I couldn't switch."

"Turn around," Sadie countered, her eyes boring into Natalie's with an intensity that sent a shiver down Natalie's back. She instinctively arched and pressed her pelvis against Sadie's thigh.

She needed this.

"I've seen you wearing—"

"Turn around," Sadie repeated slowly and with more firmness as she stepped closer.

Without another word, Natalie turned. A small squeak left her mouth when Sadie pushed up against her back, took her hands and placed both palms on the work top.

"Right now, I'm in charge," Sadie said against her ear before her tongue flicked out and licked the edge of the shell.

Her fingers then lowered and unbuttoned Natalie's trousers. The zip dragged so slowly she thought she might combust. She yanked the material down in one swift move that had Natalie gasp out loud.

"I want you." Natalie said the words, but they were barely audible. Like a wish made on a summer's day when you blew the seeds of a dandelion into the wind.

"Shh," Sadie answered. A palm wrapped around the side of her torso and rose up to cup her breasts and pull her upright and against her.

Natalie moaned at the touch, pressing herself into warm hands that expertly caressed and enfolded her flesh. Her nipples, hard as diamonds, were pinched between deft fingertips.

"Be a good girl, and don't move," Sadie whispered in her ear again, her fingertip now drawing slowly down Natalie's neck. The words, the movement, all worked to send Natalie's arousal skyrocketing.

Natalie said nothing more, but she grinned at the sound of clothes rustling as she assumed Sadie was stripping off.

It felt like a lifetime.

Just waiting and waiting.

She stood half-naked, feeling wanton and primed for something that, despite their intimate moments so far, she'd been waiting twenty-five years to enjoy again: spontaneous frolicking whenever they wanted to.

Being with Sadie was like being home. Any doubt she had around herself, her life, it all just dissipated in this woman's touch. Nothing had changed in all this time apart.

Her clit throbbed and she squeezed her thighs together. She wanted to bend at the waist and just let Sadie take her, but she would wait for further instructions.

And then she felt it, the first nudge of something familiar and hard against her backside. A backside still covered in cotton and lace. Natalie opened her eyes and looked down at her hands, now covered by a more tanned pair belonging to her lover. Sadie pressed firmly against her back, the length of the dildo between her legs, nudging frustratingly against the base of her aching clit.

Sadie's cheek pressed against her own. "Do you know what I remember most?"

"No," Natalie answered.

"I remember that little squeal you used to make when this would slide inside of you." Sadie's hips moved slowly but the intimation was enough.

"Yes."

"And I remember how much noise you would make once we found the rhythm you liked."

"Hm-mm."

"I want to hear you, do you understand?"

"Yes."

"Good," Sadie encouraged. A moment later, she stepped backward, causing Natalie to groan at the loss and then gasp as her underwear followed the rest of her clothes. "Step out and spread your feet for me."

Natalie kicked off her shoes and the clothing wrapped around her ankle quicker than anything she'd done in a long time.

"Eager. I like it." Sadie grasped her hips and tugged, backing her up until she was all but bent over the counter.

Displayed.

Natalie gave a little playful wiggle and was rewarded with an upward moving slap that sent a vibration straight to her core.

"I told you not to move." Sadie's voice was low and sultry.

It was not a tone Natalie could ever remember hearing before, but she liked it. Disobeying Sadie occasionally would work in her favour often, but she knew when to push it and when to be a good girl.

She closed her eyes as Sadie's hands returned to her torso, unable to focus as one moved higher while the other went lower. Her nipple and clit were both squeezed simultaneously.

"Sadie," Natalie murmured as she writhed under the intensity. Her hips jerked. Her chest heaved. "Please," she managed before she all but growled when Sadie's fingers moved away, and she was pushed forward again.

The hands now caressing her buttocks, spreading and massaging. Her left foot nudged to open wider. She allowed it all as her head dropped between her outreached arms and the first gentle pressure of something harder and unyielding pressed against her opening.

All the breath left her lungs, ending with the tiny squeal Sadie wanted to hear, as her body became accustomed to the wanted intrusion and the increasing thrust of her lover's hips.

Chapter Seventy-One

2024 Amberfield, Natalie's home

Natalie curled up on the sofa, her head resting in Sadie's lap, Muffy lying behind her knees.

Sadie finally flicked through the rest of the paperwork they'd collected from the flat the previous week. She smiled down at Natalie when she moved and made a snuffle sound against her chest.

It didn't feel quite so strange anymore, to be enjoying this honeymoon period with Natalie while mourning Blanca. The two emotions seemed to console and cajole each other, riding along next to each other like partners.

And maybe, this insatiable appetite for Natalie, that was absolutely being reciprocated, was an effective way of focusing her mind away from the sadness that threatened to envelop her at times.

She reached down and picked up the next batch of papers. There had been numerous old bank statements and other personal life information like her birth certificate and old birthday cards Blanca had kept. *Sentimental old fool that she was*, Sadie thought as she smiled to herself, but there had been nothing regarding her will so far, and there wasn't a huge amount left to go through.

Blanca had been organised to the point that everything was in the box, but everything in the box was not organised. Finished with one handful of papers, Sadie placed them on the floor beside the box and then delved in for the next batch.

She rubbed her face and then flicked through, stopping when she noticed a white envelope addressed to herself. Taking a deep breath, she gently nudged the edge of the stuck-down flap until she could peel it back and pull out the slip of paper that was neatly folded and handwritten. Her eyes scanned the page looking for anything that suggested she had planned her funeral. She hadn't, but she'd planned everything else.

"Holy fuck."

She sat up so fast that she didn't have the chance to consider Natalie snoozing.

Shaken awake, Natalie moved quickly, which set Muffy off howling and scrabbling, claws sinking into Natalie's calf.

"Ow."

"God, I'm so sorry," Sadie said, dropping the paper she'd been holding to reach out. "Are you alright?"

"Yes, I think so," she answered, reaching down to rub her leg. "What happened?"

Sadie reached for the letter and handed it to Natalie. "I found this, tucked away; it's addressed to me. She's left me everything."

"Oh, well that's understandable, isn't it?" Natalie blinked her eyes a couple of times to wake herself up properly.

"Yes, I guess so, I just didn't realise how – it's a lot."

Natalie took the letter. "May I?"

Sadie nodded. "Yes, maybe then it will sink in."

Natalie scanned the first paragraph before she read aloud.

"My dearest Sadie,

"If you are reading this then it is because my heart could take no more and I have died. Do not be sad. I lived the life I wanted, and made choices that weren't always the best, but I have no regrets, and you shouldn't either.

"I want you to know, that you were the daughter I never had. Meeting you all those years ago gave me hope, and a new life. I believe we found each other for a reason. I was blessed to have you all these years by my side."

Natalie clutched her chest, tears welling in her eyes as her voice choked over the words. But she continued.

"I have watched you grow and become the woman you are, and I couldn't be prouder. I just wish to one day see you fulfil your dream, and a life that no longer means detaching from the woman you want to be with. Even if you can never find her again in anyone else, find her in yourself and use this gift to make your dream come true.

"I have an account at the bank that is all yours. it's all set out in my will which is held by my solicitor Ed Thompson, a sum of £85,000. Put it towards the cottage, or anything else that makes you happy. What is left in my accounts, use to pay for my funeral and look after Muffy."

Natalie dropped her hand and the letter into her lap. "Wow, that's a lot of money." She looked at the date; it had been written three years prior.

Sadie merely nodded, still taking it all in.

"What does she mean when she says 'find her in yourself?'"

"She means you," Sadie said quietly. "She always said that I was searching for you in everyone else, and that I needed to love myself as much as I'd loved you."

"I wish I'd gotten the chance to meet her," Natalie said, placing the letter on top of the box. "She sounds like such a wonderful woman, and she loved you and looked after you when I wasn't there. But now, I can at least make her and you a promise, that I will love you like you deserve and need to be loved."

Chapter Seventy-Two

2024 Amberfield, Natalie's home

Rain lashed at the window when Natalie woke up. She stretched and smiled to herself as her body remembered the way it had been played and aroused these past couple of weeks and after yesterday, something had been reawakened within her, that was for sure.

"Harry?" she said into the phone when it rang silently but buzzed.

"Hey, just checking in. Wondered how things went after, you know?" She cleared her throat. "Thought I'd leave it a couple of days and let things settle. I didn't hear from you, so, I assume all is good?"

"Yes…all is good," she said without any conviction. Until right then, she'd forgotten about the episode surrounding Davina. Now, she wasn't quite so sure who heard what. "Did everyone—" She sat up and adjusted the pillows behind her.

"No, not everyone. I managed to shift the attention elsewhere, but…I heard."

Natalie remained quiet. What was there to say?

"So, is it true?" Harry continued. "Cos, I don't want to – if it's not, then…I mean, equally if it is—"

"It's true. What you heard, what Davina implied and…it's all true."

"So, Sadie's a…she's—"

"An escort, yes."

"Wow, I mean that's wild. And you're okay with that?"

Was she? The truth was that other than the episode with Davina, she'd not had to think about it. When Sadie decided that it was time to go back to work, that would be different, wouldn't it?

"Of course I'm okay with it. It's just a job," she heard herself say it, and felt it settle better than a moment ago. It was just a job. "We sell sex, is it any different?"

"I mean, yeah, a little bit…don't you think?"

"No, I don't think. Look Harry, if this going to be a problem for you then—"

"Hey, it's me, remember? Your best bud. I'm just checking in with you, that's all. I know how much this woman means to you and I just want to be sure that you're not ignoring something because you don't want to lose her again."

"You're right, I don't want to lose her, and I'm not going to by judging her for something she chooses to do that has absolutely no bearing on me and our relationship."

"You don't think so?"

"I do not. I accept her for who she is, and what she does is…it's for her to decide."

Harry sighed. "I guess so. I just worry about you, you know? She's sleeping with other people."

"I know, and I love you for that, but honestly…I'm okay with this. I want you to meet her. Why don't you come over tomorrow night? I'll cook."

"Okay, I'd love to. Oh, and check your email. I've sent through some images and clips from the ad."

Natalie sat up. "Really? That's wonderful. Thank you again for all the hard work."

"It's my job, remember?" Natalie could tell she'd smiled as she'd spoken. "So, tomorrow night then? Seven?"

"Yes," Natalie said. A gentle knock on the door caught her attention. "Tomorrow will be lovely."

"Alright, see you then." The call disconnected.

"Come in," Natalie said, sliding the phone under the duvet and out of sight. Her lips curled upward when the door crept open, and Sadie was beaten to the threshold by Muffy running in and jumping up onto the bed. "Morning, Muffy."

"I think she likes you," Sadie said, coming to sit on the edge of the bed, the dressing gown sliding open a little to reveal more naked skin. She reached out a hand and stroked Muffy's head quickly before her palm landed on Natalie's covered thigh. "Sleep okay?"

"I'd have slept better had I not woken up alone." Fingertips found each other and touched.

"I'm just trying to keep a level head," Sadie said.

"I don't think that's going to be possible if we keep doing things like we did last night." Natalie couldn't stop the grin from spreading, or her hand from moving to land on Sadie's thigh and inch up slowly. "And I am not complaining."

Leaning in, Sadie returned the grin. "It sounds like a plan I could really get onboard with, and I am onboard, completely. I just think a little space here and there isn't a bad thing. It leaves one wanting more, doesn't it?"

"Yeah?" Natalie teased. Her palm slid higher, inching under the silk gown. "Should we put that to the test?"

"We could."

Their lips touched, soft, tenderly moving before an urgency built and tongues met and danced. Natalie pulled the covers back. Sadie twisted until she could slide one knee between Natalie's thighs.

Sighing into the kiss, Natalie threaded her fingers up and into Sadie's hair.

"I guess so. I just worry about you, you know? She's sleeping with other people."

Natalie felt herself tense, Harriet's words echoing in her head. Was this what Sadie was like with women who paid her? She heard herself groan at the featherlight touch of her lover's hand between her legs. Her clit throbbed and ached for the touch, and yet, she couldn't get the thought out of her head.

"What's wrong?" Sadie asked. She always could read every imperceptible move.

Opening her eyes, she found Sadie staring at her. Her fingers stilled.

"Nothing, I'm fine." Natalie tried to smile, tugging Sadie's hand back to where she needed it. But she could see from Sadie's face that she wasn't buying it. "I'm fine. I promise."

Chapter Seventy-Three

2024 Amberfield, Natalie's home

"What are you doing?" Natalie asked, standing in the doorway to Sadie's room. Her lover was standing in front of the mirror in nothing more than her underwear. Her hair was immaculate, make-up perfectly applied.

Sadie spun around. "Is that what you're wearing?"

Natalie looked down at the simple summer dress she'd pulled on. "Yes, it's just Harry over for dinner, not the King."

"But I need to make an impression."

Natalie leaned against the doorframe, her arms crossed. "Do you?"

"She's your best friend, and ex-wife, and work colleague. She literally fills all aspects of your life, and she knows about me, and what I do for a living." Her hands hung limply by her side, shoulders sagging, and for a moment, Natalie thought she might actually stamp her foot. "Of course I have to impress her."

"I understand." Natalie pushed off from the door frame and entered the room. "But that also means, she knows me very well, and she knows I don't do anything I don't want to do anymore…" She stood behind Sadie and kissed her shoulder. "And she knows how much I love you; she's always known that. In many ways, she already knows you."

"That was before you knew that I was a whor—businesswoman," Sadie said into the mirror at Natalie over her shoulder.

"Trust me, Harry hasn't become this ingrained in my life by being a judgemental, mean, and rude person. I don't have anyone like Lina in my life anymore." Their eyes locked in the mirror again.

"I'm so glad that I don't have to contend with Aunt Lina."

Natalie leaned forward and placed a gentle kiss once more on her shoulder. "So am I, now please put something on that makes you feel comfortable, and then come downstairs to welcome our guest to our home." She turned to leave, letting her fingers trail down the length of Sadie's arm, until just fingertips touched.

"Our home?" Sadie gripped the fingers and stopped her from leaving.

Natalie smiled. "If you want it to be."

Sadie was not used to feeling like this: somewhat uneasy and a little nervous. It hadn't dissipated despite Natalie's pep talk. Especially when the doorbell had rung, and she'd listened at the door to the muffled greetings between Natalie and her best friend.

She slid into a wide-legged black pantsuit. She left her arms and feet bare, her hair swept up and off her face apart from the fringe. The debate on whether to go make-up free had lasted all of a minute before she was pulling out the mascara and brushing on more of the dark eyeshadow that had become her mask over the years. She realised that in the last few years, only Blanca – and now Natalie – had seen her without it.

A deep red lipstick smeared across plump lips, and she kissed off the excess with a tissue. She turned one way and then the other to check herself one last time before she headed downstairs.

"Right, Swanson, time to put on a performance and show this Harry who you really are."

Walking slowly down the stairs, mainly to make sure she didn't stumble and make the kind of entrance nobody wanted to make, she could hear laughter and conversation. Words became more focused the closer she got.

"And so, James came running down the corridor, chased by a very enthusiastic terrier who had taken a shine to his leg."

"Oh goodness, that sounds crazy." Natalie laughed. "Where did the dog come from?"

"Apparently, someone working upstairs at Pickford's brought their dog in and didn't notice it go off for a wander." Harry joined in the laughing.

Deeming it a good time to make her appearance, Sadie took a long, calming breath and then walked into the kitchen.

"Sadie," Natalie said brightly, a smile erupting onto her face in an instant.

"Hello," Sadie said, making eye contact with Harry, who despite the photo in the lounge, didn't look anything like how Sadie had expected.

"Sweetheart, this is Harry. Harry, this is Sadie."

"I gathered that." Harry grinned, reaching out a hand. "I feel like I already know you. She's talked about you so much over the years."

"No pressure then," Sadie joked. "Do you need a hand with anything?" she said to Natalie. The aroma of the lamb stew she was cooking had been permeating the house all afternoon.

"No, everything is as it should be. Wine?" Natalie asked.

"Sure, why not?"

"I'll have some," Harry jumped in. She then turned to Sadie, her face solemn as she spoke. "So, I just wanted to say that I was sorry to hear about your loss."

It took a second for Sadie to realise Harry was speaking to her. She'd been captivated by the vision of Natalie with her tongue poking out in concentration as she worked the cork loose.

"Thank you, that's very kind of you."

"I know it comes to us all in the end, but death is always such a shock, isn't it?"

"It is, yes," Sadie agreed. She turned her attention back on Natalie. "Do you need a hand with that?"

Natalie gave up trying and held out the bottle. "Yes, it's glued in."

"She never could open a wine bottle that didn't have a screw cap." Harry laughed as Sadie reached out and took the bottle.

"That isn't true…Okay, fine, it is," Natalie admitted. "I'm just not made for such intricacies."

The audible pop turned all attention to Sadie, who waved the bottle opener still attached to the cork in the air triumphantly. "There you go."

Handing over the bottle, she felt the tension within her begin to ease. She waited as Natalie poured three glasses and handed them around.

"So, I do hope you're going to tell me lots of stories about Natalie?" Sadie said, turning back to Harry.

The laugh and smile were genuine. "Oh, you bet. Come on, let's go sit down and I'll fill you in on the time she got caught with nothing more than a hat to hide her blushes."

"Harry! Don't you dare." Natalie laughed.

"Oh, she's going to dare." Sadie grinned, grabbing the bottle. "Lead the way."

Chapter Seventy-Four

Come Again headquarters

Natalie walked into the office the following day smiling to herself. She was fairly sure the previous evening had been a huge success.

The bottle of wine had been finished, and another opened. Harry had stayed over, sleeping on the sofa, and Natalie had slept, eventually, with Sadie in the guest room. In hindsight, she should have changed the sheets and insisted that Harry sleep in her room, but Harry hadn't minded.

The couch was comfortable, and Harry all but squealed when Muffy made an appearance and decided she would do for a bed partner, which was why Natalie was surprised to find her best friend up and gone already when she'd come down for coffee.

"Good morning, Natalie," Bina said as she approached her P.A.'s desk.

"Good morning, Bina. Can you send Harry in when she arrives?"

"Of course. She already called in to say she'd be a bit late. Something about having to go home and change so as not to be doing the walk of shame in yesterday's underwear."

Natalie raised her brows and chuckled. "Nice of her to be so detailed."

"I thought so." Bina grinned. "Coffee?"

"Love one, thank you."

The coffee was on her desk by the time she sat down and opened her laptop. Clicking onto emails, she groaned when she saw Davina Gorman's name listed.

The opening line read, *I'm an arsehole…*

"Yes, you are," she said aloud and ignored the mail.

"I am what?" Harry said, sauntering in wearing a freshly pressed shirt with her hair still a little damp.

"An arsehole," Natalie answered. "I thought you'd be there for coffee this morning. I got up especially early, and you'd already buggered off."

Harry pulled a chair out and took a seat. "I woke up with the sunrise. Figured I was safe enough to drive home. Then I fell asleep again and had a mad dash to get showered and dressed."

Natalie stiffened and frowned. It felt like a lie. "You've never left early before."

"No, I haven't. Well spotted."

"Then why did you leave early this morning?"

She watched Harry's face move through a multitude of considerations before it brightened under a realisation.

"Oh, you think I left because I didn't like Sadie?"

Twisting her coffee cup absently, Natalie said, "Well, that had briefly crossed my mind, yes."

"Aw, Nat. No, no way. She's lovely, I can absolutely see what you see in her." Harry's cheeks blushed. "Okay, fine, if you must know why I left…Your floorboards are quite thin."

It took a moment, Natalie frowning as she tried to understand what that meant, but then it was Natalie who flushed crimson. Her hand moved to cover her mouth as she laughed nervously.

"Oh. That's…well, it's a relief. I really thought it was because you hated her."

"To be fair, I might hate her just a little bit." She squeezed her finger and thumb together and grinned. "I've never had a woman making the noises you were last night, so I guess she's very skilled at her job. I might need some tips."

Natalie hid her face in her hands.

"Come on, it was pretty awesome, but not something a best friend wants to be thinking about with the wrong kind of pussy for company."

"Alright, I get the picture." Natalie smiled. "She is very skilled, and I won't be complaining. She just has to tell me I'm a good girl and it's like I liquify into this compliant being willing to do everything she demands."

"So, the toy box is finally getting an outing?"

Natalie picked up her mug and sipped. "Let's just say that some items are."

"Not the footlong double dildo then?" Harry giggled.

"I'm not sure I'll ever be interested in that."

"Unless Sadie demands it?" Harry quirked a brow and wriggled it.

Natalie thought for a moment. "Maybe."

Chapter Seventy-Five

The funeral

Sadie had been holding it together until the moment the hearse pulled up outside of her flat and Natalie had smiled sadly at her as she'd asked, "Ready?"

Sadie broke down in tears. "No, I'm not. I can't do this."

Reaching for her, Natalie wrapped two warm arms around her and said nothing, allowing her to just let it out until the sobbing eased off by its own volition.

Upright, she caught sight of herself in the mirror and groaned. "Jesus, now look at the state of me."

"I think under the circumstances, it's all allowed." Natalie produced a packet of tissues and pulled one free. She dabbed gently at Sadie's wet cheeks. "Why don't you go and fix this and I'll see to the chaps outside, and then we will go and give Blanca a beautiful send off."

"Alright," Sadie said without any real conviction.

She'd been trying not to get angry, but as the day had approached, her frustration had been harder to manage. Not one of Blanca's family had returned her calls. This woman so vibrant in life would not be missed by more than a handful of people. And that rankled Sadie more than she'd thought it would.

"You deserved better," she murmured aloud. "You deserved so much more than this, Blanca Alfonsa." She fixed her lipstick. "I'll do you proud."

When she made it back out into the hall, she found Natalie waiting. The door was open, and she could see the funeral director waiting outside.

"Do I look okay?" she asked Natalie, who was impeccable in her expensive black dress.

Natalie smiled and stepped forward, reaching up to adjust the tie Sadie wore loosely around her neck. "You look perfect," she answered, tucking the tie back inside Sadie's waistcoat. "Are you ready?" Natalie asked for the second time.

"Yes." Sadie nodded, appreciative of Natalie's presence in her life right now. "Let's do this."

Sadie clasped Natalie's hand tightly as they followed the coffin into the crematorium, held aloft by hired pallbearers. She'd tried smiling at the small group of mourners. People Blanca spent her days with.

There was the woman from the local café, and two men who walked their dog past the house each morning and always stopped to talk with her. The others she didn't know. They'd been listed as people to contact if anything should happen, but they all seemed sad and spoke kindly about Blanca.

"It makes me so mad that there's nobody here," Sadie whispered.

Natalie squeezed her hand. "We're here, and those she liked are here. That's all that matters."

Sadie nodded. "You're right. I know, I'm just so…she deserved better."

The civil celebrant greeted them and led the mourners into the room that felt way too big and far too empty. She walked away to the lectern and waited until the music Sadie had chosen finished playing.

Smiling easily, she began by thanking everyone for coming, and Sadie found her thoughts drifting.

"You know, I don't care for most people," Blanca said. *She pushed her Prada sunglasses up onto her head, looking around at the people milling about before her stare settled back on Sadie.*

"I get it. I prefer my own company too." Sadie nodded as she sipped Coke from a straw sticking out of the top of a glass bottle. She laughed. *"Who would have pictured us as friends, huh?"*

One brow raised and Blanca turned her face just enough that Sadie felt the stare. "You think we wouldn't be friends in any other life?"

Sadie shrugged. "Don't know. Would we have met had I not run away from my problems and come here?"

"You don't believe that the universe provides?"

Shaking her head, Sadie laughed. "No."

"Oh, you think not, uh huh." Blanca wagged her finger at her. "You'll see, you'll see. One day you'll look around and realise, you're always right where you're meant to be."

The sharp nudge in the side brought her spinning back to the present. All eyes were on her as Natalie leaned in.

"You need to do your reading."

"Oh, right, yes. Sorry."

Sadie went to stand, but Natalie stopped her.

"Are you alright?"

She sighed gently and looked closely at the woman staring up at her, full of concern, but here. Dependable. Doting. Never judging her.

"Yes." Sadie smiled. "I'm right where I'm meant to be."

Chapter Seventy-Six

2024 Amberfield, Natalie's home

It was quiet as they returned to Natalie's house. Muffy greeted them with barely a raise of her head before she closed her eyes again and went back to sleep.

"Cup of tea?" Natalie asked as she hung her coat and turned to Sadie.

"Yes, sure," Sadie replied absently. Big eyes stared at the floor, unfocused and sad.

"Sadie?" Natalie moved closer. "Sadie?" she said again, more gently. "Do you want to—"

"I think I need to go home," Sadie said without looking at her.

"Home? To your flat?" Natalie felt confused. "Okay, we can go to your flat."

Now, Sadie turned to her. "No, I think I need to go home…alone."

"Alone? I don't under—"

"It's just…this last couple of weeks have been fantastic and I don't want – I'm not ending things, I just…I need to work out what to do next, and to do that, I need some…space."

"I see." Natalie felt her heart drop. "I guess I can understand that."

"Can you? Because I want you to, I want to be sure that you understand this isn't about us…" She sighed. "I mean, it is, but in a good way. I realised today that I have something I need to work through."

"And you can't do that with me? Did someone say something?"

Sadie shook her head and pulled at her tie, getting frustrated when the knot tightened. "No, nobody said anything. I just need a few days, if you can give me that?"

Gently slapping her hands away, Natalie took over easing the tie free from the knot. "I can give you all the time you need. Just remember that I'm here, and I'm not going anywhere, and whatever you need to do…" She pulled the tie free. "We will work it out, okay?"

Sadie didn't answer with words. Instead, she leaned in and kissed her, a soft, tender press of lips.

"I love you, Sadie Swanson," Natalie said when the kiss ended.

"I love you, Natalie Shultz. I always have." Sadie smiled when the flat of Natalie's palms pressed against her shoulders and moved slowly down an inch. "I'm coming back, and to prove it…" She covered Natalie's hands with her own. "Can I leave Muffy with you?"

"Muffy?" Natalie exclaimed loudly enough that the cat in question looked up once more.

"She just seems so settled, and—"

"Of course, yes. I'd be happy for her to stay until – I want you to live with me. When you've worked everything out, I want us to finally be together. I want to wake up every morning wrapped around you, so while you're taking time to think things over…can you include that?"

"I can do that."

"Okay then. Let's get you packed up."

Natalie went to pull away, but Sadie stopped her and gently yanked her back until they were chest to chest, nose to nose.

"Let's have dinner first. I'm in no rush."

Chapter Seventy-Seven

Outskirts of Brighton, Sadie's flat

Sadie walked back into her flat with nothing more than her handbag and a small holdall she'd borrowed from Natalie. She'd left her clothes there, another signal of her intention to come back.

It all felt so different now that Blanca wasn't around. She had nobody other than Natalie to bounce ideas off, and this was a subject she really needed to work out, because it wasn't fair to put Natalie in the middle of it. She'd already been so gracious and loving about it all.

As Sadie had finished speaking about Blanca, telling the small congregation all about her, she had a sudden realisation that it was maybe time for something different for herself.

The cottage by the sea was no longer her dream. Natalie was. Being with Natalie was all that mattered. How to make that work was the question that she realised had been bothering her lately.

Natalie's world was open-minded and progressive but even so, despite all the assurances to the contrary, would they really be able to make it work in the long run with Evelyn as a third wheel?

Even more so, she needed to know, did Evelyn even exist anymore?

She'd been so wrapped up in mourning her friend and in falling in love again that she was unsure if she could switch between the two personalities now.

And there was only one way to find out, wasn't there?

A message had come through a few days ago from one of her repeat clients. Wonder Woman had reached out about a potential booking, but Sadie had ignored it. Now, however, it seemed the perfect opportunity to test her theory.

Sadie opened the website on her phone and thumbed through until she found the message.

Evelyn: Hi, I am available tonight if that works for you?

The reply came back almost instantly, affirming it was a date.

Placing the phone down slowly, Sadie puffed out her cheeks and exhaled slowly. She had three hours to get ready and transform into Evelyn.

Arriving promptly at the address she'd been to numerous times now, Evelyn pressed the button and waited for entry. The door clicked and buzzed, and she pushed it open and entered.

The long black coat hung down to her heeled feet and swished gently with each step she took towards the door that was already open.

"Come in," the bright voice sang out when Evelyn knocked gently. "I'm just opening a bottle of Merlot, your favourite."

"Great," Evelyn said, entering the cosy flat and closing the door behind her. "How have you been?" she asked, just as Wonder Woman came into view.

It was funny, she thought, how despite being told the woman's name was Rose, that she had always thought of her as the superhero character. She'd only worn that outfit once, and yet, it had stuck.

"All the better for seeing you, my dear." Rose smiled warmly.

"You look well," Evelyn said, taking the glass of wine offered. She sipped it and studied Rose. A nice, easy client. All she had to do was spend the evening talking with her, have something to drink and then take her to bed and...and what? She'd never questioned it before. Never thought anything more than what the client wanted. Natalie's face flashed across her mind.

"Yes, I'm really well. That's why I thought of you and—" She leaned in and kissed Evelyn's cheek, her palm resting easily against Evelyn's arm. "It's so good to see you."

Rose was speaking, but all Sadie could hear was Natalie. *"I love you, Sadie Swanson."* It was like an echo chamber, repeating over and over in her head. *"I love you."*

Sadie placed the glass down and stepped backwards. "I'm sorry, I…I can't do this."

"Oh, I – did I say something wrong?"

"No, no, absolutely not, it's not you – I just…" The tears spilled out; she couldn't stop them.

"Goodness, Evelyn, what's wrong? Come on, sit down." Rose was guiding her into the lounge. "Sit down, just breathe. It's okay."

It took a moment to realise that the arms around her and the shoulder she was sobbing into belonged to Rose, her client. It was unprofessional, but she couldn't stop. Tears she'd held in for decades mixed in with those she had failed to shed recently. Two huge losses in her life were now finally exploding from her.

"Do you want to talk about it?" Rose asked when finally, the sobbing had subsided into occasional hiccups and sniffs.

Realising that she was still being held by Rose, Sadie stiffened. "I'm sorry, this wasn't what you were expecting, was it?" She laughed, feeling every bit as awkward as the situation allowed.

Rose patted her knee and reached for the box of tissues on the table. She plucked one free and handed it to Evelyn. "I like to think that despite the fact I pay for your company, I am somewhat of a friend, as much as anyone else can be a friend in this situation. And if you need to be the one who talks this time, that's perfectly alright with me."

Sadie smiled. Evelyn had gone, that much she was sure of right now.

"So much has changed in these last few weeks. I guess I didn't realise how much it's all affected me." She wiped her face with the tissue and grimaced at the black stain of mascara that she was seeing a little too often lately. "And I'm sure I look absolutely stunning right now."

Rose smiled at her. "To be honest, it's nice to see your softer side. As much as I enjoy Evelyn's company, I often wonder what you're like, the real you." She pulled another tissue free and handed it over. "I'm not so naïve that I ever thought Evelyn was who you are outside of this."

"Very perceptive. I don't think many people care."

"I can imagine not. It must be a very lonely place to be sometimes."

Sadie nodded. "I…I always managed. My best friend would always be there, you know? But I lost her recently and I guess I never realised that I'd be without her…I thought we still had more time."

"Oh, I'm so sorry for your loss."

"Thank you." Sadie blew her nose before continuing, like a tap had been turned and she couldn't stop the words gushing forth. "And I've fallen in love again. Actually, I've never not loved her, but we've reconnected and now I know that she's all I want and this…I thought I could separate still, that work was work and she was home. She's been so supportive of my choices…"

"But it's not that simple, is it?"

"No." Sadie shook her head slowly before blowing her nose. "I can't be in my Evelyn headspace and not think about her, and that makes me feel like I'm cheating on her. That I'm being selfish and, honestly…I think now, maybe I need it to only be her."

Rose smiled. "I think you've found the answers you've been looking for."

"I think I have. I'm so sorry to have ruined your night and blurted everything out like that."

"You haven't ruined anything. You know me, I'm all about the company. So, do you want to finish that drink and tell me all about this woman who has captured your heart?"

"Yes, and then I'll refund you." Sadie grinned.

Chapter Seventy-Eight

2024 Amberfield

Natalie pottered around the house finding things to do. They were things that mostly didn't need doing, but she was doing them anyway.

It had been quiet the previous night without Sadie there. Just a few weeks together had transformed her life so momentously that she wondered if things would ever be the same again.

She hoped not.

Life with Sadie back in it was so much richer and more vibrant, not to mention she had a sex life again. God, did she have a sex life again.

Muffy hadn't been impressed when the hoover had appeared two days running. The loud vacuum cleaner at least drowned out the silence, but it couldn't erase the tension building in Natalie's psyche.

She was overthinking everything. What if Sadie didn't come back? What if Sadie decided she didn't want to live with her? What if Sadie…

"Oh, for god's sake pack it in, Natalie," she scolded herself and switched off the hoover. She pulled her phone free from her jeans pocket and sent the text she'd been wanting to send.

Natalie: I know you want space, but I'm wondering if we can at least say good morning and good night? Xx

The message was unread. And still unread twenty minutes later, and thirty minutes after that.

"Right, Muffy, you're going to have to look after the house while I go out," she said to the cat who paid no attention to her. "It's Saturday and that doesn't mean I need to stay cooped up indoors." She stared at the cat. "Why am I talking to a cat?"

She grabbed her bag and headed for the door.

The river sparkled in the sunshine as Natalie strolled happily along the promenade. Her bare arms felt warm and sun-kissed. It was a beautiful summer's day, and she smiled casually at people as they passed each other by.

She mused at the shop windows and considered a new outfit, deciding she'd have lunch first and come back to it. After all, she had all afternoon to herself.

Finding a table free, she sat herself down and perused the menu – not that she needed to, she ate at Aston's often enough to know it off by heart, but still it was how it worked, wasn't it?

"What can I get you?" a smiling Pippa asked. A small boy ran around with a dinosaur making roar noises. "Sorry," Pippa said, turning to him. "Max, you know you're not supposed to be out here by yourself."

He stopped what he was doing and wandered over, looking up at Natalie before he turned back to Pippa. "I'm not, you're here." His toothless grin widened.

"Very smart." Pippa narrowed her eyes at him, and he looked at Natalie smiling at his antics and giggled.

"Do not leave the seating area, do you understand me?" Pippa said, not quite sternly but firm enough that the giggling stopped, and he nodded, running to find a free table to sit at. "Sorry about that."

"Quite alright. I'll keep an eye on him while you're in and out, if you like," Natalie offered.

"Thank you. Once Georgia gets back from the cash and carry, I'll take him home. He must be bored senseless." She chuckled. "Anyway, what can I get you?"

Placing the menu down again, Natalie said, "I'll take the Greek salad and a bowl of sweet potato fries, and a lemon Fanta."

"Great, I'll get that done and out asap."

"No rush, I'm just enjoying an afternoon in the sun."

Pippa nodded and smiled once more, and then rushed back inside, leaving Natalie to enjoy the view.

She watched a paddleboarder, upright, with a long paddle, moving slowly down the river towards the bridge. Her line of sight followed until it changed direction and she looked longingly at the building that used to be Rainbow.

Her mind wandered back to the times she'd be inside sprawled over Sadie as their friends joked and danced around them. It had been such a fun time. So much of who she was now was because of those people. It was easy to understand why Sadie missed Blanca so much.

Friends were important; they filled voids you didn't know you had until they were no longer filling them. She was so lost in her thoughts that she didn't notice the person in front of her until the shadow fell over her.

"Greek Salad, chips and Fanta?" A tall, dark-haired teenager stood in front of her holding a tray between her hands. She was already placing it down onto the table before Natalie could answer.

"Uh, yes, that's me." She read the name tag on the shirt, recognising the elder of Pippa and Georgia's brood. "Thank you, Robbie."

"No problem." She smiled. "Anything else I can get for you?"

Natalie shook her head. "No, thank you, this looks perfect."

"Cool." The smile grew bigger, and then she disappeared with the tray swinging against her leg as she walked. She stopped to ruffle Max's hair and whispered something that made him laugh. Natalie smiled at the interaction.

Picking up her fork, Natalie dug in and began to eat. It was delicious, as it always was, and she was halfway through when she glanced up again at the building in the near distance that used to be such a big part of her life.

Squinting against the sunlight, she looked more closely. A recognisable figure stepped out of the bar, smiling and laughing with someone Natalie couldn't make out as they were just hidden behind a lamppost, but she was sure the person she could see was Sadie.

They stood there for a long minute or so before parting ways, and Sadie's long strides took her away from the bar, and away from Natalie.

Picking up her phone once more, Natalie checked her messages. Still unread, but just as she was about to put the phone back into her bag and begin the process of overthinking, she noticed the ticks turn blue and the word "typing" appeared.

Sadie: Hey, of course we can message. I didn't mean to make you feel left out, or to think I don't miss you. xx

Counting to ten before she opened the message, Natalie typed a reply.

Natalie: I miss you too. Are you okay? Are you finding answers? xx

She looked up and across the river, Sadie now out of sight. Her phone pinged again before she could overthink about why Sadie was meeting someone in a bar.

Sadie: I think I am. I just need a couple of days to work things out, and then…can I come home? xx

The smile that broke out across Natalie's face would have bathed the street like sunshine had it not been the hottest day of the year already.

Natalie: You know the answer to that question. XX

Sadie: I know. You don't think it's too soon? XX

Natalie: If anything, it's not soon enough. We should have been doing this for years, don't you think? xx

Chapter Seventy-Nine

2024 Amberfield, Natalie's home

Harry relaxed on the chair in the garden, sunshine on her face, sunglasses shielding her eyes. She had been summoned the moment Natalie had gotten home, when the excitement of Sadie wanting to come home had worn off enough that the anxiety of why she was meeting someone at the bar had pushed to the fore.

So, of course, she called Harry to talk her off the ledge.

"Right, so, you don't know who she was with?" Harry asked.

Natalie shook her head. "No idea. I didn't think she knew anyone around here anymore. And if she did, why would she take them to our place?"

Harry's mouth twisted back and forth before she finally asked the question, "Could it have been a…client?"

Despite Natalie wearing sunglasses herself, it was clear by how high her brows raised that her eyes were wide beneath them.

"To our place?" Her voice rose an octave. "No, I don't think so."

"Is she working again?"

"You know, I hadn't thought of that." She chewed the inside of her lip. "I don't know why I assumed she wouldn't be working."

"I mean, it probably wasn't." Harry shrugged. "Who would meet someone they intended to sleep with in a pub? That's the kind of thing you do on a date." She'd said it before she could stop it. Wincing, she added a quiet, "Sorry, not helpful."

"No." Natalie looked away to the bottom of the garden. A small water feature was gurgling away against the stark white wall. "I don't think it was a date. I trust her. I've no reason whatsoever to think that she would do anything like that behind my back."

"That's good, because I didn't get that impression from her either. She seems pretty upfront about things."

Natalie turned towards Harry again. "Yes, exactly, so why do I feel like she's up to something?"

"Maybe she is." Harry grinned. "Maybe it's something positive and exciting and all these nerves you have are just remnants left over from having an arsehole for family."

"You're probably right," Natalie agreed, lifting her glass of elderflower cordial and sipping. "And she did ask if she could come home."

"Home, eh? That's big."

Smiling again, Natalie said, "It is, isn't it?"

"I should say so. And she can move into your room, and I can have my spare room back." Harry raised her glass and winked. "Although, I want it sanitised now I know what you've been getting up to in there."

"Oh, stop it." Natalie laughed, but her cheeks flushed at the memory. "Like you've never—"

"I've never done that!" Harry joined in the laughing. She leaned forward. "Seriously though, which toy were you using? I need to invest."

"Who said we were using any toys?"

Now it was Harry's turn to look shocked. "No toys, just—"

"Hm-hm, just—" Natalie giggled.

"Fuck me."

"I'm not sure she's taking on new clients," Natalie said quite seriously before the smirk broke out and they both burst out laughing.

Chapter Eighty

1999 Amberfield

Alice was dancing with Tom. They were the only straight people in the pub, but they didn't look out of place in amongst the crowd of sweaty bodies bopping away to S Club 7.

Natalie was laughing at their antics.

From where she stood behind the bar, Sadie watched her, totally enthralled by the way Natalie could just go with it and enjoy herself regardless of what was going on around her.

Natalie must have felt the stare because she turned slowly, and Sadie found herself locked into a moment between them. There seemed to be a lot of those lately.

"Oi dreamer, stop ogling the fanny. There's customers waiting."

Sadie turned quickly to find her boss pointing down the bar towards a couple of boys waving a tenner at her.

"I know she's cute, and I'm very happy for ya, but work's work."

"Sorry, Kath." Sadie nodded. "What can I get ya?" she asked them, taking the order and pouring two pints. "There you go."

When she turned around, she found herself locked in again. Natalie was at the bar, staring at her, a little tipsy and grinning.

"Excuse me, I was wondering what time you get off shift, because I'd quite like to let you do obscene things to me."

"How obscene?" Sadie asked, leaning towards her almost close enough that they could kiss.

"Really, awfully ob—"

"Sadie, I won't tell you again!" Kath shouted.

Looking sad, Sadie pushed out her bottom lip. "See you on my break?"

"I guess so." Natalie grinned, grabbed her drink and turned on her heel. She threw one quick glance over her shoulder to make sure Sadie was still watching.

"Death of me," Sadie whispered to herself. Turning, she noticed Kath about to bellow at her again. "Alright, I'm on it."

"I know you think you run the place." Kath rolled her eyes, but Sadie saw the small grin as she twisted away to serve a customer.

Hand in hand, swinging arms between them, Sadie and Natalie walked slowly down the street. The ten-minute walk to Lina's house would take more than twenty, as they both did everything they could to draw out their final moments with each other before they'd part for the night.

"You know, I don't know what it is about you being at work that makes me feel so—"

"Turned on?" Sadie smirked, pulling on her hand until Natalie was pressed up against her front.

"Yes. Very," she admitted. "You need to be the manager, and then we can live above the bar and be together any time I feel the need to let you…"

"Do obscene things?" Sadie laughed. "Don't think I've forgotten that. I will at some point be taking you up on it."

"I hope so." Natalie leaned in. "Kiss me."

Chapter Eighty-One

2024 Come Again HQ

It had been a long day.

Getting home and putting her feet up was exactly what Natalie needed. A nice glass of Chablis, maybe even a pizza, she thought to herself.

Standing up from her desk, Natalie began to shove her things back into her bag and tidy everything. Lifting her bag to her shoulder, she was about to leave when she was interrupted by a message beeping its arrival on her phone.

Glancing at it, she smiled when she saw that it was Sadie. She sat back down to read it.

Sadie: Would you be free for a drink this evening?

Natalie: Always, but only a quick one. I am exhausted.

The reply came back instantly.

Sadie: Another time then. You go home and get some rest.

Natalie: I want to see you. Where do you want to meet?

Sadie: Okay, well if you're sure, I was thinking you could meet me at Rainbow, or Ringo's as it is now.

Natalie: Alright, well I'm just leaving work now. Is it too early?

Sadie: Now is perfect. I want to run something by you.

Natalie: Great, I'll see you in a minute then. Xx

She put the phone into her bag and went over the conversation again in her head. "Run something by me."

Snatching up her keys, she rounded the desk and left the office. Bina had gone an hour ago. Half the building was probably empty by now, but she walked quickly down the corridor to the one office she hoped wouldn't be.

Tapping on the door, she pushed it open before any response had come. Harry was typing away on the desktop, eyes squinting at the screen.

She didn't look up.

"I do wish you would get your eyes tested," Natalie said, closing the door and pulling the chair free. She sat down.

"Nothing wrong with my eyes," Harry said, still typing and not looking up.

"If you say so," Natalie said, waiting patiently. She glanced around. Harry had the least decorated office in the company, she was sure of it. Plain walls. No photos or paintings, not even a promotional poster.

When the tapping stopped, she turned back to find Harry looking at her.

"Why are you smiling like that?" Natalie asked.

"Because you look as though you're about to erupt over something that most likely isn't a big deal and I'm going to tell you so."

Natalie realised her leg had been bouncing and she made a conscious effort to stop it.

"Sadie wants to meet for a drink."

"Alright, that's good, isn't it?"

Natalie nodded. "Yes, of course, but she also wants to run something by me."

"And you've instantly decided that it will be something negative?"

"No, I – yes. Yes, that is exactly where my head's at. Why? Why do I do this?"

"Because you're traumatised, you know that. The way your father would just pull the rug out, or Lina would deliberately be mean.

Those things stick with us, and now, when you've finally got her back again, you're worried that Sadie will pull the rug out too."

"I'm being ridiculous, aren't I?"

Harry got up, came around the desk and perched on the corner of it.

"No, you're being triggered, and you probably need to go back to that therapist and do some more work on it, but in the meantime, you've got me to whack some sense into ya."

"Thank goodness for that." Natalie smiled, feeling better already.

"So, where are you meeting her?"

"At our old haunt."

"Then I imagine it's going to be good news. She's taking you somewhere that is familiar to you both, to share something I assume she finds exciting, with you."

"I hope so."

Harry stood up, checked her watch. "Well, only one way to skin a cat, as they say."

"That is a revolting saying, and Muffy would not be impressed with her new friend."

Harry grinned. "Ah, Muffy is cute, though…Muffy?"

Natalie held her hands up. "I didn't ask."

"No, probably for the best." Harry grinned, kissing her cheek and leading her to the door. "Now, go on. Go." She pushed Natalie gently out of the office.

"Thank you," Natalie said as she walked away backwards, waving at Harry.

"And let me know what it was. You know I love knowing all the details!" Harry called down the corridor after her.

Chapter Eighty-Two

Ringo's Bar, Riverside

Natalie walked in and almost did a double take. The bar was empty for a start, except for Sadie, who sat at their table smiling at her.

"You look…" Natalie was lost for words. The change was quite dramatic and unexpected, though not in a negative way.

"A bit different?" Sadie asked, still grinning. The dark hair was now back to the colour Natalie remembered: a lighter brown with a few darker and lighter streaks running through it. And the cut was softer, less severe than the asymmetrical fringe and long hair she'd been rocking previously.

"You cut your hair."

"Restyled, it's still the same length…mostly." Sadie fingered the longer strands. "Just more layers, and more me, again."

Natalie finally slid onto the chair and smiled. "I like it."

"Yeah?"

"Yes, it suits you."

Sadie inclined her head and blushed a little. "Thank you." The heavy dark eye make-up was gone also, leaving her face looking fresher, and younger. "I took the mask off," she said by way of explanation.

"I didn't realise you were wearing one," Natalie said, unable to keep her eyes off her. "You look…stunning."

Her cheeks blushed some more, as she answered, "I didn't realise I was wearing one; at least, not in my real life."

Sadie stood up and walked towards the bar where a champagne bucket held a bottle, with two flute glasses beside it. Carrying it back to the table, Sadie smiled at Natalie.

"Are we celebrating your new look?"

Sadie laughed. "No, we're celebrating my new life."

"Oh, tell me more." Natalie grinned just as the cork shot from the bottle.

When both glasses were full, Sadie sat down again, scooting her chair closer to Natalie.

"I realised over these last few weeks that something was changing for me. Finding you again, and then losing Blanca, I think I became a little overwhelmed and pushed everything down thinking I could just go on as I was."

Natalie said nothing. There was no need.

"I needed to take time out so that I could work through everything I was feeling and make sure that I was right." She glanced away. "I booked in a client."

The subtle flinch from Natalie didn't go unnoticed, and Sadie reached out a hand reassuringly.

"Loving you, being loved by you, it changes me," Sadie said. "So, I booked a safe client, one who I knew wouldn't be too upset if my experiment worked."

"Experiment? I don't understand."

"I began to think that maybe I'd been lying to myself all these years, that I did get something out of being Evelyn. I had my sexual needs met without ever having to be intimate or give anything of myself to anyone. But now, here I was with you…getting my needs met. All of them."

"So, your experiment was—"

"I thought that I was switching Evelyn on and off, that she was specifically a work persona, but I looked back at my life and saw how many other instances Evelyn took centre stage, and then I realised, she hadn't made a single appearance while I was with you."

"And why do you think that is?"

"When you left all those years ago, I swore I would never let another soul close enough to hurt me like that again, but I did. I was falling for someone and when I told them about…" She sighed. "It didn't end well."

"I'm sorry."

Sadie squeezed her hand. "So, I really swore I wouldn't let anyone else into my heart, and yet, the moment you were in front of me again, it was like all the hurt just slipped away. I didn't need Evelyn to fight a battle, because there wasn't a battle to fight."

"And now?"

"Evelyn's gone." Sadie pointed to her face. "Just me now."

"And your clients?"

Sadie shrugged. "I sold my list to an associate I know. Closed the website. Switched off the phone number and ta-da."

Natalie sat open-mouthed for a moment, taking it all in.

"Not quite what you were expecting?" Sadie asked.

"Uh, no, I guess it wasn't. I don't know what I was expecting really, but this wasn't it." She laughed almost nervously, daring herself to ask the next question. "So, what now? What are your plans?"

"Well…" Sadie picked up her glass and waited for Natalie to follow. "I figured maybe there was an opportunity to do something else that I loved." She glanced around at the empty bar. "I remembered when we came in here the other night, that Ben mentioned his dad was selling up and moving to Benidorm, so…I tracked his dad down, and we talked, and I've agreed to buy—"

"You've bought our bar? This bar? Rainbow?" The excitement shone out of Natalie as she spewed words.

"Not quite yet, but the paperwork is going through. In the meantime, I've agreed to manage the place until…"

"Sadie, that's amazing news," Natalie cut in. She held the glass up. "To new ventures."

Epilogue

2024 Riverbank, Amberfield

"You know you have to get up today, right?" Natalie said to the lump under the duvet currently sliding a tongue up the inside of her thigh.

The cover flew back, and a flushed Sadie stared at her with one brow raised. "I'm sorry, am I not keeping your mind focused elsewhere?"

Natalie laughed. "Of course you are. I am just aware that today is the big day and—"

She felt her legs grasped, her torso pulled further down the bed, and Sadie now pressed up against her and hovering above her. Her legs wrapped around her lover instinctively.

"We have hours until I need to even think about getting up..." Sadie's eyes lingered on Natalie's before they lowered their gaze to her mouth. "And we're upstairs, we haven't even got to travel...so, I plan on keeping my mind occupied on you until then."

"Okay...I can get—"

Sadie covered her mouth with her own, tongue slipping against Natalie's, hips undulating slowly.

"Do you think..." Her mouth moved to Natalie's neck, kissing and licking the skin until she reached an earlobe. "That you might..." Her lips wrapped around the soft skin and sucked. "Let me enjoy you?" Her voice was low and sent a vibration with every word.

"God...yes," Natalie gasped as fingers pushed between them and pressed firmly against her clit, hips still rocking gently against them.

Sadie smiled against her skin. "And if you're a good girl, I'll sit on your face."

Natalie groaned. "I want that."

"Good, so…you have choices…I can go back to what I was doing before being so rudely interrupted and take my sweet time, while you're begging me for more—"

"Or?" Natalie all but begged.

"Or…I can stay right here and—" Her fingers slid inside Natalie. "I can make it hard and fast until you're begging me to stop."

"That's not a fair—" Natalie arched at Sadie's movement. "Really…not a fair—" She gasped when Sadie's palm pressed against her clit.

"Sorry, you were saying?" Sadie smirked down at her, completely in control. "Would you like some input from me and what I'd like to do?"

Natalie's head nodded.

"Speak it out loud, darling, you know how much I like it when you do."

"I…fuck." She couldn't focus. Sadie had found that perfect spot and gently moved her finger back and forth against it. "Yes, like…that."

"You like that, or you like it when I ask you to use your words?"

Natalie felt her body tighten. She raised an arm and wrapped it around Sadie's neck, pulling her down until her face was mushed against her chest. With every ounce of concentration, she gritted her teeth and said, "If you stop doing that, I will make you sleep in the spare room for a week." And then she added, "With Muffy as the only pussy you'll see."

Sadie rose up enough to stare into her eyes, smiling at her. "See how easy it is when you really understand what you want?"

"I've always known what I want."

The bold tubular neon sign flashed into life the moment Sadie hit the switch. Blanca's Bar was now open for business. Huge rainbow flags flapped in the gentle breeze from the four flagpoles that hung at angles from the front of the building, which had had a fresh lick of white paint. Tables and chairs filled the small forecourt outside, but it was inside that looked the most different.

"It's like stepping back in time," Natalie said when she finally saw the finished design. The builders had been working for weeks to get everything ready for the big launch.

"Well, I admit I was a little nostalgic, but I liked the old layout. It worked," Sadie said. "Drink?"

"Of course." Natalie smiled as people followed them inside and began offering their congratulations. Realising that the drink would not be quickly forthcoming, she moved away and left Sadie to revel in her success.

Approaching the bar, she noted the framed photograph of Blanca in pride of place on the wall. The older woman was smiling, beautiful and relaxed, as though she'd just been laughing at something.

"I have a lot to thank you for," Natalie said to the image. "All those years you took care of her for me, and I have a little inkling that you helped push her back to me. So, thank you, and I promise that whatever happens from now on, nobody will come between us again. It was always her."

She felt her hand grabbed. "Hey, come on, I want you to meet Tanya."

Dragged away to meet the new bar manager, Natalie glanced back over her shoulder once more at the photo of Blanca, and for a moment, she was sure the smile had widened.

"Sadie?" she said, stopping them both before they crossed half the room. "She'd be so proud of you and everything you've achieved; you know that, don't you?"

Sadie sighed happily and looked around the room, people filling the space. Laughter and happiness were all around, as well as the colour. Half the local women's football team were there, as well as students from the local college.

It was loud, music almost drowned out by upbeat voices and laughter.

Pride reflected on every face.

"Yeah, I think I do. She'd have loved this place, and she'd definitely have loved it being called Blanca's." Sadie chuckled. "And she would have loved you." She stroked the back of her fingers down Natalie's cheek. "Not as much as me." She winked. "But she would have adored you, like I do."

Natalie took Sadie's hand and turned it to cup her cheek, covering it with her own hand.

"It was always you; you know that, right? We were meant to be."

Standing face to face, chest to chest, Sadie smiled and nodded, their eyes locked on one another.

"Yes, I've loved you since we met, right there." Sadie pointed to the spot at the end of the bar where she'd first laid eyes on the curious, naïve teenager. "And I'm never letting you go again."

"Good, because I'm not going anywhere." Natalie pulled her closer and placed a gentle kiss against her lips, lips she knew she would be kissing every day for the rest of their lives.

Because Sadie Swanson was still the one.

The End

If you enjoyed *You're Still the One* by Claire Highton-Stevenson, be sure to check out her back catalogue and sign up to her newsletter for news and updates on her next books.

Hit this button and Subscribe now!

Find Claire and follow her on social media.

Linktree: https://linktr.ee/itsclastevofficial

You can find Claire's back Catalogue here:

Claire Highton-Steven Books (itsclastevofficial.co.uk)

Printed in Great Britain
by Amazon